EXPERIMENTAL MAGIC

MYRTLEWOOD MYSTERIES BOOK TWO

IRIS BEAGLEHOLE

PROLOGUE

Dain pulled up to the old house. It was just as he remembered it, though it had been years since he'd been there. Rosemary's grandmother had warned him off, and he wasn't fool enough to mess with someone as powerful as Galderall Thorn.

Even now, he was wary of ringing the bell in case she answered and blasted him to another realm.

He parked the car and began unloading boxes.

His daughter's things.

Rosemary's things.

He knew he didn't deserve them – these women who had somehow become the most important part of the tornado of his life.

He had wronged them too many times – stole from them, lied to them, left them, only to return again and start the whole cycle over. Dain had wanted things to be different, every single time, and yet there was only so much he could control.

This was the least he could do – pack their things into boxes and drive them over here. Rosemary even said he could keep the car and sell it. She knew him too well – knew he would need the money. Dain sighed.

The last box was loaded onto the porch and he could hear them inside – Rosemary and Athena – talking. Their voices were soothing to him. They anchored him here in this world where he had no real place.

He wanted to see them, but he was afraid of the old woman, and something seemed to be holding him back.

It must be Galderall's power. She's trying to keep me away from her family...from my family.

It wasn't strong enough to stop him and his instinct was to push through, but he hesitated again, unsure whether they would want to see him or not.

Hesitation was unusual for Dain, who'd never had any particular form of self-control. *It must be the magic making me hold back,* he thought, and that was enough to get him to push through, no matter how scared he was of Granny Thorn.

He reached up to the door and knocked. Then he turned around. He could hear it. From far away, a familiar sound, roaring towards him faster than anything of this world.

Oh no...they've found me.

A swirling mist appeared, enveloping Dain in white, and he disappeared from the human world.

CHAPTER
ONE

"Mum!" Athena yelled down the stairs. "Where's my green jersey?"

"How am I supposed to know?" Rosemary called from the kitchen. "Come and have your toast before it gets cold. We're running out of time!"

Athena clomped down the stairs. "I have absolutely no good clothes and this school doesn't have a uniform like St Maria's did."

The black fluffy kitten that had been hovering around Rosemary's feet crossed the floor to greet Athena, who immediately went to the fridge to feed her.

"Little fuzzball is taking a liking to you," said Rosemary.

"When are you going to give her a proper name?" Athena asked. "She's supposed to be *your* familiar, but she definitely likes me more. Maybe I'll name her...hmm, how about Serpentine?"

"Eat some breakfast," said Rosemary, brandishing toast. "The cat can wait."

"Fine," said Athena, grabbing a piece. "What can't wait is finding my jersey. Can't you do a magic summoning trick or something?"

"You know that has only worked a few times," said Rosemary. "And only by accident when I was actually looking *at* the thing."

"Please? Just try. You should be experimenting with your magic – learning it properly."

"Oh, fine."

Rosemary closed her eyes and imagined Athena's forest green jumper. She held out her arms and willed it to come to her.

There was a rustling sound and Rosemary felt quietly optimistic for a moment, until a pillowy force smashed into her, knocking the plate of toast off the bench and sending her hurtling to the floor.

Rosemary opened her eyes in shock. "What the—?" She looked around. "Don't tell me I was just bowled over by a wall of fabric?!"

"That was kind of awesome," said Athena, peering at her mother over a pile of blankets, cushions, and throws. "I mean, I know you didn't intend to do that, but it's a bit like those really random super powers – you have control over all cloth-based materials or something."

"Oh, stop it. I do not," said Rosemary. "I just don't know what I'm doing with this magic stuff. Although it's just as well my super-strength seems to be only in response to danger or I'd have broken all the tea cups by now."

Athena sighed. "It's *so* not fair that you have all the power and can't be bothered learning to use it."

Rosemary looked around at the pile of fabric and shrugged.

They both laughed.

"You know that feeling," said Rosemary. "When you're riding high, confident and full of a sense of empowered purpose?"

"Not really," said Athena, offering her mother a hand and pulling her up. "Is that how you're feeling? Because if it is I want whatever is in your tea!"

"No," said Rosemary with a frown. "That's how I felt after I unleashed the family magic and defeated that vampire brat. I want it back. It's like just when I'm starting to think I've finally mastered this life business, I'm suddenly back to square one and Monday mornings. Why is that?"

"Neuropsychology?" Athena suggested. "But at least you don't have to go to work. You got fired, remember?"

"Don't remind me! I need to start applying for jobs. Who knows when this inheritance business will get sorted. *And* I really need to master this magic stuff before it all backfires on me in a much worse and less fabric-oriented way."

"You'll get the hang of it," said Athena with a giggle. "Besides, it worked." She held up her jersey, lifting it out of the pile. "It must have been in the parlour with all these cushions and throws."

"Well, that's something, I guess. Next time I need a wall of fabric to smash into me, I know what to do." Rosemary glanced at the wall clock. "Oh no."

"What?"

"Look at the time!"

"Let's go then," Athena said, picking up another piece of toast from the plate that had clattered very gracefully to the floor, right-side up, no doubt supported by the delightful magic of Thorn Manor.

They raced to the car. Granny's old and elegant Rolls Royce started with a purr and Rosemary drove them quickly towards the school, instructed by Athena who was following the directions on her phone to avoid her mother getting them lost *again*.

Rosemary pulled up in front of the old castle-like stone buildings.

"Seriously?" she said.

"What?" Athena asked.

"It's like you're about to join Miss Cackle's Academy or something."

"What did you expect in Myrtlewood?" Athena asked. "Because this is pretty much what I was anticipating."

"I hope you don't have to make potions with gross newt's eyes," Rosemary said. "Do you want me to come in with you?"

"I'd rather gnaw off my own arm," said Athena.

"Harsh!"

"Mum, you do realise this is my opportunity to make a first impression at a new school, right? Parents are *not* cool."

"Fine," said Rosemary. "But don't blame me if you get lost and can't find anything."

"I don't think you have a good track record when it comes to senses of direction," said Athena. "I'm probably better off without you!"

"You have a point," said Rosemary. She reached over and hugged her daughter goodbye from the safe distance of the car, so as not to tarnish Athena's reputation. She watched as the sixteen-year-old made her way towards the ornate building, sporting a significant number of towers and clad in large swathes of ivy.

She had a pang of pride, watching her daughter waltz confidently into her new school. This was followed by the sting of longing for the life Rosemary could have had if things had been different.

What if I'd grown up in Myrtlewood with Granny, rather than with my extremely religious parents in St Austell?

What if I'd gone to school here? What would my life have been like?

With a strange sense of emptiness, Rosemary drove the few blocks back into Myrtlewood village, parking next to the tea shop. She was more than ready for a pick-me-up. What she wasn't prepared for was seeing a certain gentleman sitting inside, watching her arrive as if he'd been waiting for her.

CHAPTER
TWO

"Mister Burk," Rosemary said as she entered the tea shop. Burk put down the newspaper that he was clearly no longer reading.

"Rosemary," he responded.

It took a moment for it to dawn on Rosemary that Burk, as a vampire, should surely be fizzling up into dust. She stared at him in horror. "But it's day time!"

"Indeed it is."

"Wha—" Rosemary stuttered, panicking, as she expected Burk to disappear at any moment.

"Marjie has UV resistant glass," Burk explained. "And an underground entrance through her cellar."

"Oh," said Rosemary in relief. "Of course she does,"

She looked around for Marjie, who was nowhere to be seen.

"Do you have a minute to talk?" Burk asked.

Rosemary blushed, remembering the few fleeting moments of intimacy she'd shared with the elegant vampire. Nothing had happened, and Rosemary didn't date – not with her track record. She was worried Burk was about to suggest they start something.

Her mind raced with excuses and possibilities as she recalled the awkward conversation she'd had a few days before with Liam, her old teenage flame, where he'd asked her out and she'd had to decline. Things had been weird with him after that. Liam had been distant and awkward. The last thing she wanted was additional weirdness – from her lawyer!

"Uhh...umm," said Rosemary. "I'm kind of busy."

It was a total lie. Now that she'd dropped Athena off at school, the only things occupying her were the utter emptiness of her day, her challenging financial situation, and how to get control of her magic...All things that were not as immediate as her desire for a nice cup of Marjie's special tea and a slice of lemon cake.

"It won't take long," Burk assured her. "But you could make an appointment to see me at my office if you prefer."

"Your *office*?!" Rosemary asked, shocked at what she assumed he was suggesting.

"Yes," said Burk wryly. "You know, my office, across the square where I practice law, including administering your grandmother's estate. Remember that?"

"Oh," said Rosemary. "Of course. You want to talk to me about *that* stuff."

"That stuff," said Burk, his voice dry yet amused. "Yes. I have some updates for you. It would be more professional to meet in my office, but I reasoned that since you're here..."

"So what's the news?" Rosemary asked, blushing even more at her arrogance for assuming that Burk must surely be asking her out. He was a gorgeous, educated man who wore nice suits. He had a very, *very* long undead existence ahead of him – not to mention the age gap!

Burk probably thinks of me as a little child, Rosemary thought, her blush deepening.

"Are you quite alright?" he asked. "You look flushed."

"Yes, just feeling a bit warm."

"You're not coming down with a fever, are you?" Burk said, raising his cool palm to her head in a slightly paternal gesture.

8

"No, really," said Rosemary. "I'm fine."

"There you are!" said Marjie, bustling over to give Rosemary a kiss on the cheek. "I was busy out the back. You know, now that it's spring and wedding season, I'm overrun with catering orders!"

Rosemary smiled at her Granny's old friend with the wild curly red hair, who had quickly become one of her and Athena's closest friends in Myrtlewood.

Beeping sounded from the kitchen.

"Help yourself to anything from behind the counter, dear," said Marjie. "I need to get the jam tarts out of the oven before they burn! And then I need to ice the cupcakes!"

Rosemary looked back at Burk as Marjie disappeared into the kitchen.

"You were saying?" she prompted. "What lawyerly things do you have to tell me? Please say it's good news."

Rosemary was dreading what might happen if the money from Granny didn't come through soon. She was up to her neck in debt, due almost entirely to Athena's father, Dain.

"It is, I'd say," said Burk. "The estate of Galderall Thorn is being processed now. A significant sum of money will be incoming shortly."

"Oh my gods! That's fantastic!" said Rosemary. "There seemed to be such a big delay before, I wondered if it was ever going to come through."

"Well, you've now been cleared of murder," said Burk. "That helped."

"And how exactly do you clear someone of murder when an ancient child vampire, a secret society of supernatural beings, and a giant apparition of a dragon are involved?" Rosemary asked.

Burk shrugged. "The Myrtlewood authorities have their way of doing things. It's slightly...different from the way mundane society functions, but it works."

"Well, to celebrate, I'm having cake!" Rosemary announced. "Do you want anything?" she asked Burk.

"I'm fine here," he said, waving his hand over his coffee.

"Oh, that's right, I forgot. You can't eat normal food. Erm, by normal I mean human, uhh...do you count as—never mind. It's just as well

Marjie can whip up those enchantments to make things err...palatable for you. Though I wouldn't have the faintest idea how—"

Burk cleared his throat.

"Sorry," said Rosemary, aware she had been growing redder in the face as the rambled. "I really need Athena around at times like these to stop me."

"It's fine," said Burk, looking amused. He took a sip of his beverage and Rosemary wondered briefly if his coffee had to be enchanted too, but decided it might be rude to ask. After all, vampires were very private beings.

"I'll just..." she said and got up to help herself to a large slice of lemon curd sponge from behind the counter.

She was still behind the counter, about to head back over to the table to sit with Burk and maybe convince him to divulge some more information about the timing of the aforementioned great pile of funds, when the door opened. Mr June, the mayor, waltzed in, his oily hair sticking to his forehead and his long purple cape looking slightly more crinkled than usual.

"A large slice of carrot cake if you please, love," he said, tipping his hat to Rosemary. "I didn't know you'd been hired."

"I haven't," Rosemary said, raising her hands in innocence. "Marjie just told me to help myself while she's busy icing cupcakes."

Marjie popped her head around the kitchen door at that moment. "You could help Mr June as well, dear, if you don't mind."

"Sure," said Rosemary, fetching another plate so that she could serve the Myrtlewood mayor a slice of carrot cake. She took it over to his table, and then carried her own cake back to where Burk was sitting.

"So," she said, after savouring a few mouthfuls of the delicious light, tart, and creamy sponge. "What kind of timing are you expecting?"

"Excuse me?" Burk asked.

"For the estate to be fully processed."

"It could be weeks," Burk said. "Two months, tops. It just needs to be checked by a handful of lawyers and bureaucrats. These things tend to take an unreasonable amount of time."

Rosemary nodded, feeling her heart fall. She was already skint and Athena needed new clothing, especially as Myrtlewood school didn't have a uniform and teenagers needed to have at least a few decent outfits to cycle through.

"Are you sure you're alright?" Burk asked.

"What are you, my mother?" Rosemary retorted. "I'm fine."

"Ten minutes ago you looked flushed and now you look pale. Humans as so changeable and so...fragile."

"Don't be ridiculous," said Rosemary. "I may be many things. Changeable, sure, but fragile? Certainly not. I've been through a lot in my life and I'm tough as nails."

Burk smiled and returned to reading his paper.

Rosemary tried to stifle her sigh. She wasn't fragile, exactly, but she was broke. The debt just kept piling up and her credit was so bad she couldn't even hope to get another loan to tide her over for a few months.

It took Rosemary a while of dwelling on her financial woes before she remembered she still had a few questions to ask the lawyer.

"Burk," she said, trying to be polite and maintain distance all at the same time.

"Yes?"

"When we first met...Umm, how do I say this?"

"You suspected me of killing your grandmother?" Burk suggested.

Rosemary blanched again. "Well, kind of. The thing is, you seemed to want me to sell the house – at our very first meeting. Later on, that seemed suspicious. I just wanted to know why."

Burk looked slightly embarrassed. "I simply thought you were so young and metropolitan compared to the old country lifestyle we have around here. I assumed you'd prefer to live in a city. That's all."

Rosemary spluttered as she sipped her tea. "It's funny," she said. "I don't feel young at all, but I guess by comparison..." Her words trailed off, as she wasn't sure it was polite to refer to a vampire as excessively old, even if he was. "Is that really the reason?" she asked, raising an eyebrow quizzically.

Burk sighed. "Not entirely. I also suspected there was danger connected to the house and that the Bloodstone Society was involved. I suppose I felt...protective of y—your family and wanted you and your daughter to be safe."

"That's kind of you," said Rosemary, wondering if Burk had boundary issues.

"I also suppose I felt guilty," Burk said.

"Guilty?"

"Yes. That something had happened to my client, Madame Thorn, at what I suspected was the hands of my old enemy."

Rosemary smiled in what she thought was a reassuring way.

Yes, definitely boundary issues, she thought.

CHAPTER

THREE

Athena was relieved her mother hadn't insisted on coming in with her. High school was hard enough without parents there. They'd managed to sort out her enrolment the week before, over the phone, despite the school apparently being closed for the spring festival of Imbolc. Strangely, they hadn't needed any documentation of the kind that Rosemary had been required to provide at other schools. In fact, Myrtlewood Academy had all the documentation of the Thorn family they'd needed. All Athena had to do was turn up and make herself known at reception so that she could be shown to her class.

It sounded simple, but it really wasn't.

Athena had experienced so many awkward, isolating, humiliating, and generally uncomfortable things at the various schools she'd attended over the years, as they'd moved around so much.

Every one of those bad school memories seemed to be haunting her as she walked through the courtyard between the big old stone buildings, following signs for reception.

To make matters worse, she hadn't figured out how to turn off the buzzing in her head which was interrupted occasionally by the errant thoughts of people around her. This made her paranoid that she would seem utterly bonkers to her new classmates. She'd asked Finnigan to help her master the telepathy that he seemed to understand so well, but nothing he'd said had made a difference so far.

Finnigan...

That was the other thing plaguing her mind. She kept thinking about him – the boy who had appeared in her life out of nowhere, only to make a very deep and lasting impression.

Athena wasn't used to having *feelings* for people. Indeed, she'd sometimes wondered if it was a part of her that was missing. While her peers had often talked with dazed expressions about their crushes, including celebrities they'd never met, Athena had never liked anyone in that way. She barely even had any friends, let alone romantic relationships. It had niggled at her for a long time that there must be something badly wrong with her, and the voices she heard only added to that concern.

But Finnigan understands. He's got the same ability – or curse – or whatever it is.

She wished that he attended Myrtlewood Academy, but alas, he'd informed her that his education was carried out somewhere a little further afield.

So here she was, starting a new school yet again, knowing no one, and to make matters worse, this was clearly a magical school in a magical town and she had the magical aptitude of a broken radio.

Athena entered through the doors marked 'reception' to find a big carved wooden counter. Behind it sat a rather small woman wearing a sage green cardigan over a pale-pink-and-cream polka-dotted dress. The dress had a Peter Pan collar, making the woman appear even more child-like, despite the obvious lines on her face and her grey hair. She appeared to be so busy with the papers on her desk that she didn't notice anyone come in.

Athena cleared her throat. "Excuse me," she said.

The receptionist looked up, over her horn-rimmed spectacles. "Greetings. How may I help you?" she said in a high and croaky voice, flashing a reptilian smile.

"I'm Athena Thorn. It's my first day. I was told to come here."

"Thorn...Thorn..." the woman muttered, licking her index finger with a rather long tongue and rifling through a stack of papers. "Ah yes. Here you are. Nice to meet you. I'm Marla Twigg – Ms Twigg to the students."

"Twigg?" said Athena. The name sounded familiar.

"Yes," said Ms Twigg, batting her eyelashes. "You're probably wondering whether I'm related to the famous historian, Agatha Twigg."

"Oh, Agatha. That's right," Athena said. "We met her down at the pub."

Ms Twigg looked slightly ruffled at that response, clearly expecting more awe in the recognition.

"Oh...umm," Athena continued. "She's a historian? Actually, come to think of it, I was looking at a book by A. C. Twigg the other day...and...err she came to our house for dinner once, but I didn't realise..." Athena stopped, realising she was rambling like her mother. "Uh...Are you related?" she asked.

"She's my aunt," said Ms Twigg proudly. "She's quite well known, you know. But I suppose your family is too. The Thorns are infamous in these parts."

She said all this with a generous smile, but her words only increased Athena's sense of dread.

The family is famous...but I'm utterly useless. Mum is the one with magic and all I have is a buzzing sound in my head!

"Follow me," said Ms Twigg, hopping off her rather tall chair and gesturing out to the foyer. Athena was startled to find the woman was even smaller than she'd realised, and only came up to just above her waist. She followed her along the wood-panelled hallway.

"You're very early, you know," said Ms Twigg.

"I thought I was late," Athena said. "Why are there no other students around?"

"We start mid-morning, usually."

"But the website said..." Athena stared.

Ms Twigg gave a small, shrill, laugh. "I forget we have a website. It's compulsory for all schools in the district or the country or something. It has standard information so that we don't look suspicious to the mundane folk."

"Oh," said Athena, nodding. "Of course. Does that mean school finishes late, too?"

"No, it simply means we bend time if we have to – to get through the lessons. School must finish promptly at 3:15 p.m. or we'd all be late for our afternoon tea, wouldn't we?"

"But why—?"

"Nobody likes mornings," said Ms Twigg, as if it was all perfectly obvious. "Here is the library."

Athena peered into the large high-ceilinged room filled with enormous old wooden bookshelves laden with books.

"Wow," Athena said. "That's awesome."

Ms Twigg smiled at her, clearly savouring the response. "Thank you. It is my library. I am also the librarian here."

"Cool," said Athena.

"Is it?" Ms Twigg asked. "It actually feels rather muggy in here, for February anyway."

Athena thought Ms Twigg was making a rather naff joke at first, but quickly realised there was no humour involved. The response reminded her of Ferg and other odd characters she'd met around Myrtlewood. For a moment Athena felt like she was on another planet. She chose not to explain her remark, as it clearly wasn't worth her effort. Instead, she silently followed Ms Twigg around the school, baffled by half the things the small woman said.

"The planetarium is through that way, along the eastern corridor, and I'm sure, being a Thorn, you'll be keen on the herbarium – it's around the back of the building on the southern side. Your grandmother was a maverick with herbs."

Mis Twigg continued on, gesturing around and naming half a dozen other "arium" type places Athena did not quite comprehend and immediately forgot.

"Here is your hearth room," said Ms Twigg, leading Athena to a particular door, though by this time she had no idea where in the sprawling building she was or how she'd gotten there.

"My what?" Athena asked.

"You know – the room you start the day with. Your main classroom."

"Oh...great," said Athena. "Kind of like a form room or homeroom?"

Ms Twigg gave her a blank look and then turned on her sage green heels and strode away.

Well, that was rather abrupt, Athena thought, worried that she'd somehow disappointed the receptionist-slash-librarian and dreading that there was only more embarrassment to come.

ATHENA PUSHED OPEN the hearth room door to find the room empty. It could have almost been an ordinary classroom at an ordinary school, except there were only a handful of desks arranged in a semi-circle, facing towards a large oak table laden with books, unusual vessels, and all sorts of objects bearing a vague resemblance to bizarre chemistry equipment. Behind the table there appeared to be a large pile of rags, but when Athena's eyes came to rest on them she could have sworn they were moving.

No. They were definitely moving.

The rags roared loudly, making Athena jump. She lost her balance, knocking over a desk. It clattered loudly to the floor and Athena felt creeping panic. Surely, whatever the creature in front of her was, it must have heard her.

Finding her balance, she looked back in horror at the unknown beast and watched as some of the rags slid back in the form of a hood. A very old face with a very large white beard emerged, with little bright blue eyes, blinking up at Athena in surprise.

"Oh, sorry," Athena said.

The old man cleared his throat. "Hello there," he said in a kindly voice. "And who might you be?"

Athena stuttered for a moment before muttering, "I'm Athena Thorn."

He gave her a serious, squinty look and then rummaged around on the chaotic table in front of him, which Athena realised must surely be his desk, until he found a small pair of round-lensed spectacles that reminded her a little of the Beatles.

He put these on and squinted at Athena again.

"Thorn. Hah! Indeed you are. Related to old Galdie, rest her spirit."

"That's my great grandmother," Athena said, nodding. "And I don't think her spirit is getting much rest. She's up to mischief in the spirit world, I'm sure of it. That's when she's not popping in to Thorn Manor for deep and meaningful chats."

Athena clasped her mouth, recalling that Granny Thorn didn't want people to know about her ghostly apparition.

"Is she now?" the old man asked, smiling with such warmth that Athena stopped worrying. Then his smile shifted into a slight frown. "Oh, bother. How rude of me not to introduce myself. I'm Aventurine Spruce. And I suppose I am your new hearth teacher."

"I suppose so," Athena said. "I think I'm a bit early. Oh, and I'm sorry I knocked over the desk."

"Never mind that," said Mr Spruce. "Take a seat and make yourself at home."

CHAPTER
FOUR

Rosemary stayed for too long at the tea shop. The early rush of guests had cleared out and they were well into the pre-lunch lull. She didn't feel in the mood to go home to Granny's house and be all by herself or have to confront her unpredictable grandmother's ghost. Not today.

Burk had long left for his office. Rosemary borrowed his newspaper so that she could look at the job listings. There were a few options in the next town over, but that would require driving there, probably at the exact same time she needed to be getting Athena to school. Still, she needed a job.

The money from Granny's estate would help, whenever it happened to come through, but even then it wouldn't last forever. The problem was, she didn't have any qualifications or much experience. She circled a request for grocery check-out attendants and then slumped down onto the table, not even attempting to conceal a loud sigh.

"What is it, love?" Marjie asked, coming over.

"It's nothing." Rosemary straightened up and plastered on a smile.

"Looking for work?" Marjie asked, gesturing to the newspaper.

"To be honest, I'm a little short on cash," Rosemary admitted. "I can't see any postings for jobs in Myrtlewood though."

"Oh, no one bothers with that," said Marjie, gesturing at the paper. "That's all for the mundane world, you see. If we posted help-wanted ads in the county newspapers we could get people showing up who screamed at the first sight of magic. No...here we just ask around if there's a job needing doing or a person needing work."

"Oh," said Rosemary. "So if the newspaper isn't even relevant to Myrtlewood, why would anyone want to read it?"

Marjie shrugged. "Just keeping up to date with the state of the world, I s'pose. It's good to be informed. But don't change the subject. Tell aunt-Marjie your troubles and I'll see what I can do."

Marjie came and sat down at the table, bringing Rosemary cream and jam scones and a pot of tea with her special pick-me-up charm added in for good measure.

Rosemary took one sip of the brew and instantly felt better. The shame she'd been carrying about her money problems seemed to evaporate and she filled Marjie in on the whole sorry state of affairs.

"So you'll be fine soon," Marjie said. "Galdie's money will come through and sort you out."

"Sure, for a while," said Rosemary. "But for now, I'm totally skint. Even after the money comes in, it's not going to last, is it? I'll need some kind of job, some income, to be self-sustaining. I don't want to squander my inheritance and go back to being broke again."

"Take another sip of tea, love," said Marjie.

Rosemary did as she was instructed and watched Marjie's face furrow into intense concentration.

"It seems to me," Marjie said, "that you have two problems here."

"Not just one big gaping one?" Rosemary asked.

"No," said Marjie. "You've got the problem of what to do with yourself right now, and for the next few weeks, just to get by – which is the easy problem to solve."

"Easy?! How is it *easy*?" Rosemary asked. "Do you know something I don't?"

"Oh Rosemary, we love you in this town, and I'm sure there's plenty of work. Ferg's got plenty of jobs, I'm sure he has a few he can spare. What are you keen on?"

"Honestly, I'll do anything," Rosemary said, feeling her problem halved already, simply by sharing it with Marjie.

"How about here?" Marjie asked.

"The tea shop?"

"Sure," said Marjie. "It's the busy season for me – like I told you before. If you don't mind donning an apron then I'd love to have you here to keep the customers served while I potter around out the back. You could even help me cook if you like. I know you're gifted in the kitchen."

"Won't it be a bit crowded out the back with Herb around?"

"Oh pish," said Marjie with a dismissive wave. "Herb has been too busy with his blighting model train club. They're staging an exhibition. He's been of no use to me. You'd be perfect."

"Really?"

"O'course," said Marjie. "You've already served the mayor, and I've seen what you can do in the kitchen. You can start tomorrow, if you like. Simple as that."

Rosemary sighed – but this time in relief and delight. "That's wonderful. Thank you!" She threw her arms around Marjie. "You're a lifesaver, and I couldn't think of a lovelier job."

"See – that speaks to your second problem," said Marjie.

"What's my second problem?" Rosemary asked, baffled.

"You might not be ready to hear this," Marjie warned.

"Oh no. You can't do that! You can't tell me I have a problem and then keep me in suspense. What is it?"

"Long-term thinking," Marjie said sagely. "You're too used to living week-to-week – never risking getting your hopes up about the future."

Rosemary nodded. "I haven't had that luxury."

"True, but it's also something you're afraid of, I'd wager."

"You're probably right," Rosemary replied, resting her cheek in her hand, elbow leaning on the table in a manner in which her conservative parents would have told her off for. "It's easier not to think about the future. When I do, there's just this big scary void of unknowns and potential failure."

"You can put that in the past now," Marjie said, gently patting Rosemary's shoulder. "You're home with us, in Myrtlewood, and we take care of our own."

Rosemary smiled. "Thanks. That's lovely of you to say."

"It's just the truth, is all," said Marjie matter-of-factly. "Now, you can stop worrying and start asking yourself, like that famous poet says: What is it you want to do with your one precious life?"

Rosemary groaned. "I've been asking myself the same question. For years, actually. It all just seemed so impossible before, but you're right. Now that I finally *do* have enough freedom in sight, it's terrifying!"

It was Marjie's turn to sigh. "That it is, love. To be sure, not feeling we have any choice in our destiny is tough, but having the power to choose, well that can be even harder."

"It's a lot better, though," said Rosemary. "Having a choice over my life is far preferable over not having any power."

"But...?" Marjie prompted.

Rosemary rested her head in her hands. "But I'm scared that if I do try to do something new I'll just mess it up and get into more terrible debt and we'll be back to square one. Or I'll make the wrong choice and miss out on what I really should be doing. Or...or..."

"I understand, love," said Marjie. "You have an enormous case of what the young people call FOMO – fear of missing out."

"Athena says young people don't use that anymore," said Rosemary. "Now that older people know about it. Perhaps it's more FOF."

"Foff?"

"Fear of failure," said Rosemary. "Though I'm not sure anyone calls it that. But yes...a bunch of fears and a bunch of unknowns."

"Well, you know what the good thing is?" Marjie asked.

"What?"

"You're safe, and well, and you have Athena who's just going to flourish here, I know it. You don't have to figure it out all at once, and in the meantime you can help me out at the shop."

"You're right," said Rosemary, smiling again. "Thank you, Marjie."

"It's no bother, dear. I'm just so chuffed to have you home in Myrtle-wood after all these years." And with that, Marjie got up to serve a customer, humming happily to herself as she did so, leaving Rosemary to ponder her hopes and fears.

CHAPTER
FIVE

A thena sat anxiously behind a desk, examining her dark purple chipped fingernail polish. Mr. Spruce had fallen back to sleep and was snoring rather loudly. She didn't want to disturb him and she didn't know what else to do.

She kept her head down as the other students started to arrive.

"Who in Hades are you?" A shrill voice interrupted Athena's thoughts.

She looked up to see a blonde girl with a long neck and pointy nose, her hair pulled tightly into a high ponytail.

Athena glanced around the room to see a few more faces. All eyes were on her.

"I'm Athena Thorn," she said.

The girl's blue eyes bulged in recognition.

Apparently everyone knows our family name. Athena felt the weight pressing down on her, of all the expectations that the name seemed to carry with it.

"I'm Beryl Flarguan," the girl said in an icy tone. "I come from an old witching family, and I'm top of the class."

Athena gave her a puzzled look. "Okay."

"You might come from a well-known family, but I'm better," Beryl continued. "You're not going to beat me." She then turned, with her nose high in the air, and stormed to the other side of the class, taking the desk closest to Mr Spruce.

Athena looked around to check how the other students were reacting to Beryl's display.

Are they all going to be that horrid?

She was relieved when the cool-looking kid next to her wearing an oversized hoodie shot her a sympathetic look. Meanwhile, a couple of others in the room burst out laughing. Athena eyed them warily, unsure if they were laughing at her or Beryl.

One girl had bright blue hair in a pixie cut. She smiled warmly at Athena. The guy next to her, who was also laughing, was tall with rather a lot of black hair. Athena wished she could tell what either of them were thinking. Her head was buzzing with static, but there were no clear thoughts coming through, which was the usual case when she was surrounded by people.

Athena cursed her power, which was literally more of a headache than an asset. It would be much more useful if she could hone it somehow so that she could hear specific thoughts. She made a mental note to ask Finnigan about this.

A tanned boy with dark red hair and a slight build entered the class-room. His eyes fixed on Mr. Spruce.

"Sprucey's asleep again," he said mischievously.

"No way, Felix," said the girl with the blue hair. "Don't you try anything."

"Just a little charm," he replied, taking a glowing blue ball from his pocket and setting it on the desk in front of Mr Spruce.

Athena looked around, anxiously wondering what was going on. All eyes were on Felix as he bent to whisper something over the ball and then stepped two large paces back. The charm whirred and fizzed, and blue smoke burst from it, causing Mr Spruce to sneeze and stand up in alarm.

"Huh! Emergency! Emergency!" he cried.

The class giggled and clapped and laughed, all except for the blue-haired girl and the kid in the hoodie next to Athena, who seemed to be taking this all much more seriously.

"Felix!" Mr Spruce bellowed. "I take it this was another one of your pranks."

"Guilty as charged," said Felix with a twinkle in his eyes.

Athena breathed a sigh of relief. At least the prank was just for show, no real harm done.

"A new kid, eh?" said Felix, swaggering over to Athena and sitting down next to her. "Well, fancy that. Fresh blood."

Athena blanched, feeling slightly queasy, and looked at her hands again.

"Order! Order!" Mr Spruce said.

"We're not in court, sir," Felix said casually.

"Felix, do I *have* to give you detention again?"

"It's not detention if I don't show up," Felix replied.

Mr Spruce's voice took on a tone of authority. "Alright. I'll send you to Ms Twigg."

There was a hush around the room.

"Please don't!" Felix said, sitting up straighter in his chair and crossing his arms. "I'll be good. I promise."

Athena wasn't sure if Felix was playing the clown, but from his tone she sensed he was genuinely scared of the tiny librarian.

"Very well. Class, let's get started," said Mr Spruce. "Take out your homework. If I recall correctly, you were to memorise a chant to the Moon and then write three paragraphs on what it meant to you. If you'll all begin..."

The class began reciting a chant that, of course, Athena had never heard before. She felt incredibly out of place.

She'd never been particularly good at ordinary schooling, but now she was so totally out of her depth that she didn't know how to respond.

She felt perplexed about how any of this could possibly fit into the national curriculum or qualify as a useful education.

The buzzing in her head had become a right headache, and her sense of dread only worsened. The next class was History and Folklore, taught in the library by none other than Ms Twigg, who, like Ferg, appeared to have far too many jobs for one person, although unlike Ferg, hers all seemed to revolve around the school.

Athena didn't know where to start with ancient fairy texts. The other students all seemed to know exactly what was going on. She kept to herself and tried not to interact with anyone, though Beryl kept shooting her sly looks, clearly enjoying Athena's obvious discomfort.

It was painfully clear that Athena had no clue what was going on and the teachers were far too odd and unsettling to be of much help.

The other kids didn't seem to be quite so awful, but Athena didn't want to take any chances with them either. Though some of the students seemed helpful and even friendly, she felt safer keeping to herself. There were too many unknowns.

At lunchtime she hung back in the library and tried to make sense of the thirteenth century texts written by visiting Welsh nuns about the local pixies.

She was tempted to pull out her phone and search online to see if she could find an explanation for some of the concepts that made no sense to her, though she doubted Wikipedia would have anything so obscure. Besides, she doubted Ms Twigg would approve of phone use in the library.

Ms Twigg stood behind the desk keeping a close watch on everyone in the room and looking mildly threatening. Athena was still slightly unnerved about why Felix the prankster was frightened of the small woman.

AFTER LUNCH WAS ART CLASS. At least that one was relatively similar to the kind of curriculum Athena was used to. The teacher was old and petite, wearing a tartan suit. She introduced herself to Athena as Ms Tabitha Coin. "But please call me Tabby," she added.

The class began and Athena was paired with Sam, the kid in the oversized hoodie, who had a nose ring, and shortish scruffy dark hair streaked with purple.

Athena smiled awkwardly. "Hi," she said. "I'm Athena."

"I'm Sam, but you already knew that from Tabby...Err, but before we start, you should probably know that I...err, I don't have a gender. Like pixies."

"Pixies?" Athena asked, baffled.

"Let me try this again," said Sam. "What are your pronouns?"

"Excuse me?" Athena replied as they sat down, wondering if this was another magical thing she was oblivious to.

"Your pronouns. You know...? I prefer people to call me 'they' or 'them'."

"Oh!" Athena said. "You're non-binary?"

Sam looked slightly surprised. "I suppose I am," they said.

"That's the term people use in the non-magical world," Athena explained.

"Non binary," Sam repeated. "I like that. I normally just explain it to people in terms of the faerie creatures that are genderless, like pixies, though I hear they prefer "it" pronouns, which they use for everything... which of course is *not* an okay thing to call most people."

"I...have no idea about pixies, but in terms of pronouns, she/her, I guess," Athena said. "I haven't thought about it that much."

Sam shrugged. "Most people don't if they don't have to." They gave Athena an uncertain look, as if trying to gauge her reaction.

"Thanks for telling me about your pronouns, and also about the pixies. That's all good to know," said Athena. "It's kind of cool that the magical world understands."

"For the most part," said Sam. "I mean, there are also plenty of gods who change their genders all the time, and other creatures too. But some humans are still strange about it."

"I'd never thought about gender-fluid gods," said Athena.

"Gender-fluid!" Sam crowed. "I love it!"

Athena smiled. She hadn't previously been particularly aware of Sam's gender. But unlike magic, this at least was something Athena understood. There had been several diverse gendered students at her old high school.

Sam beamed at her. "We've got to draw each-other," they said.

Athena and Sam sat on opposite sides of a desk, each trying to capture the other's likeness on the canvas boards they'd been given by the art teacher, Tabby.

Sam was quite friendly, if a little timid, but Athena could relate. She didn't feel particularly boisterous herself.

Felix kept interrupting the class, making jokes about the blue-haired girl, Elise, whose locks progressively changed colour to red as he drew her.

Athena tried not to stare at Elise's flame-coloured hair.

"She's like a mood ring," Sam said.

"What?" Athena asked.

"You know, her hair changes colour depending on how she feels."

"Oh, wow!" Athena said, surprised. "I'm...I'm not really used to the magical world."

"I can tell," said Sam. "Don't worry. You'll get used to it. Like Ash."

"Ash?"

"Ashwagandha, over there," Sam gestured to a beautiful dark-haired girl who Athena guessed was of South Asian descent. "She moved here from Surrey with her parents last year after they discovered her powers. They heard Myrtlewood was the best place for a magical education."

"Oh, that's interesting," said Athena, feeling more confidant as the conversation progressed.

"At least you *have* power," said Sam.

"Not really," said Athena. "My mum does."

"You've got loads of it. I can tell," Sam insisted. "Even if it hasn't manifested yet. I'm probably the only one at the school who doesn't have much of anything. I just live here. My family practice folk magic, but I'm nothing special, not like these other kids."

As they continued to draw each other, Sam became flustered, using the eraser more and more frequently.

"What is it? Athena asked.

"I just can't seem to capture you. It's like...you're not even there." Sam's words shocked Athena.

She was even more surprised when Sam showed her the vague and blurry face they'd drawn of her in comparison to the very lifelike sketches in their notebook of other faces and animals.

"There's something strange about you," Sam said. "It's not just the power. There's something else."

Athena felt herself withdrawing back into her shell again. Even at a magical school there was something wrong with her. Even among freaks, she didn't fit in.

To make things worse, the trouble maker, Felix, wandered across to them at that very moment, staring at Sam's sketch and then at Athena.

"I wouldn't say the likeness is uncanny," he said. "But there is something odd about you, new girl."

CHAPTER
SIX

Rosemary made her way home to Thorn Manor a little before midday, buoyed by several additional cups of Marjie's special tea.

As she drove up the driveway, admiring the glimpses of the sea along the Cornish coast, she felt slightly more confident about her future. She had a temporary part-time job to tide her over, after all. Working in Marjie's tea shop would be a lovely way to get to know more people around town, and she'd get to spend time around delicious food all day which meant she'd be in her element.

She parked the car out front, and looked up at the house. It was her home and that felt wonderful after so long hopping between different terribly run-down flats and shared houses without any real sense of grounding.

She stood back and admired Thorn manor. The old stone building held a certain presence, with its excessive (and dusty) rambling wings and its romantic (but inaccessible) tower. They had searched again but still had been unable to locate the entrance to the mysterious tower. An odd feeling came over Rosemary as she looked up at the house. She had the sense there was something different about it. Something had changed since she'd last been home, a few short hours before.

The last time Rosemary had had a feeling like this, there had been a giant gaping void inside the front door, and that was enough to made her gut tighten.

For the past few days she hadn't been thinking about the dangers they still likely faced. She'd been avoiding worries – as much as possible, anyway – about that blasted secret society and their ploy to get hold of her family magic.

It was hard to believe how much had happened in the short time Rosemary and Athena had been back in Myrtlewood. The Bloodstone Society's attack had only been a few days ago, and though Rosemary had managed to vanquish their small vampiric leader, she couldn't help but wonder now, what about the rest of the group? Had they really dispersed as she had hoped, their power depleted?

Her own power had surged during the confrontation when she'd finally unlocked it, along with the previously bound Thorn family magic, but since then it had ebbed and only seemed to work quite randomly, with unintended consequences like that morning's fabric avalanche.

She eyed the house suspiciously, wondering if there might be intruders lurking inside.

Even if I don't have complete control of my power yet, I'm sure it will come to me if I need it, Rosemary reassured herself. No one busts into my house without consequences!

She got out of the car and stormed towards the house. She heard an anxious mewl and saw the kitten emerge from a cat door that the house had graciously added of its own accord. Fuzzball the yet-to-be-properly-named ran for a little while and then paused before stalking off into bushes nearby. Clearly even the cat didn't want to be inside the house at this point.

"If you're in there – whoever you are – you've got another thing coming!" Rosemary called out as she tried the door handle. It was still locked, so she used her key, fumbling clumsily with it in a way that was not as intimidating as the impression she was trying to give off.

The door opened and everything looked...normal.

Rosemary wondered if she had just been paranoid, moments before.

It was understandable to be a little on-edge, given everything they'd faced in the past week and a half, but she had been sure *something* was different about the house.

She checked the main living area and upstairs for signs of intruders, but everything seemed to be in order. She was tempted to examine the entire house, but that would take quite a long time and she was already in need of another cup of tea to calm her nerves.

She sat down at the kitchen table while the kettle boiled and rested her head in her hands. Now that the sense of danger had passed, she was back to feeling unnerved about the future again. A part of her even wondered whether she had unconsciously imagined something being different about the house just to distract herself from that empty unknown.

Rosemary didn't make tea, after all. She turned the stove off, removed the kettle, and went upstairs feeling utterly exhausted at the prospect of having to think seriously about what she really wanted.

Myrtlewood had been so welcoming to her and Athena, but she had big shoes to fill, left by Granny Thorn, a notorious witch, highly involved in the community, and generally well-liked.

Rosemary had no control over her magic, so she could hardly offer magical services to the town, and she felt half her life had already been wasted. All of these circular thoughts just added to her tiredness and sense of uselessness.

To deal with this proactively, she decided to have a nap, but she only made it as far as the upstairs hallway.

Something *was* different. Only, it wasn't an intruder.

It was a *door*.

Right next to the hall table, laden with its usual doilies and decorative plates, ornaments, lamps, and crystals, was a door Rosemary had never seen before.

It might well have been there when she did a quick sweep of the main part of the house, scanning for potential assailants from the Bloodstone Society, but it surely hadn't been there earlier on. It was a smallish door, made in the same oak wood as the panelling that lined the walls. It had a large rose carved on the front and was edged with gold leaf.

Surely, I would have noticed a door edged in gold leaf, sitting right outside my bedroom! Rosemary approached the door cautiously.

It wasn't overly surprising that something in Thorn Manor would change by itself. The house had a wonderfully convenient habit of fixing and cleaning itself, after all, at least in the main living areas. But this, she had not expected.

A door has to lead somewhere...and a door like this has to lead somewhere interesting!

It bore a tarnished golden lock, one that would fit an old-fashioned style of key. Just like many of the keys on the keyring of her master set.

Rosemary felt a lump of tightness in her gut. She *needed* to know what was behind that door, as if called towards it by fate itself.

She reached out to touch the golden lock. It shimmered, the tarnish disappearing, just like the front door lock had when Rosemary and Athena first arrived back at Thorn Manor.

She ran downstairs to fetch her keys, hoping the door wouldn't disappear. She returned moments later, relieved to find it was exactly as she'd left it.

Rosemary fumbled with the keys until she found a small old-fashioned golden key with a rose stamped into its end.

This must be it!

Rosemary took the tiny key and placed it into the lock. As she turned it, she sensed something click into place, internally.

It felt a bit like levelling up in a video game, the kind she used to play with Athena to pass the time when they'd had nothing much else to do in one of the old shared houses they'd lived in.

The door swung open and Rosemary hesitated. The house had always looked after her and Athena so far...but was this the house's doing or something more malicious? She took a deep breath, trying to sense through her magic to see if she could intuitively tell if she was walking into some kind of trap or not.

She wished her grandmother was around to ask, but even Granny Thorn's ghost seemed to be keeping her distance recently.

Nothing *seemed* evil in the air around her. Nothing about the door seemed out-of-place, despite its sudden appearance.

And besides, if it was bad, why would Granny have given me a key?

She took a tentative step through the open door to find a spiral staircase.

The tower!

Rosemary felt a thrill of excitement. She and Athena had searched for the entry to the tower when they'd explored the house to no avail. Rosemary had assumed it must be somewhere in the dusty west wing of the house, but she'd given up looking for it after too many sneezing fits.

She felt slightly guilty, coming up here alone for the first time. Athena had gotten all misty-eyed at the romantic idea of the tower when they'd first arrived and insisted it would be her bedroom, but Rosemary figured she might as well check it out and therefore, be better able to manage Athena's expectations, as it was likely the tower would be quite dusty and small, and in some state of disrepair.

Rosemary made her way up the staircase to find that the top room of the tower was actually huge – at least double the size of the parlour, with panoramic views out to sea, over the forest, and across to Myrtlewood village. Rosemary had never tried to look for Thorn Manor from the township and she wondered whether it would be visible. Or was it perhaps magically disguised?

This room certainly *was* magical.

From the outside, the tower looked tiny.

It wasn't dusty as she'd expected, either. The wooden panelling under the windows gleamed, carved with rosebushes, and edged in more gold leaf. The velvety blue ceiling was painted with gold and silver stars to look like the night sky. The dark hardwood floor beneath her feet seemed to be etched with gold to resemble a map of the earth.

Rosemary took a deep breath and admired the beauty of the room, but she could tell it wasn't here for show. This was a working room. A large cauldron sat in the centre, surrounded by an assortment of green velvet chairs. A bookcase stood to one side bearing a collection of books that looked to be very old. There was also a large ornate wooden desk and a table covered with interesting looking potion bottles and contraptions.

So this was where granny did her magic!

Rosemary had never been up here before, even as a young child, and now that she saw the space she felt she understood her grandmother a little better. Granny Thorn was an enigma, a secret hidden within another secret like stacking boxes.

She walked the circumference of the room, examining things, and then flopped down in one of the armchairs and sighed.

She was delighted to find the tower room, but after the initial wonder wore off she found her previous exhaustion creeping back in.

"Oh bother," she muttered. Myrtlewood had been so welcoming, but was that because they expected Rosemary to be some kind of amazing witch? The Thorn magic was legendary in this town, for good reason. Whatever Rosemary did, she'd be in Granny's shadow, and if she failed... Well, she could lose everything.

"What's that dear?" Granny's voice asked.

Rosemary jumped.

She looked across the room to see a large standing mirror, framed in dark wood, next to the bookshelf. She hadn't noticed it there before. Whether it had merely escaped her notice or had suddenly appeared was anyone's guess. What *was* clear, though, was that Granny Thorn was in the mirror glass, reflected as plain as day, wearing one of her signature black dresses and with her wild white curly hair tied up in a bright red scarf.

"Granny?"

"Of course. Who were you expecting? Dolly Parton?"

"Not in particular," said Rosemary. "But I haven't seen or heard from you for days. I thought you might have..."

"Moved on?" Granny Thorn asked, with a little cackle.

"Yes," Rosemary admitted, wondering if that was a rude thing to assume about a ghost. Supernatural creatures had their customs, after all, and though she was largely unfamiliar with them, she was trying her best to show respect. "I did wonder whether releasing the binding might have..."

"Sent me packing?" Granny cackled again.

"Something like that."

"It'll take more than a gigantic blast of magic to cast me off into the nether regions."

Rosemary laughed. "Well, you certainly haven't lost your sense of humour. You look much clearer that you did last time. Your cheeks are even rosy!"

"Why, thank you, dear."

"What have you been doing?" Rosemary asked. "I mean, what's it like over there?"

"Oh, well I've had meetings with the Counsel of Elder Souls, and I have business with a few spirit guides who want my opinion on some documents in the Akashic Records. Quite busy, really. I'm glad you released that family magic though. It's given me a real boost. I'm so proud of you, dear."

"Thank you, Granny," Rosemary said, flushing with pride, which only reminded her of how little praise she'd received before in her life. Much of that had come directly from the woman in ghost form she was currently speaking to.

"So, dear, I've been meaning to ask. What are your plans now?"

"If only I knew!" Rosemary said, flailing her arms in the air dramatically. "Marjie has offered me some part-time work in her tea shop to tide me over."

"Tide you over?!" Granny asked, outraged. "I left you plenty of money. It's a shame you always refused to take it while I was alive."

"It hardly seemed fair to scrounge off a pensioner," said Rosemary.

"Hah!" said Granny. "That's where your poor judgement gets you. So what's happened to my fortune?"

"Well, your – I mean my – inheritance is apparently coming through shortly."

"Tell that stud muffin vampire of a lawyer to get a move on," Granny said. "I don't pay him good money to muck around. What's the big delay?"

"It didn't help that we were caught up as potential suspects in your murder," Rosemary said, glaring a little. "You didn't exactly make it easy for us to figure it all out."

"I did what I could," Granny said dismissively. "Oh well, you'll get by, then. Make some tea and serve some cake until the money comes in. Then what?"

"Why does everyone keep asking me that?" said Rosemary. She slumped back down in the chair. "Actually, that's what's got me into a funk. I'm scared of finally trying to do something with my life and then failing. Everyone knows our family here – knows you were a magnificent witch. And me? I can't even summon a jumper without creating chaos."

"You'll grow into your powers, dear," said Granny reassuringly.

"I don't know if that's who I am, though," said Rosemary. "I can feel my power – even though I can't control it yet. But I feel like a teenager at the career counsellor's office: totally lost on what to do, but with magic thrown in! Plus, I'm already middle-aged."

"Hah! Thirty-nine is *not* middle aged. If that blasted vampire child hadn't snuck up on me with her stupid dragon I'd have lived well past a hundred and seven."

"You were a hundred and seven?" Rosemary asked. "But you were so spry."

"Give or take a few decades," said Granny. "You lose count after a while. I'd probably been a hundred and seven for a few years, come to think of it."

Rosemary sighed. "At least we have longevity in the DNA. So what you're saying is, I may well have a whole lot more time in which to not know what to do with my life?"

"Pish posh," said Granny. "First, you complain you're too old, now you complain you're too young. Age is a mere figment of the limited physical concept of time. It's no big deal."

"Oh, and I suppose stretch-marks are just organic tattoos?"

"If you like," said Granny with a grin.

"Can't you see I'm trying to mope around to avoid making hard and scary decisions about my future?" Rosemary said, only half joking. "Everything has changed for us within the last fortnight and I'm taking a while to adjust. All I need is my dead grandmother telling me to pull my head in!"

"Good, pull your head in!"

"Fine!" said Rosemary, folding her arms in a mock huff. She couldn't stop herself from smiling at her Granny. "I've missed you."

"I've missed you too, poppet. And come to think of it, I have a little gift for you."

"Really?" Rosemary said, and then frowned. "Please tell me it's not something cryptic, like a music box with a very secret manual locked inside which can only be accessed through a key hidden inside your smelly old dancing shoes!"

Granny laughed and clapped her hands. "Oh, you!" she said affectionately. "You always were my favourite. And no, it's not cryptic this time. It's really quite simple."

"What is it?"

"Look inside the box."

"What box?" Rosemary asked. "Not another mystical object that will transport me to a disorienting alternate dimension where an ancestor will give me lessons in how to unlock family magic, because I've had quite enough of that!"

"It really has been a busy fortnight, hasn't it?" said Granny. "But no. The box on the desk, silly."

"There is no..." Rosemary said, glancing at the old writing desk, which now did indeed have a small metal box sitting on top. "That wasn't there before."

Granny gave her a mischievous look.

"This better not be a trap," said Rosemary.

"I promise it isn't," said Granny excitedly. "Just look inside."

"Oh, alright."

Rosemary walked over to the desk and reached for the box. She opened it and breathed a sigh of relief when nothing unusual happened. Then she gasped in wonder at what was inside.

"For me?" she asked.

"That's what I told you," said Granny.

Rosemary admired the gleaming emerald pendant, set in gold, that seemed to glow with its own light.

"Can I...touch it?" Rosemary asked.

"Of course you bloody well can," said Granny. "Put it on. What else do you think it's for?"

"What I mean is, will it do anything weird?"

"If by weird, you mean magical – which is quite offensive, actually – then yes, it certainly will do something *weird*."

"Haven't you ever heard of informed consent?" Rosemary asked. "Oh, and I'm sorry, I didn't realise calling magic weird was offensive."

"Actually it isn't," said Granny.

"What? But you just said."

"Weird comes from 'wyrd'," Granny explained. "It is a sacred word, speaking to the mystic interconnectedness of all things, and it's offensive to use it in a non-magical way."

Rosemary sighed. "Oh, whatever."

"Just put the necklace on, dear," said Granny.

"Not without knowing exactly what it'll do," Rosemary insisted.

"This is the pendant of Elzarie Thorn."

"Who?"

"Your great, great, great, great grandmother," said Granny.

"That's lovely," said Rosemary. "So, it's a special family heirloom. And it does what, exactly?"

"It'll help to stabilise your powers – that's all," Granny said. "It'll make you feel more centred, more comfortable in your own skin. That way, it'll help with mastery."

"That actually sounds pretty good," said Rosemary.

"Put it on then, my dear, go on."

"It's not going to make me breathe fire or poo chocolate buttons or anything?"

"No – it'll just centre you. I promise."

"Alright," Rosemary said, tentatively.

She picked the necklace up and felt her fingers instantly tingle in a pleasant way that made her giggle.

"It's lovely, isn't it?" Granny said. "I wore that necklace every day for many years. It passes on the maternal wisdom of our line, you see."

"I thought you said it would centre me," said Rosemary.

"Exactly," said Granny. "Go on. Put it on. Stop dawdling."

Rosemary lifted the necklace up, carefully placing it around her neck. The pendant was drawn to her, like a magnet, lighting on her sternum. The clasp practically fastened itself.

"How does it feel?" Granny asked.

"Good," said Rosemary, drawing in a breath that felt like refreshing mountain air.

"Is that all?"

"It's...it's like I'm more...all in one place instead of feeling scattered from worrying about this or that. I'm...I'm present."

"See," said Granny. "I told you I had a present for you!"

"Very clever," said Rosemary, rolling her eyes at her grandmother's ghost.

"And with that, it's time for me to go," said Granny.

"Sorry," said Rosemary. "I mean, thank you. I promise to behave myself and stop being cheeky and sarcastic."

"Oh no you don't!" said Granny. "You keep being your vivacious self. As for me, I only have so much energy to expend in the physical plane and I have other matters to attend to. But do give us a yell if you need anything. I'll pop in if I can."

"Thanks Granny. There's...there's so much more I wanted to talk to you about. To ask you. Like, what's going on with Athena. Why is it she can hear thoughts?"

"Oh that," said Granny, though her voice was growing quieter as her image began to fade out. "That's something you should talk to her father about."

"Dain?!"

"Yes – that troublemaker. He knows a lot more than he ever told you, I'd wager."

"Seriously."

"Seriously. The only trouble is, he's missing, isn't he?" Granny said, barely visible as she continued to fade.

"What are you talking about?"

"You'll figure it out, soon enough," said Granny, and with that, she disappeared.

CHAPTER
SEVEN

Rosemary returned downstairs, locking the special door to the tower behind her, as it seemed prudent to protect Granny's special space.

Little fuzzball yawned from the window seat and then stretched and lazily made her way over to Rosemary for a pat.

Rosemary scratched the purring animal behind the ears and then made her way to the kitchen to finally sort the tea she'd been planning on having earlier. She also made some simple toast with sliced tomatoes, black pepper, olive oil, and basil for lunch, to compensate for the overly rich cake she'd had quite a lot of earlier.

She sat on the window seats, sipping her tea and nibbling her toast, looking out at the light drizzle that had started falling outside. Wearing the necklace did make her feel better – not in the bubbly way Marjie's tea did, but calmer and more centred, just as Granny had described. It did not, however, remove all her worries or her errant thoughts, which her grandmother had only added to.

What happened to Dain?

The last she'd heard from her wayward ex, he'd agreed to deliver all their measly worldly possessions from the run-down flat in Stratham to

Thorn Manor. Rosemary had asked for the favour as Constable Perkins wouldn't let her leave town while 'under investigation'.

Dain had come through, despite generally being unreliable. In the past, he'd had a bad habit of erratic behaviour, such as taking off with the contents of Rosemary's wallet.

It had always puzzled Athena that her mother never properly got angry at Dain, considering everything he'd done. Rosemary's frustrations with him never seemed to last. Athena had often commented that he must be possessed with a strange power over her – and indeed, over almost every woman he met, but Rosemary never considered the possibility that it was a magical ability of any sort.

She wanted to text him, to see if he was okay...to check whether Granny was right about him being missing, but Athena would hate that.

Athena had no time at all for her father – to the point where she'd gotten Rosemary to make a protection charm to ward him off, lest he weasel his way back into their lives.

Is that why he's gone missing?

A lump of guilt formed in Rosemary's abdomen. They'd intended for the charm to ward him off and stop him from getting his slippery hands on the Thorn family fortune.

Had they, instead, sent him somewhere else entirely? Or addled his brain so that he couldn't make his way back to wherever it was he was living these days in the general vicinity of Stratham?

Two weeks before, Rosemary would've scoffed at all these ridiculous thoughts, but now they seemed common sense. Magic was real. She did not yet comprehend how it worked or what the boundaries were, but she had accepted it as the only possible explanation for all the unusual things that had happened to them in Myrtlewood.

Had their attempt at warding against him made Dain disappear entirely?

How stupid of me to meddle in something I don't understand!

She clutched the necklace, which sent a ray of reassurance through her, but it did not entirely quell her anxiety.

Rosemary texted Dain, knowing that her daughter would be mad about it. Perhaps Athena didn't need to know about that little detail, but someone certainly needed to check to see if something had happened to her father.

She waited until the tea went cold, but there was no response.

Rosemary kept checking her phone as she paced around the house. The rain was falling more heavily outside, which gave Thorn Manor a sense of tense ambiance.

Though Rosemary felt more certain of herself, she was unnerved by Granny's final words to her upstairs. Her phone remained dormant, until a phone call came through.

Athena calling.

"Bollox!" Rosemary cried, checking the time. She answered the call. "I'm so sorry, love."

"Sorry...as in you totally forgot about your only child on her first day of school and left her to wait in the rain?"

"Pretty much. I've uhh...I've had some distractions."

"That's just great," said Athena darkly. "And are you going to distract yourself from those distractions and come and get me RIGHT NOW?!"

"Yes," said Rosemary, grabbing her jacket. "I'm on my way."

"Good, because my only half-decent outfit is getting soaked!"

Rosemary ran outside through the rain she hadn't noticed earlier. She jumped into the Rolls Royce, grateful that it was a hundred times more reliable than her rusty bomb of a car. *The one that Dain had driven over here...*

Come to think of it, what happened to the old car?

It had been there one night and she hadn't seen it since.

The spectre of her old vehicle plagued Rosemary's mind all the way to Athena's school. *How could I possibly have forgotten about it? How did I not realise it was missing?*

Her anxiety was so strong, edged with shame about forgetting to pick her daughter up on time, that it counteracted any calming balancing affect the emerald pendant might've otherwise had.

By the time she pulled up outside Myrtlewood Academy, Athena looked thoroughly soaked. The tree she was standing under had not been sufficient protection from the downpour.

Athena did not make eye contact with her mother as she got into the car.

"I'm sorry, love," Rosemary said.

"Don't talk to me," said Athena. "I'm not in the mood."

Rosemary sighed, her guilt swallowing up all her other scattered thoughts for the moment. "Do you feel like going to the pub for some mulled mead?"

"No."

"Marjie's for hot chocolate?"

"No. I want to go home."

"Okay," Rosemary said, giving up on peace offerings and guiding the car back towards Thorn Manor.

Once home, Athena went straight to her room.

Rosemary had been looking forward to telling her about the mystery door, and showing her the gorgeous – and unexpectedly large – tower room, but she decided to let the teen cool off first.

Rosemary decided she, too, needed to relax. She went upstairs and ran a bath in the large claw-footed tub, adding in Granny's rose geranium bath salts and a splash of bubble mixture.

Before she got in, she remembered to take off the special necklace so as not to tarnish it. She draped it carefully over the bench.

As soon as it was off, Rosemary's energy lapsed, and she felt scattered. The psychological disturbance of returning to her normal state of mind, however, was temporary. As soon as she got into the bath, her anxieties melted away and she was left feeling lovely and serene amid the sweet rosy scented bubbles.

Everything will work out, Rosemary told herself, feeling more optimistic than she had in a long time.

Things have already gone so well...Apart from the secret society coming after us, and the murder investigation, and that giant dragon thing, and the break-ins, and the ancient tiny vampires...and...actually all of that went surprisingly smoothly, considering.

We're at home here, and we're settled for the first time in a long, long time. And I even have a job.

I don't have to worry about money. Athena might be mad now, but she'll come around.

There was a loud knock at the bathroom door.

Rosemary rocketed out of the bath and almost slipped over on the tiles, reaching out for the towel rack for support. *Did I forget to lock the front door?* she wondered. *Has someone just wandered in, looking for me?*

"What is it?" Rosemary asked.

"How long are you going to be?" Athena asked, her voice taking on a demanding tone. "I should be the one having a bath. After all, it was your fault I got soaked. Didn't you even think to run one for me?"

"Actually, it did cross my mind," Rosemary replied. "But you'd already refused all my other offers and told me not to talk to you...so."

"Fine!" said Athena.

"I won't be long," Rosemary promised. "I'll run you one as soon as I'm done."

"Never mind," Athena said, retreating back down the hallway.

Surely, this bad mood isn't just because I forgot to pick her up on time, Rosemary thought with a sinking feeling. *I bet the first day at school did not go well.*

She got back into the tub and washed her hair, contemplating what kind of thing she might say or do to support her daughter who was clearly having a very bad day.

Rosemary decided she would run Athena a bath, after all, and then make her a special meal. She quickly finished up in the tub and then ran a fresh bath with extra bubbles. It seemed to take quite a while for the water to fill up, and Rosemary wished it was faster because her mind began to race with great ideas to help Athena feel better. While the water was still running, she popped downstairs to get started on a special spiced hot chocolate.

She hummed to herself as she blended the herbs in the mortar and pestle, and then mixed them in a saucepan with milk, cocoa, and dark chocolate, which she put on to simmer.

"Ah, Mum?" Athena called from upstairs.

"What, love?"

"Why is the hallway wet?"

"Oh drat!"

Rosemary raced back upstairs to see water flooding out from under the bathroom door.

"You left the bath running!" Athena shrieked.

"It was for you," said Rosemary. "It was filling so slowly. I wasn't gone long."

"I told you I didn't want one. Uhh..."

A STRANGE GURGLING sounded from behind the door in question. Rosemary tentatively tried the handle and the door swung open to reveal a wall of warm, bubbly, rose-scented water which immediately rushed towards them, sweeping them along the hallway and all the way down the stairs.

Athena spluttered, wiping bubbles from her face. "What was that?"

Rosemary was so shocked, all she could do was laugh. To her great surprise, Athena joined in and they both lost themselves in cackling giggles for at least ten minutes. They laughed until their abdominal muscles ached and then they lay there, slumped at the bottom of the staircase.

Fuzzball approached them to investigate, took one sniff of the water, and strode away with an unimpressed look on her face.

"That was so weird," Athena said. "There's no way all that water came from overfilling the bath. It must have been your magic."

"Or yours," Rosemary suggested. "You sounded quite mad before when you demanded a bath."

"I don't really have magic, remember," said Athena. "I just have annoying voices in my head that belong to the minds of other people."

"About that..."

"What?"

"I spoke to Granny Thorn today," Rosemary said, relieved Athena seemed to be feeling much better so that she could finally talk about the matters at hand. "Well, I spoke to her ghost, anyway. She told me something strange and troubling that you probably should know about."

"Why didn't you tell me earlier?" Athena asked, sounding concerned.

"You didn't want to talk to me," Rosemary replied. "And you hardly seemed to be in a mood for any more troubling news."

"What's that?"

"Well, the news is..."

"No, wait, what's that you're wearing? That necklace. It's gorgeous." Athena pointed to Rosemary's neck.

Rosemary reached up to feel the shape of the emerald pendant there.

"That's strange," she said. "I could have sworn I took it off before I had my bath."

"Can I have it?" Athena asked.

"Maybe one day," said Rosemary. "Granny Thorn gave it to me. It's supposed to centre my energy and make me more present."

"And how's that going for you?" Athena asked with a cheeky grin.

"Well, I'm...here," said Rosemary. "It's been a heck of a strange day."

"Tell me about it," said Athena, pushing herself up off the floor and pulling her mother up too.

"I'll tell you all about it over cocoa," said Rosemary. "Oh blast! I forgot I left the cocoa on!"

She and Athena raced to the kitchen to find the oven had been turned off and two cups of perfectly brewed cocoa sat on the bench next to a pile of fresh, clean clothes for each of them.

"Thank you, house," Rosemary said, chuckling.

"Hey, you don't suppose the house was to blame for that whole bath-water incident, do you?" Athena asked as they wandered back up the noticeably dry staircase to go to their rooms to change.

"It wouldn't surprise me," said Rosemary. "Maybe it was trying to shake you out of your grump."

"I guess it was successful then," said Athena. "There's nothing like a bubbly rose-scented tsunami to blast away a foul mood."

They came back downstairs in fresh, dry clothes, and headed to the parlour with their hot chocolates, to sit on the comfy sofas there. The fireplace spontaneously lit itself as they walked in, creating an even cosier atmosphere.

Rosemary patted the wood-panelled wall in appreciation of the house and then sat down to enjoy her hot chocolate.

"So, tell me what this news is, then," said Athena.

"Well, the troubling part is..." said Rosemary, and then hesitated, wondering how much her daughter needed to know.

"Dad's gone missing?" Athena asked.

"Hey, stop reading my mind," said Rosemary. "I'm trying to be a good parent and censor things for you."

"Really, Mum," said Athena. "I'm almost an adult. I think I can handle it. Besides, I need to practice using this stupid telepathy and your mind is the only one simple enough for me to read."

"Simple?" said Rosemary. "Who are you calling simple?"

Athena laughed.

"It's a serious situation though," said Rosemary. "Your father—"

"So he's gone and got himself into trouble. Big deal. It's hardly out of character for him, is it?"

"Only...the car disappeared too."

"What car?" Athena asked.

"Our old car," said Rosemary. "Remember, it was parked outside when the boxes turned up on the doorstep, and then...well, it must have vanished."

"Or someone drove it away," Athena suggested. "That's strange. I forgot all about the car."

"Don't you think it's weird we didn't notice?" said Rosemary. "And Granny knew about it, somehow. I have a feeling it was magical. I can't help worrying that our charm to ward him off backfired and blasted him into a different dimension or something."

"I don't think that's likely," said Athena. "But even if it is it's probably a good thing not to have to worry about him anymore."

"Athena! I know you have no time for him, and I accept that, but he's still your father. And here's the thing – Granny said he knows something about your mind-reading ability."

"What?!" said Athena, looking livid. "Did you tell him?"

"No. Not like that. Granny wasn't exactly detailed in her description, but she implied your power is to do with *his* side of the family."

"But he's not magical," said Athena.

"Not to our knowledge. But it kind of make sense when you think about it. He always had a strange power over people – specifically women – and that's not all. Remember how I never even got mad at him no matter how many times he messed me around or stole from me? That's not normal."

Athena was silent for a moment, then said, "I don't want it."

"What?"

"This gift – or curse – or whatever it is in my head. I don't want it if it's from him."

Rosemary sighed. "You may not have a choice if it's genetic."

"But Finnigan..."

"Finnigan what?"

"Finnigan is like me. He can do it too. I don't need to ask Dad about it. I can just ask him."

Rosemary gave her daughter a curious look. "Don't you think it's a bad idea to get involved with someone like your father?"

Athena glared at her and threw a cushion, which narrowly missed Rosemary's head.

"Hey! Watch it!"

"Don't ever say anything like that to me again," said Athena. "Anyway, we are not *involved*. That's such an old-person way of thinking. I haven't even seen him since after that...that incident with the dragon and the nasty little girl vampire on Saturday."

"But have you heard from him?" Rosemary asked.

Athena was silent.

"I suspected as much."

"Stop it, Mum. Let me have some privacy."

"Fine," said Rosemary. "But I do want to know about your first day at school – at least the basics. Whatever you want to tell me without invading your privacy."

"It sucked."

"That bad?" Rosemary asked. "Was it the kids or the teachers?"

"The teachers are fine, the kids are nice...mostly."

"So what's the problem then?"

"I am!" said Athena. "It's all magical and I know nothing. I suck."

Rosemary sighed. "Don't be so hard on yourself, love. It's your first day. You'll catch up in no time."

"Easy for you to say, you don't have to go to school. You don't even have a job. Speaking of which, how are we going to get by? I need new clothes urgently!"

"Actually," said Rosemary, "I have some good news on that front."

"Really?"

"Marjie offered me some part-time work in the teashop while she's busy catering spring weddings, so we'll have some cash to tide us over until the inheritance clears. I also ran into Burk there, who said it might only be a matter of weeks..."

Rosemary didn't want to bother her daughter with the other thing that had been troubling her – the uncertainty and fear of failure she felt regarding what to do with her life.

"That's great!" Athena said. "And don't worry about that other stuff, Mum. You'll figure it out soon enough."

"I told you to stop reading my mind!" Rosemary said. "Didn't you just say you value privacy?"

"You're my mother. You have no privacy. Anyway, whatever you do – it has to involve food. Marjie's tea shop is a great place to start figuring things out."

"Why are you so sure about that?" Rosemary asked.

"Food was your first love," Athena said, batting her eyelashes at her mother. "You always wanted to be a chef, didn't you?"

"I suppose I did, once upon a time. But now that I've inherited all this from Granny, including the family magic, I feel like I need to become some kind of epic witch so that the town isn't disappointed in me."

It was Athena's turn to sigh, or at least groan and roll her eyes. "Mum, that's silly."

"Is it, though? I would love to be able to go to magic school. Do you think they take adult enrolments at Myrtlewood Academy?"

"Don't even think about it," said Athena. "I'm already embarrassed enough about being a total newbie without having to worry about having a parent at school! Anyway, Granny wouldn't want you to try to become like her or anyone else, and neither does the town expect that. Just be yourself and stop being so neurotic."

"I'll stop being neurotic if you stop being such a wise-arse," said Rosemary.

"Deal," said Athena. "Actually, you already seem a bit less neurotic – your thoughts are clearer to read too."

"It must be the necklace," said Rosemary. "And hey! I told you to stay out of my head!"

"Not going to happen."

CHAPTER

EIGHT

Athena smiled across the table at her mother, feeling much better after all the laughter earlier, and enjoying the home-cooked meal of spaghetti Bolognese that Rosemary had managed to quickly whip up for dinner.

Rosemary was thinking about culinary herbs, and occasionally her mind darted to her new job in Marjie's tea shop or concerns about her daughter's new school. Athena listened to all this with quiet interest, not wanting to show her mother exactly how much mind-reading she was now capable of.

"This is good," Athena said. "You should cook more often."

"While I was making dinner I was thinking about what you said before," said Rosemary. "I do love food. Do you really think I should go into the restaurant business?"

"Maybe," said Athena. "Though that does sound rather stressful. Isn't that what they say about chefs – they're always so stressed that they swear a lot and throw plates?"

"Hmmm, true. Maybe it's good I never finished culinary school, then," said Rosemary. "The last thing I need right now is more stress."

"You seem pretty calm actually," said Athena.

"The necklace must be helping."

"How did you get it, again? Did Granny's ghost just pop up and hand it to you?"

"Funny you should ask," said Rosemary, setting down her cutlery on her empty plate. "I got home and there was something different about the house."

"Oh no, not again!" said Athena.

"It wasn't actually a bad thing," said Rosemary. "Though, I was suspicious at first."

"What was it then?"

"There was a new door."

"A what?"

"A new door, upstairs. Come on. I'll show you."

Rosemary got up from the table and led Athena upstairs.

"Wait," she said, looking at empty wall space. "It was right here."

"Are you sure?" Athena asked. "Is it hidden or something."

"It was glaringly obvious before – all carved and gleaming, and edged in gold leaf. But come to think of it, I didn't notice it again when we got home."

Athena gave her mother a sceptical look. "I've never seen anything like that around here."

"Neither had I, but believe me – it was here."

"So there was a door," said Athena. "And...?"

"It led up to the tower."

"No way!" said Athena. "Not fair. That's supposed to be my new bedroom."

"I think Granny's still using it," Rosemary said.

"What do you mean?"

"It's huge, for one thing – way bigger than how it looks from outside – and there are all these special-looking magical things, including a big cauldron. Anyway, Granny appeared to me in a mirror up there. We had a good long chat and she gave me the necklace."

"As in, handed it to you?"

"As in, the desk was empty one minute, and the next thing I knew a box was sitting there with the necklace inside. Apparently it belonged to my great, great, great times a million greats ancestor Elzarie Thorn. That was how Granny gave it to me. She insisted I put it on right then and there."

"Interesting," said Athena. "You know, if you'd told me all that a couple of weeks ago..."

"I know, I never would have believed it either."

"It's weirding me out to think that Dad might know about all that magic stuff – that he might have known about it for years."

"It is a strange thought," said Rosemary. "Granny also told me off for misuse of the word 'weird', which is apparently a sacred term or something."

Athena shrugged. "Who would have thought?"

"Anyway, it does bother me if your father is missing, even if you don't give a bat's claw about it."

"Do bats even have claws?" Athena asked. "I mean...sure, I don't want him to come to any serious harm, just like anyone else. But he's hardly even a father to me, is he? What has he done for us other than cause trouble?"

"I get it, kid," said Rosemary.

"Don't call me that," Athena grumbled, then yawned. The day was catching up to her and so was her curiosity, but she didn't want to tell her mother what she planned to do next. "I might go to bed," she said. "It's been a long day and it's only Monday!"

"Fair enough, love. You go to bed and I'll go downstairs to clean up, if the house hasn't beat me to it."

Athena hugged her mother goodnight, picked up the kitten which she was clearly trying to claim as her own, and made her way to bed. It was nice having a whole large room to herself with a big queen-sized bed. She put the purring kitten down near her pillow and made her way directly across the room to what had – that very morning – been a large window, only to find it was now a set of French doors, leading out to a small balcony.

"Thank you, house," Athena whispered. The house had clearly been reading her mind. Athena had been daydreaming earlier about sneaking out the window, wondering whether the thick ivy that clung to the side of Thorn Manor was sturdy enough to hold her.

The doors opened easily and a crisp breeze blew into her bedroom. Athena grabbed a soft woollen blanket, scuffed on her slippers, and slipped outside into the cool, dark night.

Finnigan, she called out. Finnigan, if you can hear me, please come here. I need to talk to you.

Athena looked out into dark forest surrounding the Thorn Manor. She could hear the hoot of owls and the swish of ocean waves. The moon was beginning to peek above the horizon over the sea, in the distance. It was possible she was simply talking to herself in her head. Finnigan could be miles away, and yet, he'd told her that he'd come if she called. She'd thought of him often, but had resisted the urge to call until now. Now, she had a good reason. She needed to understand what was going on inside her head – regardless of what her father had to do with it. She needed to understand herself.

Athena. Finnigan's voice rang through her head. *You called.*

I wanted to talk to you, Athena replied. Can you come?

Not tonight. I'm...far away.

Athena wondered how far their telepathic voices could possibly be travelling.

I'll be back soon, he continued.

How soon?

Tomorrow night or the night after.

But, wait...

I have to go. Take care of yourself, Athena. Until next time.

Athena frowned. Finnigan obviously had more important things to do than talk to her. She felt a bit confused and cross, not because he was busy, but because he seemed so aloof.

What's really going on? she wondered.

CHAPTER

NINE

Rosemary woke up bright and early the next morning and rose from her little single bed in the room Granny had kept for her as a child. She knew it was odd, a fully grown woman sleeping in a child's room, but it was *her* room and she hadn't gotten around to redecorating, given the chaos of the last few weeks. She prepared herself mentally to ferry Athena to school and get herself to work, only to find her daughter still fast asleep in bed.

"Come on, love. You'll be late if you don't get up soon."

Athena yawned and groaned. "School doesn't start until mid-morning," she grumbled, and pulled the covers over her head.

"That's ridiculous!" Rosemary said.

"No, it's true. You can even call them to find out."

Rosemary did, in fact, call them, only to be told that Athena was right.

"I told you so," Athena said, clomping downstairs in her dressing gown.

"Sure," said Rosemary. "But it sounded like wishful thinking to me. How am I supposed to get you to school now? I told Marjie I'd be in at nine. I suppose I can call her and tell her it will be more like ten thirty."

"Don't be silly, Mum," Athena said as she poured herself some tea. "I can just walk. It'll only take about twenty minutes."

Rosemary handed her daughter a plate of toast. "I suppose that'll be alright. Don't get into any strange cars or talk to any wolves in the forest or anything like that, though."

"I'm old enough to walk across the village unchaperoned," Athena said.

"It seems like you're feeling better about school, too. I haven't heard any more complaints."

Athena shrugged as she sat down at the kitchen table. "I *want* to feel better about it. Anyway, it's not the school that's the problem. It's just that I don't know the first thing about magic and the whole curriculum is based around it."

"How do they get you ready for national testing, you know A-levels and so on?" Rosemary asked, emptying the teapot into her own cup.

"They said they have their way of helping us learn the basic mundane curriculum without actually studying it specifically," Athena said, between bites of toast. "The qualifications carry across in case we want to go on to other non-magical academic pursuits. But I have no idea how that works."

"It sounds fabulous," said Rosemary, feeling a little envious. "Much, much better than the strict religious school I had to go to when I was your age."

Athena put down her piece of toast and sighed.

"It *would* be fabulous if I had even an ounce of your magic. It's so not fair."

"I can try asking Granny about that," Rosemary suggested. "Next time she pops in, whenever that is."

"Please do," said Athena with a pleading look. "I need all the help I can get."

Rosemary left for work while Athena was still eating toast in her dressing gown, complaining she had nothing to wear. Promises were made regarding a weekend shopping trip.

As she drove the short distance to Myrtlewood, Rosemary hoped the second day at school went much better than the first. Athena had always struggled with school. She wasn't particularly interested in a lot of the curriculum and making friends had been hard in the past, especially as they'd moved around so much. This school was particularly important, as it seemed they would be in Myrtlewood for the foreseeable future.

Rosemary parked up near the tea shop and found it buzzing with activity. Three people stood waiting at the counter to be served and most of the tables were already full.

"Thank goodness you're here!" Marjie called out.

"I've never seen this place so packed," said Rosemary, making her way around the shop and behind the counter.

"I suspect you have a little something to do with that," said Marjie as she served a piece of chocolate orange torte and a beef pasty to a vaguely familiar looking woman with dark hair and a red coat.

"Me? Why?" Rosemary asked.

"News travels fast around here. Everyone wants to come and meet the descendant of Galdie Thorn, especially after what we all saw in the sky over your house!"

Rosemary stifled a groan as the customer smiled at her. When the woman left for one of the few remaining tables and the other customers' orders had been taken, Marjie gave Rosemary a big hug and handed her a bright green apron covered in red roses.

"This one's for you," said Marjie. "It will bring out your eyes."

Rosemary smiled. She put the apron over the plain black-on-black t-shirt and jeans combo she was wearing and instantly felt at home. Working in the tea shop and serving the customers was easy, though she had to pay careful attention to the money side of things. She'd never been particularly strong with numbers and Marjie's system was much more manual than the automated grocery store checkout she was used to.

Many of the customers did, indeed, want to meet Rosemary and introduced themselves to her enthusiastically, telling her all about how marvellous her grandmother had been. She heard numerous stories of how Galdie had helped them out with a wayward pet or a mysterious ailment. This was a little overwhelming for Rosemary as she already felt a weighty burden to fill Granny's shoes and had no idea how to. She clutched her emerald necklace for a little extra centredness.

The necklace itself did not go unnoticed. Marjie was the first to remark on it – remembering that Granny had worn it for years.

"I always envied that pendant, I did," said Marjie wistfully.

Various customers remarked on the emerald, as well. There was quite a mix of clientele that day. Some only wanted take-away tea and cake, whereas others seemed to while away the morning, much like Rosemary had done the day before. One of these customers was the dark-haired woman with the red coat that Rosemary had noticed multiple times before.

As Rosemary was clearing one of the tables, the woman caught her eye and smiled again. Rosemary smiled back.

Just then, a familiar face entered the tea shop. Detective Neve wore a smart navy jacket over a plain cream silk shirt and dark blue jeans. The stylish outfit complemented her perfectly straight jet black hair.

"Rosemary," Neve said, grinning.

"Hi," said Rosemary, smiling. "Thanks so much for your support last week. It made a huge difference to us."

Detective Neve had helped to resolve the rather outrageous issues with Granny's murder investigation, the secret Bloodstone society, and the tiny-but-ancient vampire who had tried to steal the Thorn family magic.

"You are the one I should be thanking," said Neve. "I'm so pleased we got to the bottom of things, but I'm not sure how far I would have gotten without you stopping Geneviève."

Rosemary smiled. "I just did what I had to do at the time. But really, thanks for getting Perkins off my case." Rosemary hesitated, then asked, "Do you think it's safe now? I mean, the other members of the Bloodstone society are still out there somewhere." She looked around the tea shop suspiciously.

"There's no sign of Despina," said Neve, lowering her voice. "And it seems the other members have disbanded for now, since the society's power has waned, but stay vigilant."

Rosemary frowned, worrying that she perhaps shouldn't have let Athena walk to school alone. The threat from vampires seemed less severe in broad daylight at least, but the evil secret society seemed to have all kinds of other magical members who were perfectly comfortable in the sun, including animal shapeshifters.

"It's just as well," said the woman with the red coat as Neve took a seat next to her at the table.

"Oh, excuse my manners," said Detective Neve. "This is my partner, Nesta Divine. Nesta, meet Rosemary Thorn."

"It's nice to finally meet you properly," Nesta said.

"Nesta Divine!" Rosemary said. "What a wonderful name. Are you another kind of police officer, then?"

"Hah! No," said Nesta. "Not that kind of partner. We live together."

"Ohhh, sorry!" Rosemary said, blushing a little at her error.

"It's a common mistake." Nesta smiled warmly. She began pulling her long, wavy black hair into a tight bun as Rosemary went to clear a table.

As Nesta went to lower her hands, her fingers collided with the tea tray Rosemary was attempting to carry to the kitchen, knocking over a tea pot and sending a half-full cup of oolong careening over. The contents spilled all over Rosemary's apron.

"I'm so sorry!" Nesta said.

"It's no problem," said Rosemary, mopping up the spill with a spare napkin.

Nesta looked embarrassed. "Really, I'm mortified. How clumsy of me not to see you there."

Rosemary smiled at her reassuringly. "I'm usually the clumsy one, so it's actually a refreshing change. I'm not sure how I managed to last all day without spilling something on myself."

"I'm sure that's not true, you seem so comfortable in the kitchen," said Nesta.

"I do love food," Rosemary admitted gleefully.

Nesta and Neve both nodded enthusiastically. Rosemary was enjoying their company so much that she didn't really want to go back to cleaning up behind the counter, and fortunately there was a lull in customers, so she decided to take a break. It struck her that she missed hanging out with women roughly in her own age bracket.

"That's a lovely necklace you're wearing," said Nesta. "It looks special."

"Thanks," said Rosemary. "It's a family heirloom. I quite like it."

"I hear you're new in town," said Nesta. "And you've already been through so much! I bet that's a tough adjustment. It's a very welcoming town, but it takes a while to make new friends anywhere. Why don't you come over for dinner sometime?"

"That's nice of you to offer," said Rosemary. "Sure, why not? As long as I can bring my teenage daughter, she's sometimes grumpy but is often good company."

"Of course," said Nesta and Neve at the same time.

"Neve was saying she wanted to invite you both over anyway," Nesta continued. "She's always trying to get me to socialise more. I work over in Burkenswood or from home. It's a long commute when I do go into work, whereas when I'm at home I tend to be quite isolated, so I don't have too many friends here either."

Rosemary could empathise with that. She hadn't had many friends, either, until recently.

"Just let me know a day and time," said Rosemary. "We don't have a lot of other plans at the moment, so I can probably make it anytime."

"How about a Thursday later this month?" Neve suggested. "Nesta works from home Mondays and Thursdays, so she won't be too exhausted from the commute that day."

"Sounds good," said Rosemary. She thanked both women and then left to carry the dishes to the kitchen and do some more tidying up.

As Nesta and Neve got up to leave the tea shop, Rosemary felt happy about the possibility of making new friends. Detective Neve was brilliant and smart and exactly the kind of person Rosemary would want to have as a friend, and Nesta seemed lovely. She hoped Athena didn't mind her accepting a dinner invitation without discussing it first.

She felt another pang of guilt about Athena walking alone, but when she called the school on her break to check if her daughter had arrived safely, the receptionist only gave a little laugh and said, "Of course she did," in a slightly mocking way.

Rosemary put down the phone and sipped her tea, painfully aware that Athena would be mad at her for that little intrusion into her school life. She decided to stop being quite so over-protective of her daughter, but it was hard to let go, knowing that members of the Bloodstone Society might be lurking out there somewhere, no doubt biding their time before launching another attack.

Just then, the door burst open and a small bundle of energy bearing blonde ringlets raced in.

"Mum, Mum, Mum! Ooooh, look at the cakes! Look at all the cakes!"

"Yes, dear," said the harried looking woman, following tightly behind the child. "Which one do you want?"

"Just one?" The child sounded seriously disappointed.

"Yes, of course, Gretchen. You are always allowed just one cake. What do you think we'd do with more than one?"

"Eat them!"

"Just a minute, Prue," Marjie called from the kitchen.

"Nooo!" said little Gretchen.

"It's alright. I'll help," Rosemary said, getting up from the table. "I'm about finished my break anyway."

"It's fine," said Prue. Though she did seem slightly relieved when Rosemary insisted it was no trouble to serve the energetic young Gretchen who Rosemary guessed to be about four or five years old.

"Which will it be?" Rosemary asked in a tone that she hoped matched the child's enthusiasm.

"Chocolate!" said Gretchen. "No...strawberry! Oh please, can't I have both?"

"How about half a piece of chocolate and half a piece of strawberry?" Rosemary asked.

"Yes!" said Gretchen. "Then I really get two pieces."

"You don't mind?" Prue asked.

"Not at all," said Rosemary. "I'll take the other halves home to share with my daughter."

Gretchen smiled. "Can she come over to play?"

"I'm not sure," Rosemary asked. "She might be a little bit too grown up."

"Oh bother," said little Gretchen, causing Prue, Rosemary, and Marjie to all laugh.

"What's so funny?" Gretchen said suspiciously.

"You're just a bit clever," said Rosemary. "Aren't you?"

"I am," said Gretchen. "I know all my alphabets."

"How remarkable," said Rosemary. "Here you go."

She handed over the slices of cake to Prue, who helped Gretchen carry the plate safely to a table. As Rosemary watched them walk away she could have sworn she felt a tingling sensation in her necklace. It came with a feeling of foreboding, as if something big was about to happen.

CHAPTER

TEN

Athena arrived at school later in the morning for her second day. There were more students of various ages milling around the courtyard, though not very many overall. As the only school in the village, Myrtlewood Academy started with young children and went all the way up to the end of high school.

For the size of the old school grounds there didn't seem to be many pupils on the roll. When Athena had mentioned this to Miss Twigg the previous day, the tiny reptilian-like teacher had merely shrugged and muttered something about "ebbs and flows."

Athena pulled out her timetable. First up was Alchemy, which she guessed was supposed to be the equivalent of chemistry. The class was in the East Wing of the main building. She put her timetable back into her bag and tried to orient herself.

Her sense of direction wasn't quite as bad as Rosemary's, though it was a close second.

"Hey," a voice called out. Athena continued on, hoping it wasn't directed at her.

She was intending to avoid as many people as possible.

"Hey, new kid. Athena, is it?"

Athena couldn't very well avoid such a direct address. She turned to see the blue-haired girl from yesterday who she recalled was named Elise.

"Hello," Athena mumbled as the girl approached.

"I just wanted to apologise for yesterday."

"What for?" Athena asked.

"Well, mostly for Felix," Elise said. "He's out of control. He can be such a cad sometimes."

"Why are you apologising for him?" Athena asked.

Elise shrugged. "I'm just sorry if you had a hard time. It must be strange starting a new school, especially when it's as bizarre as Myrtlewood Academy."

"It is a bit strange," Athena admitted, allowing herself to smile. Elise seemed friendly, at least a lot friendlier than Beryl, who appeared to be glaring at the pair of them from across the courtyard.

"Don't mind her," Elise said, giving a little wave in Beryl's direction. "She's so stuck up, she's practically on the ceiling."

Athena laughed. "What's wrong with her?"

"Her family are all a bit like that, I think," said Elise. "They have high expectations and Beryl's always trying to impress them by being top of everything."

Athena smiled. "She's not going to have much competition from me. I've never been top of the class in my life."

"You never know," said Elise. "It's a different school and by the sounds of it you've got loads of magic."

Athena blushed. "I really don't. My mum does, even though she doesn't know how to use it."

Elise gave Athena a quizzical look. "You're not just human. Are you?"

"What?" Athena responded. "What do you mean?"

"You must have something else in you, something otherworldly."

"I don't know about any of this stuff," said Athena dismissively. "Weird things have been happening over the past couple of weeks and I have no idea what's going on, but I'm pretty sure I'm just a mostly-regular human."

"Well, I'm happy to be your friend," Elise said, holding out her hand to shake. "If you'd like."

Athena smiled, not detecting anything nasty in Elise's demeanour or indeed in her thoughts. She shook Elise's hand.

"Is this normally how you make friends?" Athena asked. "It seems awfully official."

Elise giggled. "I don't know. I just do whatever I think makes sense at the time, really." She held up her hands and waved them playfully in the air. "Come on, it's Alchemy class now, right?"

Athena smiled and walked with Elise towards the classroom. Maybe, just maybe, school wasn't going to be as bad as she'd previously thought.

Athena sat next to Elise in Alchemy class in rapt attention. The class turned out to be loads of fun. The teacher, Perran Graveolum, seemed young and energetic and liked to make bold statements about the nature of the universe and then back them up with magical experiments which he then got the class to replicate.

Today's activity was creating a tiny galaxy in a cup of tea. There was a particular spell involving what Mr Graveolum referred to as *cosmic dust* which one sprinkled into a pot of freshly brewed English breakfast tea and then recited a chant over.

Athena partnered with Elise and Sam and they had a lot of fun. First they blended the cosmic dust in the mortar and pestle. It made a funny clicking sound which was oddly satisfying. Then they brewed the tea, which Athena was an expert in by now given her family's excessive tea habits.

By the time they'd turned the teapot three times and poured the tea out into the glass teacup, theirs was the sparkliest galaxy.

"Perfect grade," Mr Graveolum said. "A microcosm of the macro-cosm." He held up his hands. "I present you a prime example of how we're all both very, very big and excessively small at the same time." He crowed with laughter.

Beryl glared at the three of them. In comparison, her galaxy hardly sparkled at all. In fact, it looked simply as if she'd dropped a thimble of milk into a weak cup of tea.

"She's not going to be happy about this," Sam said quietly.

"Don't worry about her," said Elise. "She can't be the best at everything all the time. Nobody is."

"Well, Beryl is, most of the time," said Sam. "She doesn't like competition."

"She's gonna have to learn to live with it," said Athena. "The three of us combined are obviously fabulous at magic."

Elise laughed. "I told you, you're powerful."

"It's the magic of teamwork," Athena said sarcastically.

Sam giggled.

"What's so funny?" Beryl asked, walking towards them with a cold expression.

"We were just talking about teamwork." Elise flashed Beryl a sassy smile. "And how wonderful it is to work with people with such a sense of camaraderie. Wouldn't you agree?"

"Absolutely," said Mr Graveolum. "Sensational. I'm so pleased you're getting on board with a bit of collective spirit."

Beryl blanched and returned to her own desk. She'd refused to work with any of the other students, saying they'd only ruin her experiment.

"What are you doing for lunch?" Elise asked.

Athena shrugged. "Maybe the library...reading?"

"Nonsense, come and hang out with us," said Elise. She gently pulled Athena by the wrist of her cardigan as they walked out of the class and towards the far corner of the courtyard.

Felix and another boy were already sitting there.

"Not them, really?" Athena whispered.

"Felix isn't that bad when you get used to him, and Deron is lovely," Elise insisted.

Athena eyed the taller dark-haired boy sitting next to Felix. He was built like a thug, but he did have a warm, friendly smile on his face.

"But if you really don't want to we could sit somewhere else," Elise continued.

"It's fine," Athena said and followed Elise and Sam over to the corner of the courtyard.

"New girl!" said Felix. "Come to hang with the cool kids?"

"I think you should apologise to her actually," said Elise.

"What for?" Felix lowered his eyebrows.

"For subjecting her to your idiocy,"

"Hey," said Felix, scowling and then grinning. "Oh fine. I apologise for my immense wit and wisdom, my sparkling personality, my strong character, and my excellent tenacity."

"Felix, what kind of apology was that?" Deron asked.

"It's fine. You don't owe me any kind of apology," said Athena.

"See, I am perfect." Felix raised his arms in triumph.

Athena sighed and sat down next to Elise. She pulled out the lunch she'd brought from home. It was a sandwich made with bacon and eggs.

"That looks good," said Sam. "I bet it doesn't to Elise though. She can't eat animal products."

"Are you a vegetarian or a vegan or something?" Athena asked.

"No, it's more like an allergy," Elise said.

"Elise is a dirty rotten pixie," Felix teased, scrunching up a piece of paper bag and throwing it at the blue-haired girl.

"I'm nothing like a pixie," said Elise.

"Close enough," Felix replied. He opened his own lunch box and began scoffing food. Athena watched in astonishment as he gobbled down several large pork pies.

"He always eats like that," said Elise.

"Not a pixie," said Felix, returning to the subject after abruptly finishing his enormous lunch. "That's right you're a water nymph or something."

"I told you," said Elise. "My mother is a naiad. That is all."

"A what?" Athena asked.

"Similar to a water nymph...I guess," Elise conceded.

"Nympho," said Felix, giggling.

"Shut up." Elise glared at him. "Nymphs and Naiads are nature spirits, a bit like faeries. Mum comes from the family that creates rainbows. That's what's wrong with my hair."

"Your hair's cool," Athena said. "And that's amazing. I don't know about anything like that. I have so much to learn."

"Don't worry," said Felix. "I'll show you all there is to know about being magical."

He put down his lunch box and stood up. Immediately, red fur started sprouting from his face.

Athena gasped in horror as the beard spread to his hands and he shrunk down to the ground, transforming into a large fox and running around in circles in the courtyard.

"He loves to surprise people with that trick," Sam said.

Felix turned back to his human form. "It's not a trick," he said.

"You're a shapeshifter?" Athena asked.

"So you do know about my kind?" Felix seemed disappointed that Athena wasn't impressed or amazed.

"We did have an encounter with a particularly bad seed up at the house..." Athena said.

"We heard something about that," said Elise. "What really happened?"

"It's a long story," said Athena. "Too long for a lunch break."

She turned back to Felix. "I was wondering about something. What happens to your clothes when you change forms?"

"You mean, why don't I lose my clothes and end up naked somewhere?" He winked at her. "I guess it's part of the magic. It kind of absorbs anything I'm wearing and then spits it out again when I change back. It's quite handy really, so I don't get caught out butt naked in public."

"That's really just as well," Athena said, laughing.

"Of course. I wouldn't want to blind everyone with my outrageous beauty," said Felix.

The bell rang and they made their way to Folklore and History. Athena walked down the passageway lined with eclectic paintings and old black and white photographs. Her eyes came to rest on a familiar face.

"No way," she said, approaching.

"Someone you know?" Elise asked.

Athena nodded. She couldn't tear her eyes away from the face. It was Finnigan, his dark hair falling across his forehead in the way it always did, his eyes sparkling.

"An old family member?" Sam asked.

"No, a friend, but I'm surprised to see him here. He goes to another school."

"It can't be. That was one of the students who disappeared over eighty years ago," said Sam.

"What?"

Sam pointed to a plaque sitting next to a row of portraits.

In commemoration of our cherished pupils, Eloise Staggart, Ferin Soot, and Finnigan Marsh, who went missing on the 21st of March 1938.

Chills ran down Athena's spine and she glanced back to the photograph of Finnigan.

"Maybe your friend is a relative?" Sam suggested.

Athena shrugged. "Maybe," she said. Though, examining the portrait even closer only made her surer that it was really him. She sighed.

Finnigan, you have some explaining to do.

CHAPTER
ELEVEN

By the time Rosemary finally sat down for a bite of lunch, she was famished. Her first day working at the tea shop had been incredibly busy, and it wasn't over yet.

The bell above the door tingled as she took the first bite of the beef and mustard roll that Marjie had made her especially. She looked up to see Ferg enter the shop wearing a bright orange jumpsuit that somehow suited his wire-rimmed spectacles.

Orange must be his colour for Tuesday, Rosemary thought, recalling Ferg's odd insistence on wearing set colours for each day of the week.

"Ah! Rosemary," he said. "Just the person I wanted to see."

Rosemary looked up at him, perplexed, then narrowed her eyes. "Really? Why?"

"I'm looking for volunteers to help organise Ostara."

"Organise what?"

"The Spring Equinox, of course," said Ferg. "Traditionally it was called Ostara, the celebration of the Goddess, Eostre. You may be more familiar with the term 'Easter'," he said, making the double quotation marks with his fingers in the air.

"Easter, as in when Jesus died?"

Ferg chuckled in surprise. "What do you think he died from? Eating chocolate eggs...or did he lay chocolate eggs? That's a trick question, by the way."

"You're saying that chocolate eggs are an ancient pre-Christian religious thing? Because I don't think cocoa was even on this continent until the end of the Middle ages," Rosemary said.

"No, traditionally they were proper chicken eggs, but painted."

"I'm no good at crafts," said Rosemary. "Just ask Athena. I'm sure I'd sooner break the eggs than paint them."

"Children paint the eggs, Rosemary," said Ferg in a very serious tone. "I need your help with the ritual. I reasoned that since you're new in town it would be the perfect opportunity to get to know people and dive into something exciting."

"Oh," Rosemary said. "But didn't we just have the spring festival?"

"We had Imbolc," said Ferg. "That's the festival to signal the end of winter. Next is the Spring Equinox and after that there's Beltane, which is more about the beginning of summer."

"Why so many festivals?"

"Because they are magnificent," said Ferg simply.

"Umm, thank you for thinking of me," Rosemary said. "But I've got rather a lot on my plate at the moment with starting a new job here and supporting Athena with her new school. I don't think I can take on anything else right now."

"Nonsense!" said Ferg. "You'll be perfect. There's not all that much to do – if you know how to delegate, that is. Here."

He held out a small booklet entitled: *How to Celebrate the Spring Equinox*, by A. C. Twigg.

"Ferg," said Rosemary. "I said no."

"Oh," said Ferg, hanging his head. He looked dreadfully disappointed. "I see."

"Sorry," Rosemary said. "I might be able to help a little bit, but I'm not signing up for any more responsibility just yet."

Ferg looked up at her, an innocent expression on his face. "What is it about responsibility that scares you?"

Rosemary was floored. She didn't know how to respond. She only knew that his words had cut straight to the heart of her current struggle regarding what to do with her life and that her emerald pendant had started humming.

"That's a lovely necklace," Ferg said after a while.

"Thank you," Rosemary replied, attempting to return to her lunch. She took a big bite of her roll, hoping it would help to end the rather awkward conversation.

"How about I'll just leave the book here, and you can think about it?" Ferg said. "Have a read and let me know if you change your mind."

Rosemary was still chewing her food and didn't get a chance to respond before Ferg skipped away.

She sighed and picked up the booklet. At least it would give her something to focus on while she ate to distract her from other more serious worries.

The equinoxes, when the night and day are equal, are about finding balance. They are the times of year when the veil between the worlds is the thinnest, it read.

"What have you got there?" Marjie asked, coming over to the table, her white apron covered in chocolate stains from the hundreds of cupcakes she'd been icing – and then magically duplicating – for a very large wedding party. "Oh, it's Aggie's wee booklet."

"It is?" Rosemary asked.

"Yes, Agatha Twigg. You know – she gate-crashed your dinner party."

"I didn't know she was a writer."

"Actually, Aggie is a very famous historian," Marjie said. "She knows all about Myrtlewood and magical histories around here. Has Ferg roped you into helping with the equinox, then?"

Rosemary smiled. "Ferg is trying his best, but I said no."

"Oh bless!" said Marjie. "Good on you for having boundaries. I know he can be a demanding chap."

"So demanding that he left this book here so I could have a read and think it over," said Rosemary.

Just then, the bell sounded above the door and the mayor walked in, looking ruffled. Even his hair was somewhat scruffier than usual and his customary black and purple cape looked like it had been dragged through a bush backwards.

"The usual, please, Marjie," he said, sitting down at a table by the window and glancing around suspiciously.

"Are you alright there?" Marjie called as she bustled back to the kitchen.

"Fine, fine," Mr June said. "Why wouldn't I be?"

Marjie shot Rosemary a puzzled look from the kitchen. "I'll make your tea," she called out. "Rosemary, can you get Mr June a large piece of carrot cake with extra cream on the side?"

"Sure," said Rosemary. She had finished her lunch and was ready to get back to work anyway.

"Oh, you're properly working here now?" Mr June asked, taking in Rosemary's apron and raising an eyebrow.

"I'm helping Marjie out, since it's her busy season," Rosemary said. "I just started today."

"Interesting." Mr June stroked his goatee. He turned his attention to a small notebook which he fished out of his pocket and began writing in, occasionally glancing around to check if anyone was watching.

Rosemary served the carrot cake and carried it over to the table. As she placed it down in front of the mayor, he glanced up and his eyes locked on her necklace.

"That!" he said, pointing at the emerald pendant that hung from Rosemary's neck. "Where did you get that?"

Rosemary was taken aback. The pendant had drawn a lot of attention, usually from people who commented on how nice it was, but there was an entirely different tone in Mr June's voice that she couldn't quite place. Was it anger or fear?

"My grandmother gave it to me," Rosemary said, clutching the pendant reflexively.

"She did, did she?"

"Yes."

"I'll have you know that pendant is property of the town of Myrtle-wood and belongs in the museum!"

"Err...well, it was in my house, and Granny said it was hers."

Mr June gave her a dubious look. "How much do you want for it?" he muttered, lowering his voice.

"I...I don't want anything for it," Rosemary said. "It's a family heirloom. Granny said it belonged to my great, great, great, great grandmother or something. Maybe you're thinking of a different emerald necklace?"

He narrowed his eyes at her. "There is no other like it. Come on. Five thousand quid. I'll write you a cheque right now."

Rosemary was flummoxed. She'd assumed the pendant was worth money, being old and made of gold and emerald, but she'd never thought of selling it. And even though it might be tempting to have a bit of extra cash, Mr June's reaction to seeing the family heirloom was so bizarre. His whole manner seemed off. She simply couldn't take the offer seriously.

"Here you are," Marjie said, bringing the tea over to Mr June's table. She caught Rosemary's eye and added, "Dear, can you come out the back and help me with something?"

Rosemary gladly followed Marjie back to the kitchen. "What was all that about?" she asked.

"Something is not right with him today," Marjie said.

"You're telling me!" said Rosemary. "He seems to be so obsessed with my necklace. I'm actually worried he's about to try to fight me for it."

Marjie sighed. "It happens from time to time."

"What happens?" Rosemary asked. "The mayor picks fights over necklaces?"

"He just goes a bit...well, a bit strange. My theory is that has an obsession with eternal youth, you see. He's always off to see one quack doctor or another, filling himself with potions. He's even tried to get *turned*."

"Turned?" Rosemary asked.

"Into a vampire," Marjie explained in a whisper. "Only it's not so common, these days. Vampires don't tend to like the idea that they might crowd out the world too much, living so long and all. They're very selective about who they'll turn. It's usually only a desperate act of love. You know, if they can't live without someone."

"Oh," Rosemary said, taken aback. "I'd never thought of that. It must be lonely, outliving almost everyone else."

She wondered about Perseus Burk and how lonely he might have been over the decades or centuries...however old he really was.

"Anyway," Marjie continued. "The potions make him a bit wild, sometimes. And he's always wanting to collect special magical talismans, like your necklace."

"He said it's property of the town," Rosemary said.

"Oh, pay him no mind," said Marjie. "He's a babbling lunatic when he's like this."

"Isn't that offensive, to call someone a lunatic?" Rosemary asked.

"Not around here, it's not," said Marjie. "The moon does things to people. Especially shifters. We all know it."

There was a lot more Rosemary wanted to ask about shifters and vampires and all sorts of other magical things, but Marjie looked busy wrestling an enormous piping bag over a large chocolate wedding cake. She glanced back out to the main part of the shop to see Mr June walking out.

Rosemary decided to get on with her work. The mayor had hardly touched his carrot cake, but he'd left no sign of coming back either. She tucked it behind the counter, just in case, and wiped down his table.

The bell sounded again. Rosemary looked up, expecting to see Mr June back to re-claim his cake. She was startled when Athena bounded in instead.

"Oh no!" Rosemary said. "What's the time? Did I forget to pick you up again?"

"Relax, Mum," said Athena. "You're fine. They just let us out early from school."

Rosemary breathed a sigh of relief, but as she inhaled again potential dangers flooded her mind. "You should've called me to come and get you."

"Don't be silly," said Athena. "It's hardly a ten minute walk into town, and the weather is nice today."

"The weather might be nice, but I spoke to Detective Neve earlier. They still don't know what's happened to the Bloodstone Society members. They could be back at any moment."

"Mum, I can't live my life in fear just because of some stupid secret society. Anyway, it's bright daylight. At least the vampires won't be around to get me."

Rosemary was silent for a moment looking at the floor, considering this, then she glanced up at her daughter to see her smile.

"You're in a good mood," Rosemary said. "I take it today went better than yesterday?"

"It did!" Athena said.

"Marvellous!" said Rosemary. "How about a piece of cake, to celebrate?"

Athena's eyes scoured over the cabinet. "I want that chocolate orange one,"

"Blast," said Rosemary. "There's only one piece left and I was hoping to have that myself."

Athena smiled. "Get two forks, then. We can share it."

"Are you sure?"

"I don't need the whole piece by myself," said Athena, warmly. "And if I'm still hungry afterwards I could always have that strawberry torte. I hope Marjie doesn't mind us tucking into her cake cabinet, though."

"Tuck away!" Marjie called out from the kitchen. "It all needs to be eaten."

Rosemary made a pot of Earl Grey tea and carried it to their usual table, along with the last slice of chocolate orange cake and two forks. She also brought over the two half slices of cake left from little Gretchen's earlier appearance, for good measure.

Though the danger was still tugging at Rosemary's mind, she couldn't help but smile at Athena's especially good mood. While she waited for the tea to brew she took a little bite of the chocolate orange cake.

"Ooh...this is delicious," she said, closing her eyes to savour the rich, tangy aromatic flavour.

"See," said Athena.

"See what?" Rosemary asked.

"Whatever you decide next, it has to be focussed around food. You *love* food – especially chocolate."

Rosemary took another bite of cake and sighed in delight. "Maybe you're right," she said. *I should put that cheffing training to good use, one way or another.*

She closed her eyes to better experience the taste and texture of the wonderful cake. As she did, an image popped into her mind: a little chocolate shop with a red-and-white-striped awning, its front window display filled with fabulous confectionary, including an enormous mermaid made of chocolate.

Rosemary pictured shelves lined with all kinds of hand-made chocolate bars of different varieties, a cabinet of speciality truffles, and a hot-chocolate bar where she could whip up her favourite indulgent recipes.

As her fantasy ran away with her she imagined that she could refine her magic for delicious purposes – that each confection she invented could have a distinct property. She could serve customers a pick-me-up orange bergamot cream if they came in feeling down, a spiced dark chocolate truffle for a little boost of energy, or a chocolate dipped Turkish delight if they needed something soothing and heart-warming. The possibilities were endless.

"Earth to Mum," Athena said, jolting Rosemary from her daydreams.

"Sorry," Rosemary said, "I was just imagining... Well, it was nothing really."

Rosemary was suddenly embarrassed by everything she'd just dreamed up. It was impractical, of course. She had no control of her magic, and though she could make a fine hot chocolate and was a dab hand at basic truffles, she had no mastery over proper chocolate making.

"It can't have been nothing," Athena said, her voice lilting. "Not with that smile you had on your face. Were you thinking about that handsome vampire?!"

"Shhh," Rosemary said. "And no, I absolutely was not. If you must know I was just indulging in a little daydream about what it would be like to have my own chocolate shop."

"That's perfect!" Athena said, her tone both excited and deadly serious. "You have to do it."

"Don't be ridiculous," said Rosemary. "I'm no chocolatier."

Athena beamed at her. "You make the best hot chocolates. I'm sure you'll get the hang of the other stuff. How hard can it possibly be?"

"Quite tricky, I think," said Rosemary, taking a sip of tea. "It's an artform – an entire culinary specialty!"

"So learn," said Athena. "Or simply buy in all the things from other chocolate makers that you don't know how to make yourself."

"That would defeat the purpose a bit. In my fantasy I was making chocolate with magical properties."

"Even better." Athena took another bite of cake before adding, "you'll figure it out."

"Figure what out?" Marjie said, coming out from the kitchen, covered in chocolate stains.

"Oh, nothing," said Rosemary, not wanting Marjie to worry about the possibility of an imaginary chocolate shop as competition.

"It's not nothing, actually," Athena said.

Rosemary tried to kick her gently under the table to get her to be quiet, but Athena simply moved her legs and continued.

"Mum has figured out her true vocation...as a magical chocolatier!"

"Marvellous!" said Marjie. "That's perfect, that is! When will you get started?"

"Hold on," said Rosemary, though she couldn't help smiling at Marjie's enthusiastic support. "I don't even know what I'm doing yet. Any potential shop would be a long way off."

"Well, you just tell me what you need, dear," said Marjie. "And I'll do whatever I can to help."

Athena grinned at Rosemary from across the table as they both took another big bite of the delicious cake in front of them. Rosemary closed her eyes again and allowed herself to dream just a little more about the possibilities her future might hold – a little chocolate shop where the flavours make people feel things – feel better.

That's my kind of magic.

CHAPTER

TWELVE

Rosemary arrived home, tired but happy, with Athena in tow. Work was more fun than she'd anticipated. The teashop was a great way to meet people and keep her finger on the pulse of the town. She even felt safer, knowing that whatever nefarious things the members of the Bloodstone Society might be up to, she was sure to hear about them through the gossip that happened all around her during an ordinary day.

"I'll make tea," Athena said as soon as they got in. Her good mood seemed to be continuing. "What's for dinner?"

"I thought I'd be too tired to cook after a long day. So Marjie gave me a couple of beef pies and some coleslaw."

"Sounds good," said Athena, smiling.

Despite Athena's recent positivity, Rosemary had a distinct feeling her teen was hiding something again.

Athena had been silent on the drive home and Rosemary wondered if whatever was occupying her was just an ordinary teen issue, like a crush, or whether it was more magical in nature. Whatever it was, Rosemary hoped it wasn't dangerous. They'd already had more than enough danger in their lives recently.

"Aren't you going to tell me about school today?" Rosemary asked. "What happened that significantly lifted your spirits?"

"Do I have to tell you every little detail of my life?" Athena asked, her voice teasing.

"No, just the highlights and lowlights," Rosemary replied. "And the bloopers reel, please. I need some light entertainment."

"Actually, it's been surprisingly less embarrassing than I'd feared," said Athena. "And...most of the other students were nice to me. I don't want to jinx it but I might even be making new friends."

"That's wonderful, love," said Rosemary. "Tell me about them."

"Oh fine. If you must know," said Athena. "Sam is quite shy, and really cool! They are non-binary, you know? And they have a nose ring. They come from a less magical family than lots of the other students. Sam says their parents practice folk magic – like home remedies and little charms and things, but nothing powerful. It kind of makes me feel less alone because I don't seem to have any kind of magic aside from the annoying head radio. Lots of the other students are amazing with magic. Elise is really talented – and her hair changes colour with her mood!"

"Amazing," said Rosemary.

"I know. I'm quite jealous of that," said Athena. "She's some kind of Naiad, like in a fairy tale. She's really nice, though. She invited me to sit with her friends at lunch, and it was pretty good actually, even though Felix was there."

"What's wrong with Felix?"

"I guess he's like the class clown, really over-the-top and chaotic. He likes to play tricks on the teachers and he's so full of himself it's nauseating."

"Sounds like a real charmer," Rosemary said, rolling her eyes. "I know the type."

"Elise says he's not that bad when you get to know him. But guess what he did at lunch?"

"What?" Rosemary asked tentatively.

"He turned into a fox!"

"No way!"

"Yes. One minute he was standing there and the next, he just...was a fox!"

"So he's a shapeshifter, like that crow guy?" Rosemary asked.

"I guess so," said Athena.

"Maybe keep your distance from him, then."

"Mum, just because we met one dodgy shifter it doesn't mean they're all like that. You told me vampires aren't all bad. Like Burk – you trust him, right?"

"I suppose I do, to an extent," said Rosemary.

"Or is it just that you *like* him?"

"Athena! No, that's not it. He's like a thousand years old, and plus, he's a lawyer. That's uncomfortably similar to being an estate agent, don't you think?"

"Excuses, excuses. I know you like him," Athena said, batting her eyelashes.

"Even if I did like him, I don't date and I don't intend on starting any time soon. Besides, if I did date, then Liam has already asked me out and he's much closer to my age, and more...normal. Given how bizarre my life has become, I think I'd hypothetically be looking for a nice *normal* relationship."

"Mum, you can't use me as an excuse not to date much longer. You'll become one of those old people with tons of cats and a house full of old junk."

"That's fine by me," said Rosemary, taking a seat at the kitchen table. "I already have *one* cat. That's progress!"

"Seriously," Athena continued, as she rinsed out the tea pot and began to fill it with fresh leaves. "I'm practically an adult now and I don't care if you see people."

"I'm surprised you'd say such a thing when you know about my terrible taste in men. Anyway – we were talking about *you* and *your* social life."

Athena carried the tea pot to the table along with their favourite cups. "It's actually nice to think I might *have* a social life for a change."

"What about Finnigan?" Rosemary asked carefully. "Is he no longer in the picture? I thought you were going to ask him about the head voices and try to find out more?"

"He's...well, he's away, I think. But I'll try again tonight. And I guess I should ask him what he knows about Dad, too, even though it might not be a totally terrible thing if he's magically disappeared."

"That's right, Dain!" said Rosemary, as Athena passed her a cup of freshly brewed Earl Grey. "How did I forget about him again!? It's like there's a mysterious hole in my brain when it comes to him. Granny said he's disappeared...and I just forgot all about it!"

"You're not exactly known for your stellar memory."

"Maybe not, but that is the kind of serious thing I would normally remember and worry about at every opportunity, and it just kind of fell out of my head. It's a bit like the car vanishing. How did I forget about that? It must be something magical."

"It could be," said Athena, shrugging. She took the last sip of her tea and her tummy grumbled. "Can we have dinner already?"

"Of course," said Rosemary. "But I'm still worried about Dain and the possibility that my memory is being magically interfered with...again! I think I should tell Detective Neve."

"Alright, fine," said Athena. "You call the cops, I'll get dinner heated."

Rosemary went upstairs. She intended to make the phone call straight away but, upon realising how filthy she was after a day in the kitchen, she decided to shower first.

She turned on the shower faucet to heat up while she undressed and took off the emerald pendant, placing it on the bench by the bathroom sink. Then she stepped into the shower and let the warm water run over her, easing away the worries of the day and cleaning her mind just as she cleaned her body.

A LOUD CLANGING noise startled Rosemary from her shower trance. She turned off the faucet and immediately smelled smoke.

"Athena!" she called out, wrapping herself in a towel and racing downstairs.

A large plume of smoke bulged out from the oven. Athena was racing around, opening the windows.

"I burned dinner!" she cried. "The oven must be magically fast. I thought it would take ages to heat them. Sorry!"

"It's alright," Rosemary said, extracting a tray containing two very burnt pies from the oven and throwing them out through the open front door so that they landed, gracelessly, in an overgrown flowerbed. "Have a look in the fridge and see what's there. We can always just have beans on toast again if all else fails."

Athena went to the fridge, only to find it completely bare. "What?" she said. "It's almost always full of food. How is this possible?"

"She moves in mysterious ways," said Rosemary, patting the house kindly.

"Mum!"

"What? The last thing we need is to lose favour with our sentient abode. Check the pantry."

"The only thing in here is Jaffa cakes and the packet of crisps I made you buy the other day," said Athena. "Do you think she's glitching or something?"

They looked around at the house. Everything else seemed to be in order.

Rosemary shrugged. "Dinner at the pub, then?"

"Sounds good," said Athena. "But you'd better get changed first."

"Oh...yes." Rosemary clutched her towel. She ran back upstairs to her bedroom and threw on the first clean items of clothing she could find. Not only was she starving at this point, but she didn't want Athena getting hangry because that only ever ended in tears.

She was on her way back downstairs when she heard voices, which only made her rush faster, and that, in turn, meant that she tripped on the stairs and landed painfully on her knees.

"Gah!" Rosemary cried.

"Mum, what's wrong?" Athena asked, running towards the staircase.

"I'm fine." Rosemary groaned as she pushed herself up. "Just a little accident. I heard voices. Who's here?"

"It's only me," said Sherry, coming over to help Rosemary as she hobbled down the last few stairs. "I thought you two might need a break from cooking, so I brought over some of my famous Guinness stew and rye bread. Liam's minding the pub tonight because it's my night off."

"How sweet of you," said Rosemary, smiling. "You actually have no idea how well-timed this is."

"That's right," said Athena. "I just managed to burn our dinner and we were on our way to the pub anyway."

"Well, let me bring the pub to you!" said Sherry. "Though I didn't bring any drinks with me or anything."

"We'll supply the wine!" Rosemary eyed the big containers of delicious smelling food Sherry was carrying. "Won't you join us for dinner?"

"That would be lovely," said Sherry. "I brought more than enough to go around and it saves me having to dine alone at home with only the cat for company."

As they sat down for dinner, Rosemary had the disconcerting feeling that she'd forgotten something important, but she couldn't remember what it was. She made a mental note to ask Athena about it later, but as she chatted with Sherry she managed to forget that too.

Sherry was full of the best kind of town gossip – not malicious, but fun and interesting news and titbits about the goings on that she'd picked up by osmosis just from working at the pub.

They learned about rumours that Neve was about to propose to Nesta – or was it the other way round?

"How exciting!" Rosemary said. "I met Nesta today and she's great. They both seem so good together."

"They do make a great pair," said Sherry. "Not all is well in town, though. Mr June is having issues!"

"He was in at the tea shop today and behaved very strangely," said Rosemary. "Marjie said he's on a quest for immortality."

"There was a rumour floating around that he's also being investigated for embezzlement, something to do with his tax return," said Sherry.

"What? Oh dear, I didn't know Myrtlewood had to follow the same laws as everyone else in the country," said Rosemary. "It feels like such a cloistered little bubble here."

"Of course we do," said Sherry. "We've all got to pay our taxes and do our bit. Anyway, Mr June is a bit of a worry. No one else wants to be mayor, but no one particularly wants him to be, either."

"He certainly is an odd character," said Rosemary. "Though there are plenty of them around. Ferg, for instance. Has he always been so strange?"

"Of course he has," said Sherry.

"Is he married or anything?" Rosemary asked. "I can't picture it."

"Why. Are you interested?" Sherry asked.

Rosemary laughed. "No. It's not that he's bad looking or even unkind. It's just he's…"

"He's Ferg," said Sherry. "The whole town actually assumes he's not the romantic sort. He doesn't seem to have relationships at all."

"He's probably asexual or aromantic," said Athena. "There's a whole spectrum of that kind of thing. You shouldn't judge."

Rosemary smiled. "I suppose I should stop being so nosey."

"You're so knowledgeable!" Sherry said to Athena. "Tell me, how is school going?"

"It's actually not too bad," said Athena. "Surprisingly. Though I don't understand much about magic and that's the entire curriculum."

"I'm glad it's not too bad, then!" said Sherry. "Who's in your class?"

"I don't know all the names yet," said Athena. "There's a kid called Sam."

"Oh yes, little Sammy Jenkins," said Sherry.

"And there's Elise – with the blue hair."

"Elise Thornton?" Sherry asked. "I didn't realise she went to school here."

"What do you mean?" Athena asked.

"Oh, you know, her mother's a Naiad. They often have different ways of doing things. Like other fae folk, they aren't from this realm, originally."

Athena and Rosemary looked at each other.

"No, we don't really know," said Rosemary.

"Are you saying there's another...world?" Athena asked.

"Sort of," said Sherry. "It's here, but not here. Kind of like the layers of a cake. All the layers are on top of each-other and happening simultaneously, but they're also at different vibrations of energy or something, so we don't see those that are beyond the veil unless they come through into the physical plane."

"That's fascinating," said Athena.

"It is," said Rosemary. Hearing Sherry speak of different planes of existence was reminding her of something that felt urgent and important but she couldn't remember what it was. The effect was infinitely frustrating.

"Myrtlewood is located across ley lines," said Sherry. "That's why there's so much magical energy here and why otherfolk flock to these parts."

"Otherfolk?" Athena asked.

"Yes," said Sherry. "People like us. People who don't fit in, in the mundane world."

"Oh," said Rosemary with a sense of recognition. "I didn't realise that's how I'd always felt. No matter where we lived, I couldn't make things work. We never seemed to fit in."

"I never made any proper friends," said Athena. "Even in Stratham where I had a few friendships – none of them were really close."

"Well, you're here now," said Sherry. "And this is where you belong."

Rosemary felt her frustrations ease at Sherry's words. It was nice to finally belong somewhere.

"I've been meaning to ask you," Rosemary said. "What do you think has happened to the other members of the Bloodstone Society? There seemed to be so many of them when they attacked us, but they were all wearing dark hoods. I wish we knew who they are. Do you have any ideas?"

Sherry exhaled slowly. "There are lots of rumours about that. But it's hard to tell what to believe. It seems like every second punter at the pub has said something or another – usually the accusations are baseless. They're just trying to dob in someone they don't like."

"How do you know they're baseless?" Athena asked.

"Well, if I believed every rumour I heard, just about the whole town would be a member of that society and up to no good."

Rosemary sighed.

"If it's any consolation, the rumours are pretty consistent on one thing," said Sherry. "Everyone is saying that now the Bloodstone power has dispersed, all the members are free. Apparently, many of them are glad to be free of it and have gone off to do their own thing now that they aren't under Geneviève's thumb anymore."

"That is good news," said Rosemary.

"Let's hope none of them bother coming after us, then," Athena added.

"You shouldn't totally let your guard down," Sherry said. "But remember, your family power is massive compared to theirs right now. You're like a lion and they're an itsy bitsy spider."

"That would be a great analogy if you'd used an ant or something instead of a spider," said Rosemary. "I don't fancy any venomous bites, metaphoric or otherwise."

"That's what I mean by keeping your guard," said Sherry. "You're much more powerful, but there are still risks."

"It's good to know that their power is so depleted though," said Rosemary.

Sherry smiled and took a big gulp of her wine, then excused herself to use the bathroom.

"See, there's nothing to worry about," said Athena once Sherry had left the table. "The Bloodstones have all gone off to do their own thing. I can walk to school. I'm safe even with no real magic."

"You have magic," Rosemary said. "Remember, you made those charms? They were powerful – one took care of the creepy crow man."

"Anyone can follow a recipe," said Athena.

"Not everyone can," Rosemary reminded her. "You know I'm no good with instructions. Besides, if a non-magical person followed those recipes I doubt they'd get anywhere near that kind of result. Actually – that's an idea. Mix up some more charms. I'll feel a lot better about letting you go off to school with those in your pockets."

"Fine," said Athena. "As long as you write me a note to explain my magical pocket arsenal."

"Done," Rosemary replied. She gave her daughter a quizzical look. Something was not right. "Wait. What is it you're not telling me?"

"I don't know what you're talking about," said Athena, taking a bite of food.

"Don't lie," said Rosemary. "Want to swap powers so I can read your mind?"

"I gladly would if I could," said Athena. "It's a crappy power." Then she narrowed her eyes at her mother. "Although I don't want even more invasions into my privacy!"

"Am I interrupting something?" Sherry asked.

Rosemary and Athena both looked to where Sherry was entering the room. "No!" they said simultaneously.

"I best be going, anyway," said Sherry. "Thank you both for a lovely evening."

Rosemary and Athena bid Sherry a good night and started cleaning up.

"You know what's funny?" Athena said, standing at the open fridge, ready to put the leftovers in.

"What?" Rosemary carried a pile of plates in from the dining room.

"The fridge is fully stocked again," said Athena. "And the pantry is too."

"That is very odd," said Rosemary. "I'll have to ask Granny about that the next time I see her."

Athena yawned.

"You go to bed, love," said Rosemary. "I'll finish the washing up."

"Okay, good night," Athena said and gave her mother a quick hug.

Rosemary watched her teen disappearing upstairs and frowned.

Her spidey-sense was tingling. There was definitely something else going on with Athena, but for now, it remained a mystery.

CHAPTER
THIRTEEN

F*innigan,*
Athena called out in her mind. She was standing on the balcony outside her room which the house had mercifully kept intact.

Finnigan! She tried to call louder. He said he would come tonight.

She shivered into the night, wondering if she should go back inside to wait. Surely, even if he could hear her, it would take him quite a while to get here. She might as well be wrapped up in her warm bed, napping, since she was actually feeling quite tired.

She turned towards the house only to jump at the sight of a shadowy figure standing right behind her.

It was all Athena could do not to scream as arms reached out for her, resting on her shoulders, reassuring her. She looked up into a familiar face.

"You called?" Finnigan asked.

"You!" she said in a shrill whisper. "You scared me!"

"My apologies," he replied. "I came as quickly as I could."

"You were very quick," Athena admitted. "Almost as if you were waiting out here for me to summon you." She gave him a suspicious look.

"I promise you, I was not," said Finnigan with a cheeky grin.

"So you used magic, then?"

"Something like that."

Finnigan raised his arms for a hug.

Athena allowed herself to lean into him – allowed his arms to wrap around her. He smelled like peppermint and fennel and jasmine all mixed together. Sweet and spicy and fresh. She savoured the hug, even though she wasn't sure she should.

If Finnigan is like my father, how can I possibly trust him?

"I can assure you, I'm nothing like your father," he said.

"Don't poke around in my head," said Athena. "Anyway, how do you know my father?"

"I don't, personally," said Finnigan. "But I've heard of him. Is that why you called me? To ask about your father?"

He took a step back, a guarded look crossing his face.

"Not at all," said Athena dismissively. She walked to the edge of the balcony and leaned on the railing, looking out to sea. "I don't want to talk about him at all, unless you can tell me how he disappeared. But what I really want to ask about is the telepathy. I need to learn how to use it... And there's something else."

"What is it?" Finnigan asked.

"I'm going to school at Myrtlewood Academy, and there's a picture on the wall. An old-fashioned picture which was from the 1930s. The boy looks exactly like you. The plaque said he went missing."

Athena had been thinking about this all evening. She'd been sure the photo was of Finnigan when she was looking at it, but since then she'd had second thoughts.

"Was it...a relative maybe?" she asked.

"No. Not exactly," said Finnigan.

"Then what...?" Athena asked.

"It's a long story."

"Don't tell me. You're a changeling or something?"

Finnigan's expression darkened, as did his tone. "No. Who told you that?"

"Sorry," said Athena. "I don't mean to offend you. I don't understand any of this stuff. You're implying that changelings do exist, whatever they are? People have mentioned fairies around here, but I still can't quite believe..."

Finnigan laughed. "I assure you that I'm no changeling."

"Then what?"

"You'll find out," he said with a wink.

"But it doesn't make sense. People must see that photo all the time at school and then see you. You're around town all the time, surely someone would have noticed the uncanny resemblance?"

"They can't see my true face," said Finnigan.

"They can't?" Athena asked. "So what can they see when they look at you?"

"It's like an impression of me, but not me, exactly. They match my features up to other features that they're familiar with and they see something a little different, depending on who they are."

"But they don't see you? Is that what's happening with me too?" Athena asked sceptically. "I'm looking at you but only seeing an impression that just happens to look like that boy in the old photo."

"No, Athena. That boy in the photo was me, a long time ago."

Athena felt goosebumps raise on her skin that had nothing to do with the cold night air.

"So...you were alive all those decades ago. Doesn't that make you very old?"

"It does not. I wasn't really in this world most of that time."

"Now you're talking about another world? Wait a minute," said Athena. "You're saying I can see your real face and other people can't?"

"That's exactly what I'm saying. Just like you and I can read the minds of other people."

"We're the same?"

"Similar."

"What are we?"

Athena turned back towards Finnigan, only to find him gone. As she glared in frustration at the empty air a single word echoed through her mind: *Fae.*

As Athena lay in bed that night, her head swam with the revelation and all the possibilities that came with it. The word had come to her, not from Finnigan himself, but from somewhere else. Still, it could not be dislodged from her mind and she was certain it was true.

I'm fae...

I am fae...

What does that mean?

There were so many things that didn't make sense to her. Finnigan hadn't been in this world, so had he been in the realm of the fae? Where was it and how did he get there?

Then, there were the questions about her heritage. She was sure whatever faery genetics she might have couldn't come from Rosemary's side of the family, which could only mean one thing. Athena wasn't quite ready to think about that. Though it was true she didn't know anything about his family of origin, she refused to have anything to do with her father. Given his utter uselessness and inability to function in life, she was wary of what being fae might say about her...or Finnigan.

If Finnigan is fae too, why did he disappear all those years ago? What does that mean for me?

There were too many questions, the answers to which evaded her. She didn't have enough information to make sense of any of it, but she knew someone who might be able to help.

CHAPTER
FOURTEEN

Rosemary awoke the next morning feeling as if she'd had one too many glasses of wine the night before, though she'd only had one and a half over dinner with Sherry.

She groaned. Why does getting older mean I can barely have a drink without earning myself a hangover?

She looked around at her childhood bedroom, noticing how sad-looking the peeling wallpaper was. She wanted to go back to sleep, more than she wanted almost anything in the world at that moment, but as her mind became clearer and she remembered all her obligations, she resigned herself to the fact that she had to get up. She groaned again and pulled herself out of bed.

She could hear Athena clattering around in the kitchen downstairs. The realisation that she'd out-slept her teenager on a school day made Rosemary check the time.

She groaned for a third time.

"So late!"

She threw on the first clean items of clothing she could find – drawing on an even more limited selection than she'd found the night before – and clambered downstairs.

"Why didn't you wake me up?" Rosemary grumbled as she entered the kitchen.

"That's not my job. Oh gosh. What on earth are you wearing?" Athena asked.

Rosemary looked down at her outfit – a pink ruffled skirt with a red halter and a bright green cardigan.

"Go and change this instant!" said Athena.

"No time! I'm late for work," said Rosemary, scoffing down a piece of buttered toast from the plate in front of Athena.

"Hey – that was mine!" Athena said.

"Thanks," said Rosemary. "I hope you don't mind too much seeing as you start so late and I'm insanely jealous of that fact right now."

"It's fine," said Athena with a sigh. "Though I really do wish you'd change out of that clashing nightmare."

"The apron will cover most of it," said Rosemary. "Got to run!" She kissed her daughter on the cheek and scampered out the front door.

"We are *so* going shopping for clothes as soon as you get paid!" Athena called after her.

Rosemary drove to Marjie's tea shop as quickly as she could, without breaking any obvious laws, though she wasn't exactly sure what those were in Myrtlewood. She suspected they might be somewhat different from anywhere else, but she decided to err on the side of caution. She had already gotten on Constable Perkins' bad side too many times, and the last thing she wanted was that bothersome and suspicious old copper breathing down her neck again.

She was already parked outside Marjie's shop by the time she remembered she wasn't wearing her special emerald necklace.

Oh bother. Well, I guess I'll see how I do today without it.

Marjie greeted her, full of smiles as usual. She clearly didn't care a jot about Rosemary being late but did eye her outfit with a curious expression before handing her a bright green and red floral apron.

"Are you sure?" Rosemary asked, looking at the apron.

Marjie sighed. "It sort of matches your outfit. As well as anything possibly could, anyway. Interesting look you've got there."

Rosemary looked down at the hot pink, red, and green assortment of clothing she wore. "Laundry day, I guess," she said. "Plus, Athena and I both need to go clothes shopping when we can afford it. We're badly in need of new clothes."

"Why didn't you say so?" Marjie asked. She walked out the back and came back with a floral printed envelope. "Here!"

Rosemary examined the envelope to find it filled with crisp cash. "Oh...no I couldn't," she said.

"Nonsense. I was going to pay you on Friday," said Marjie. "But you might as well take it now."

"Really, I can wait," said Rosemary.

"Take it now. I don't want you scaring the customers off with whatever your next even-more-desperate outfit is! Besides, I'm sure I can count on you not to skip town before you've earned it back."

"Of course you can," said Rosemary. "It's just..."

"What is it, dear?"

"You've been too kind to us. I already feel as if I'll never be able to pay you back for all the lovely things you've done."

"Your happiness is compensation enough," said Marjie. "Stop feeling guilty about generosity and accept it in the spirit in which it is given. Which is freely!"

Rosemary smiled. "Thank you, Marjie."

"I'm serious," said Marjie. "I don't do nice things for people just to make them feel bad. I expect the opposite, in fact."

Rosemary kissed Marjie on the cheek and handed her back the envelope. "Give this to me on Friday," she said. "I'm determined to maintain as much self-respect and integrity as I can, and if that means waiting until payday to go clothes shopping, so be it."

"Self-respect and integrity in that outfit?" Marjie asked, giving Rosemary a cheeky grin.

A velvety laugh sounded behind them. Rosemary turned to find Burk at the counter. She hadn't realised her conversation back in the kitchen had been in earshot of any of the customers.

I guess it is true that vampires have super hearing.

She glared at him as she approached the counter.

"Sorry," he said. "I didn't mean to butt in."

"You both should be sorry," Rosemary said. "Athena is usually the only one who makes fun of my outfits. But I suppose it's warranted this time."

"You look...great," Burk said.

"Don't lie," said Rosemary. "Now how can I help you, need a cup of blood-enchanted coffee or something?"

"Keep it down!" said Burk in a rushed whisper.

Rosemary blushed. "I guess it's my turn to be sorry. I keep forgetting it's rude to...out your kind."

"It's just private information," said Burk, shrugging. "I'm sure no one wants details about their health or personal activities spread around town. Besides, there's still a lot of prejudice against...our kind. And no, I'm not in for refreshments. I came to tell you that the money has come through."

"Really?!" Rosemary asked. She stepped out from behind the cover and threw her arms around Burk, who didn't seem to quite know how to receive a surprise hug. He stood there awkwardly, patting her on the back.

"Yes, really," he said. "Well, a big lump sum has gone through, the rest of it is in a trust belonging to you and Athena. She will get a sum when she turns seventeen, and you can draw on the trust for a range of different things. Galderall Thorn set specific criteria so the money can only be used for education and investments in your future."

"Why didn't I hear about this trust before?" Rosemary asked.

"It was all in the fine print," said Burk. "Something tells me you're not one for details." He grinned.

"I suppose not," Rosemary admitted.

"It seems your grandmother didn't have confidence in everyone in your life and wanted to ensure the bulk of the money was protected from them."

"She had a point," Rosemary said. "But...well, that's wonderful! Athena and I can go shopping for clothes today after all."

Burk nodded solemnly. "I can see why that might be necessary."

"Won't everyone just stop making jokes about my outfit already?" said Rosemary in mock exasperation. The truth was, she didn't care if she was wearing a fully-fledged clown suit right at that moment.

She was free of the crushing weight of debt she'd been carrying around for most of her adult life. The sense of lightness made her feel rather high. Rosemary was so excited that she had to restrain herself from flinging her arms around Burk again.

"Thank you!" she said.

"I'm just doing my job," he replied, but his expression revealed that there was more to the story. Instead of wondering what that might be, Rosemary went to find her phone and check her bank balance.

She gulped.

A sizeable sum had indeed been deposited. It was more than enough to cover her debts, and there was a tidy amount left over that sent a tingle of anticipation through her. Suddenly her dreams didn't feel so fanciful.

I could really do it...

I could have my own chocolate shop!

CHAPTER
FIFTEEN

Athena arrived at school early, hoping to catch Elise before class. Her blue hair was easy to spot across the courtyard. Elise was standing next to Deron, holding a stack of old books. Athena waved her over hoping to talk to her alone.

"Hey," said Elise, smiling as she approached. "How's it going?"

Thankfully Deron hung back.

"I'm alright," said Athena. "I just...I wanted to ask you..."

"Ask away."

"The other day, you told me there was something otherworldly about me, and I think I know what it is."

"Oh really?" Elise said. "You were so sure I was wrong."

"I was then," said Athena. "But something happened. I won't go into the details. The thing is, I think..."

"Go on," said Elise.

"I think I might be fae, at least partly."

"Interesting," Elise said, looking at her with curiosity.

"Why is it interesting?" Athena asked.

"Well, it's very rare for the high fae, at least, to...to breed—"

"Gross!"

"You know what I mean – with humans. I think it's forbidden."

"That doesn't sound too good," Athena said. "And what does it mean 'high fae'?"

"Well, fae encompasses a whole subset of existences, even my family are considered part of the fae kingdom, but usually when people talk about the fae, they mean one particular species. I suppose they are kind of the rulers of the fae realm," Elise went on. "I don't know much about them and they're very secretive. I'm not sure exactly why they can't br—"

"Do you think I might have been lied to?" Athena interjected, thinking of Finnigan and hoping it wasn't true.

"Probably not," said Elise. "I've heard that the fae can't lie. So unless somebody else is tricking you into believing that..."

"But I can lie," said Athena.

"That's a good point," Elise replied. "Though you've never gone to the fae realm, so you're not fully under the grip of their magic. I'm actually not sure if humans with fae heritage can lie, anyway."

Athena wondered whether Finnigan always told the truth. He hadn't told her very much to begin with.

"How did you find out about this?" Elise asked.

"I have this friend...I guess he's a friend," said Athena. "I was talking to him last night and I got this idea in my head that he...we might be fae. He couldn't tell me much."

"That's probably because of the vampires," Elise said.

"The what? Why we talking about vampires now?"

"They've been at war with the fae for thousands of years. The vampires hunted them to the point of endangerment, at least in the human world. Fae have come up with a lot of magical protection mechanisms in response."

"What kind of protections?"

"All sorts," said Elise. "But they're really not obvious. I've heard there are some clever disguises in fae DNA that will stop them from being recognised for who they are."

Athena felt a tingle of recognition. That must be why Sam couldn't draw me.

"What about humans? Do the protections work against humans?"

"Probably some of them," Ellie said. "Humans might be a risk too. They could be in league with vampires, or under their control. I'm not an expert about fae, so don't take my word for it. Nobody really talks about them. There's not much in the library either, not about high fae, just catalogues of local pixies and dryads and so on. Wait, so you think one of your parents...?"

"Well, it's clearly not from my mother's side, and I don't really want to think about my dad at all."

Elise gave her a sympathetic smile. "Let me know if there's anything I can do to help," she said, just as the bell rang for class.

CHAPTER

SIXTEEN

Rosemary sat at her favourite table by the window, browsing a list of chocolatier courses to find one she might be able to enrol in online. The tea shop had reached its post-breakfast lull and there were only a few quiet customers left.

That morning, she'd helped bake the Ostara buns and Marjie even let her have a go at making chocolate eggs. It took a few attempts to get the luxury compound chocolate in and out of the moulds, but it was rewarding, and delicious too. The experience had given her more motivation to make progress towards her dream.

"Why are all the best courses in London?" she muttered to herself.

"What's that, dear?" Marjie asked from the kitchen. She was holding an enormous pink piping bag.

"Nothing," said Rosemary, not wanting to reveal anything to Marjie just yet.

The door burst open and all eyes turned to see the woman standing there, tears running down her cheeks. It took Rosemary a moment to recognise Prue, the slightly harried mother she'd met the day before.

"She's disappeared!" Prue said.

"What's that, dear?" Marjie asked, coming out from the kitchen with a smear of pink icing on her cheek.

"My little girl. Gretchen. She's gone!"

"What happened?" Rosemary asked, her mouth suddenly dry.

She got up from her table and gently led the trembling Prue back to sit down, as the woman was clearly too upset to speak readily.

Marjie brought over a tray of her special tea, with shortbread. After a couple of sips of the enchanted brew, Prue began to explain.

"We were just at home, this morning. I was busy putting the washing out and Gretchen was playing in the back yard, over by the rosebushes."

Rosemary and Marjie nodded encouragingly.

"One minute I could hear her," Prue continued, "and the next it was silent. So, of course I looked around wondering what kind of trouble she'd gotten herself into. Only she was...she was gone!"

"Oh," said Rosemary, not knowing what else to say.

"Of course I looked for her, high and low, all around the garden. I knocked on all the doors nearby and no one had seen her. I even went out back to Fin's Creek to see if she'd wandered away down the valley, but there was no sign of her. None at all."

"Have you called the police?" Rosemary asked. "And if not, would you like me to?"

"I tried," Prue said. "But Constable Perkins said it wasn't an emergency until she'd been missing a whole day. Fancy that! A child? Children of that age don't just go off partying."

Rosemary bit her tongue to protect the poor distressed woman from the string of expletives at risk of coming out over her rage at the incompetent police officer.

"Let me call Neve," Marjie said. "She'll give him what for."

"Thank you," said Prue. She took a big gulp of tea, draining her cup. Rosemary immediately filled it again, unsure how else to help the poor woman.

"Just let us know if there's anything else we can do," Rosemary said.

"I don't even know you," Prue replied. "But thank you for your kindness."

"It's nothing," said Rosemary. "I have a daughter too and I can't imagine what it would be like to lose her."

Prue gave a big sob and tears began pouring down her face again.

"Sorry," said Rosemary. "I didn't mean to upset you...Just know that we'll do whatever we can to get Gretchen back."

"Neve's on her way," said Marjie.

Several minutes later, Detective Neve arrived and led Prue away.

"Let us know if we can help with the search party," Rosemary said as they walked out the door. Detective Neve gave her a curious look and then turned her attention back to Prue as they walked away.

Rosemary returned her attention to Marjie who had gone oddly silent.

"What's going on, Marjie?"

Marjie had a distant look in her eyes. "I think I'll just close up the shop early, for today."

"What?" Rosemary asked, but Marjie was busy closing up and seemed to be in no mood to talk.

CHAPTER

SEVENTEEN

I t was as if a strange spell had fallen over the town of Myrtlewood.
People's expressions became grim or vacant. No one spoke. Rosemary helped to wipe down the counters and sweep up, but by the time
the tea shop doors were locked and she'd made her way back to her car,
she was feeling deeply unsettled.

It was too early to pick Athena up from school, so Rosemary drove
around in circles, thinking far too much for her own good.

*Why is everyone acting so strangely? Is it just the news about the little girl
going missing, or could it be that they've been bewitched somehow? Why aren't
we all out looking for her?*

*None of it made sense and Rosemary couldn't help but think it must be
part of some grand magical conspiracy. Has the mayor started abducting children to use in his magical pursuit of eternal youth? Or is it something even
more sinister? Could the mayor be a member of the Bloodstone Society? Does he
have the whole village under his spell?*

Rosemary couldn't take it anymore. She didn't know where the
mayor lived, and she was sure that the local law enforcement would be
of no use, after Neve's odd reaction. She decided her best bet was to find

Marjie again and get her to snap out of whatever spell she was under and tell the truth about what was going on.

It had been decades since Rosemary had visited Marjie's cottage, but she managed to navigate to a place that looked like the correct address, using sheer stubborn intuition.

Rosemary parked in front of the small whitewashed stone building, complete with red shutters and a rambling garden. She wandered up the driveway towards the front door past masses of over-grown rose bushes, only to find a sign that read: 'go 'round the back.'

Rosemary wandered around the side of the house, feeling somewhat less determined and more confused than she had moments before.

She passed a shed with the eclectic remnants of Marjie's former businesses in the window, including boxes of recyclable toilet paper that had not been the hit their creator had expected.

Rosemary couldn't help but smile at her quirky but unflappable family friend. Surely Marjie would be able to explain things.

"Oh, hello," said a familiar voice, decidedly unlike Marjie's.

Rosemary was startled, especially since the voice didn't appear to be coming from anyone. The back garden was full of vegetable plots without a person in sight.

"Ferg?" Rosemary asked, sure it had been his voice.

"Correct," said Ferg, saluting as he popped up from behind a trellis of vines that looked suspiciously like beans, despite it being far too early in the year for them. He was wearing purple overalls so violently neon that they almost hurt Rosemary's eyes.

"What are you doing here?" she asked.

"My job, of course," said Ferg.

"Another job?!"

"Yes," Ferg said simply. "I take it you didn't come here just to distract me from the brassicas."

"Oh no," said Rosemary, taken aback. "I'm after Marjie."

"Rosemary?" Marjie's voice said from the back door of the house. "What a nice surprise. Come in, dear!"

Rosemary wandered in to find Marjie in the kitchen, looking a lot more lively and less vacant than she had done earlier. This helped Rosemary to feel more at ease. She joined Marjie for a cup of tea in her doily-filled living room, while Herb dozed in a stuffed armchair, snoring rather loudly.

"Pay him no mind," said Marjie. "He's always like that after a train expo."

Rosemary smiled and took a sip of tea.

"So, to what do I owe the honour of a visit from Rosemary Thorn?" Marjie asked.

Rosemary took a deep breath, telling herself to be calm and level-headed and to speak deliberately and concisely. Instead, she blurted out the entire contents of her rambling and slightly paranoid thoughts.

Marjie looked troubled. "I'm so sorry to have caused you worry. You must understand that Gretchen going missing is painful for us. For the whole town, in fact."

"Are you saying that's what explains it?" said Rosemary. "That's why everyone went quiet? You're sure it's not a spell?"

"Quite sure," said Marjie with a patient smile.

"But everyone was just so strange. And Neve just looked baffled when I mentioned the search party."

"That's because there won't be a search party," said Marjie.

"What? Why not?" Rosemary asked.

"Half a dozen of Prue's neighbours would have already performed seeking spells by the time Prue even arrived at the shop. I even cast a quick one, myself, in the kitchen."

"Oh gosh," said Rosemary. "You're not saying the girl is dead?"

"Of course not!" said Marjie. "If she was dead we could find her."

"Why can't she be found then?" Rosemary asked. "Why aren't your spells working? Why would a search party be no good? Ohhh..."

"She's not *here* anymore," said Marjie, her eyes clouding over with grief. "She's gone somewhere else, beyond the veil."

"This has happened before, hasn't it?" Rosemary said.

"It has happened before, yes, to other children. Fin's Creek is known for disappearances," Marjie replied.

"Sherry told us about the fae and the other planes of existence."

"Sherry would know," said Marjie. "She was one of the ones who disappeared, once upon a time."

Rosemary gasped. "She did? When was that?"

"I don't recall exactly. A few decades ago, when she was a wee lass."

"And she just came back somehow?" Rosemary asked.

"I don't recall all the details, dear," said Marjie. "You'll have to ask her yourself."

CHAPTER
EIGHTEEN

Rosemary's head was spinning after the upsetting disruptions to her day. She was definitely not happy for Athena to walk home alone, and had rung the school to check in about what time they'd be finishing that day.

"You're very fixated on time, aren't you, dear?" Ms Twigg had said.

"I'm afraid so. Sorry for the inconvenience," said Rosemary, barely masking her sarcasm.

"It looks like they'll finish up around three."

"Thank you," Rosemary said. "Can you please get a message to Athena? Tell her to wait out front for me, where everyone can see her."

"Very well then," said the prim voice.

Rosemary arrived outside the school just after 3:00 p.m., relieved to find her daughter standing there.

"Ms Twigg told me to wait out here. What's this all about?" Athena asked. "Did someone die?"

"Not yet," said Rosemary.

"Uhhh?"

"Get in. I'll explain on the way."

"Where are we going?" Athena asked. She sounded miffed.

Rosemary hesitated and then remembered about the money coming through. That should surely lift any teenager's spirits. Before I have to tell her about everything else!

"Clothes shopping," said Rosemary.

That was all the persuasion Athena needed to jump quickly into the car. Rosemary drove them to the nearest shopping centre, which was in Cobbleston, the next town over. On the way, she filled Athena in on the missing child.

"That's awful," said Athena. "But I don't see what that has to do with me."

"You're a child," said Rosemary.

"I'm hardly a child, Mum. I'm almost an adult."

"Well, you're my child and I'm not taking any chances."

"Come on, Mum!" Athena said, crossing her arms.

By the time they got to the shopping centre, Athena was clearly fuming, but Rosemary was insistent that there had to be stricter rules, at least while children were going missing around town.

Athena was only distracted from her huff when she found out that the money had finally come through, meaning they could afford whole new wardrobes. Athena's mood brightened, but she insisted Rosemary keep her coat on the whole time at the mall, to hide her bright and clashing outfit from innocent bystanders.

"This is the best!" Athena said as they walked through what Rosemary considered a young-people-looking-cool shop. Athena was delighted that she could choose any item of clothing she wanted for a change, rather than being confined to absolute bargains and second-hand stores.

"We can afford a little splurge now," Rosemary said cautiously as Athena loaded herself up with black jeans and floaty-armed tops in a range of different colours. "But we will still have to be careful not to waste all our money so that we're okay in the long run."

"As long as you don't talk yourself out of doing something important with the money," Athena said. "You *have* to start that chocolate shop. It would be such a shame not to."

Rosemary sighed. "I do really want to. I even found a few courses I could enrol in to learn to be a proper chocolatier."

"Great!" said Athena. "Ooh, this one's for you. Try it on."

She held up a black velvet lace-up top that looked a bit like a corset with long droopy sleeves.

"It's too low-cut," said Rosemary. "Besides, where would I wear something like that?"

"It is not, and anywhere," said Athena. "Come on. At least see what it looks like when you wear it. You're a powerful witch and you should start looking the part."

"Shh," said Rosemary, looking around the shop.

Athena grinned at her. "You really think we'll get ourselves in trouble for talking about magic when no one here will believe in it at all?"

"Fair point," said Rosemary. "Fine!"

She grabbed the top and stalked off to the fitting rooms, feeling like she was the teenager in the situation.

By the time they finished shopping, Rosemary had bought not only the black velvet top but a number of other items that Athena had suggested along with several things the teen had pronounced frumpy or tasteless but Rosemary considered practical. Athena had selected double that amount of clothing for herself and seemed to be in a much more cheerful mood than earlier.

Rosemary, however, was still feeling shaken by the situation with the missing girl. Her mind spun with awful possibilities. She tried to call Sherry as soon as they arrived home but only got the answer phone.

Of course, she's probably busy at work.

"How about we go to the pub for dinner?" Rosemary suggested to Athena, who had spread out her clothing haul on the window seats and was busy matching outfits.

"Sounds good," Athena replied.

Rosemary went upstairs to change out of the clashing clothes she'd worn to work and into something new and clean. She put on the black lacy top that Athena had chosen and a new pair of jeans, then she washed her face and reapplied her lipstick. All the while her mind raced around in circles about the missing girl, trying to figure out some way she could help.

It took Rosemary a few more minutes of circling inside her own mind before she remembered the pendant. Surely that would make her feel better. She glanced down at the bathroom bench, recalling that she'd left it there when she'd showered the day before.

The bench was empty.

Rosemary stared at the clear marble surface, puzzled.

My memory might be terrible, but I'm sure I left it right there.

She looked around the bathroom floor, hoping that it had just fallen somewhere, but it was nowhere in sight.

Someone must have taken it.

"Athena!"

Rosemary stormed back downstairs.

"What?" Athena asked.

"Have you taken my special emerald necklace?"

"No," said Athena, somewhat defensively. "Why would I?"

"You were admiring it the other day. You said you wanted it."

"Sure, I was admiring it," Athena said. "But I'm not a bloody thief! If I'm going to take your stuff, I'll tell you first."

"Then what happened to it?" Rosemary asked.

"Stop getting so wound up," said Athena. "It'll turn up."

"You know, I am actually feeling *quite* wound up that an irreplaceable and valuable, not to mention useful, family heirloom given to me by my dead grandmother's ghost has somehow vanished."

"Well, how do you think I feel being accused of stealing a stupid family heirloom by my *own* mother?!" Athena yelled and stomped upstairs.

"Athena, I'm sorry," Rosemary said, following after her.

"I don't care," Athena said.

"What about dinner?" Rosemary called, but Athena didn't reply.

Rosemary sighed and collapsed on the window seats, feeling a pang of guilt about the argument. Athena's moods were all over the place recently. Rosemary had put it down to regular teenage moodiness.

Throw in magical powers coming in and the mix was far too chaotic to comprehend.

She pulled herself up and went to the pantry to find a tin of tomato soup to heat up for dinner, humming to herself as she prepared the simple meal with a side of buttered toast.

She served some for Athena and set it on one of Granny's silver trays, but when she took it upstairs and knocked on the door, Athena still apparently wasn't speaking to her and didn't respond. The soup was left to go cold in the hallway instead.

Rosemary ate her own dinner in silence at the kitchen table, her thoughts circling around the things she could not control until she felt utterly frantic. She longed for the centring power of the emerald pendant, but clearly, she was going to have to calm herself.

Rosemary decided to focus on the things that were within her power, or would be soon: the plans she could make towards the chocolate shop. She went up to bed, dreaming dreams of cardamom apricot swirls that soothed the nerves and peppermint crisp bites that refreshed the mind.

Chocolate makes everything better.

CHAPTER
NINETEEN

Athena stood on her balcony, taking in the cool night air and the atmospheric clouds brewing on the dark horizon. This time when she called out to Finnigan, he arrived straight away.

"You have a lot of explaining to do," she said.

"I do?" Finnigan asked.

"Why are you always being so cryptic? Don't I have a right to know about what I am?" A pang of unfairness hit her, and she held back tears.

"Yes, of course you do."

"Then tell me. What am I?"

"You already know," Finnigan said.

"Fae..."

He merely nodded in response.

"What does it mean to be fae?"

"You deserve to know," Finnigan said. "But all I can give you here are words, and words can't explain it. You have to come with me."

Athena's neck prickled with fear. "Come with you, where?"

"I think you know where," Finnigan said, turning away from her.

"I can't just leave my mother," said Athena. "And what about school?"

"It's not like we're going away forever. You'll be back before you even know it."

"Can you guarantee that?" Athena asked. "Clearly, time works differently on the other side of the veil, or you'd be ancient. What if I disappear for twenty minutes and come back in fifty years? I'm not just going to leave my entire life behind."

"It's not like that," Finnigan said. "Once you know how to work things you can come back and forth like I do."

"Can't you at least tell me more? I'm pretty sure this is nothing to do with Mum's side of the family. It's my dad isn't it? He's one of them, one of you."

"In a manner of speaking," said Finnigan.

"So I'm half..."

"Wow."

"What?"

"Athena, you're fae. You're not half fae. It's not like a percentage thing. It's more universal. You are human and Fae."

"And you?" Athena asked.

"Yes, me as well. My father was human. He had a relationship with my mother which was forbidden. She had to return when I was a baby. I never knew her when I was a kid. My dad raised me until...well. It was an equinox a long time ago."

"But not a long time for you, then?" Athena asked.

"Yes and no," said Finnigan. "I suppose I've only aged about a year. Maybe two. It feels like a lot longer though. I come back here to visit, to check on things...when I'm asked."

"Does that mean you are on reconnaissance or something?"

Finnigan looked away.

"You're a dirty spy!" she said, not bothering to hide the accusatory tone.

"So what if I am?" Finnigan asked.

"I honestly don't know," said Athena. "I know so little about any of it."

"There are things you are better off not knowing. Your father..."

"I don't want to know about my father. I told you."

"That is probably for the best for now," he said with a dark look.

"See – so cryptic!" said Athena, stepping away from the boy and looking out over the balcony towards the horizon.

"You just told me you don't want to know."

"Not about him." She crossed her arms.

"But you do want to know about yourself," said Finnigan, taking a step closer to Athena.

"Of course I do," she said.

"I've told you just about all I can in words."

Athena sighed in frustration. "Can you at least explain to me how to use this stupid brain psychic radio power?"

"I can show you if you come with me."

"That's not fair!" Athena said, gripping her elbows, tightly.

"Athena, believe me when I tell you the fae do not reveal their secrets in this world."

"Not even to me?"

"Not even to our own kind if they live in the earthly realm."

Athena's frustration was quickly turning into anger. "Why not?"

"We simply can't," he said. "It's a magical bind. Surely you understand that."

"I don't understand anything right now," said Athena. "But sure, I've heard of magical binds if it's like when Granny couldn't tell us who killed her."

"Similar," said Finnigan. "It causes me pain, even to have this conversation."

"Pain?"

Finnigan grimaced. "This is at the very edge of what I'm capable of revealing."

Athena looked at him more closely, noticing how tense his muscles were.

"I'm sorry," she said. "I didn't mean to cause you pain."

"I'm aware," said Finnigan. "I must leave now. Call me if you want to take up my offer."

Athena sighed and glanced back towards the house where her infuriating mother was sleeping. By the time she returned her gaze to Finnigan he was gone without so much as a "goodbye."

As Athena lay in bed, later that night, her thoughts drifted into dreams of what it could be like to leave the mundane world behind and embrace her fae heritage. Some of the dreams were frightening, but some...were delightful.

CHAPTER
TWENTY

Rosemary arrived at work the next morning, her whole body aching with exhaustion. Athena had been silent, barely speaking all morning. She hadn't even protested when Rosemary insisted on driving her to school early so she could get to work, and didn't say goodbye.

Silence was exhausting.

As Rosemary entered the tea shop, Marjie looked up from behind the counter where she'd clearly been going through the ledger.

"Oh, you're here!" Marjie said, sounding surprised.

"Of course I am," said Rosemary, smiling. "I work here, remember."

Rosemary had a moment of panic. Had Marjie subtly fired her yesterday when she'd paid that impromptu visit to her cottage? She'd seemed fine about Rosemary's appearance, but perhaps she was just being polite.

"Don't get me wrong," said Marjie. "I'm happy to have you here. I just thought that now, with the money coming through and all–"

"I didn't think you knew about that," said Rosemary. She hadn't told anyone except Athena, mostly because she'd been so distracted by her own worries.

"Hard not to overhear things in here," said Marjie with a sad shrug.

"Actually, I'd almost forgotten in the chaos of yesterday," said Rosemary as she went into the kitchen to find her apron.

"Yes, with poor Prue. And little Gretchen."

"Yes," said Rosemary, frowning. "That's my main concern. And my necklace has also gone missing."

"Don't fret, dear. It's just a necklace," Marjie said sadly. "Enchanted or not."

"You don't understand, Marjie. Without that necklace my head's a mess. Granny wanted me to have it because she knew it would help."

"Be that as it may, you are perfectly capable of sorting out your own head. You don't need to rely on magical props for that. In fact, it's all the better if you get there on your own."

"Sure, in an ideal world," said Rosemary, worrying again about Marjie's mood. "But in reality I don't know how to deal with my own brain, let alone learn how to use my magic properly. I'm a hopeless case."

"Nonsense," said Marjie. "Magic is second nature to you Thorns. After you get over the speed wobbles you'll be right as rain."

"It doesn't feel that way," said Rosemary. "I'm totally overwhelmed."

"Oh dear," said Marjie. "Is there anything I can help with?"

"I don't think so," said Rosemary.

Marjie had a slightly pained expression. "Well, you just do what you need to do, dear. Don't let me hold you back."

"What is it, Marjie?" Rosemary asked. "You seem out of sorts. Is it about the girl going missing or something new?"

"It's nothing, dear."

"Marjie?"

"Oh fine. It just sounds so petty, is all."

"What does?"

"Well, yesterday I was happy for you when you found out Galdie's money had come through...and you came over to the cottage."

"Sorry about that," said Rosemary. "If I was intruding–"

"Nonsense," said Marjie. "You actually cheered me up."

"I don't understand," Rosemary muttered.

"After you left I was feeling a little brighter," said Marjie. "Then I remembered what I'd heard about your inheritance and it hit me – you won't need to hang about here anymore. And you know Herb is too busy to help out at the moment. Too busy with his bloody trains, and besides, he's not the best conversationalist. We were getting on so well with you here."

"Marjie..."

The older woman turned toward the cake cabinet, her eyes downcast. "You don't have to stick around just on my account. You're young and I'm sure you have much better things to do than spend all your time with a lonely old woman like me."

"Don't be silly," said Rosemary.

Marjie gave her an unimpressed look. "Well, you don't have to be rude about it."

"No, I mean, I really like hanging out with you and helping at the shop. Right now it feels like it's the only thing keeping me sane!"

"Is that so?" Marjie asked, a smile twitching at the corner of her mouth.

"Of course it is," said Rosemary. "I want to stick around here for a while and help you out, but also, I'm learning a lot about how to run a food business, so all this will help me with my long-term goal."

"You mean the chocolate shop?" Marjie asked, beaming. "You're really going to do it?"

"Yes," said Rosemary. "That's the plan, anyway. I have a lot to learn about how to be a chocolatier and also, how I can use my magic – deliberately – so that my chocolates are special, a bit like your charmed tea."

"Well, that's marvellous, dear."

"I might have to slowly cut back my hours here if I start studying," said Rosemary.

"Of course! Not a problem," said Marjie. "Oh! I just had an idea. You know the shop two doors down is empty?"

"Is it?" Rosemary asked. "I hadn't noticed."

"Well, why don't we go and check it out when business quietens down here. The lease hasn't been filled for months, maybe even years, so there's no rush, but wouldn't it be lovely if your shop was close to mine?"

"It certainly would!"

"Oh!" said Marjie, bursting with excitement. She rushed over to Rosemary and wrapped her up into a big warm hug.

Rosemary hugged her back, but as she pulled away another thought tugged at her mind. "Marjie, you don't happen to know how I can track down my emerald pendant, do you? I'm sure I left it on the bathroom bench at home but maybe it's been stolen. I wondered whether you had a clue as to where it might be."

"I've no idea, sorry," said Marjie. "I can try a finding spell for you later if you like, though it may not do much good if the blighters were careful."

"Yes, please," said Rosemary. "I'd appreciate that very much."

THE MORNING at the tea shop went past in a flurry of cakes and customers and cups of tea. They didn't even experience the usual pre-lunch lull, and Rosemary had to scoff down a few mince savouries just to stop herself from getting hangry. Despite the business, the disappearances were weighing heavily on her mind.

It seemed everyone in town wanted to come in and talk about the missing girl and lament about her poor mother and what she must be going through, and share rumours about the upcoming equinox, and most of them wanted to do this over cup of tea and a piece of cake or a pasty.

At first, the hum of gossip had interested Rosemary but, by and by, she realised there wasn't a ring of truth to much of what was said. A woman with a blonde bob who introduced herself as Crystal Cassandra 'the town psychic' enthralled a group of older men and women, clustering around the table at the front of the shop. Apparently, she sensed Prue was really at fault and that all would be revealed soon.

Marjie rolled her eyes at that, and Rosemary shut off from the spurious rumours that followed, as they had a toxicity to them that made her skin crawl. Marjie had been so sure that the girl had been taken to another realm, but still, Rosemary wondered whether that was really the case, or could it be a cover for something else entirely? After all, it struck her how convenient it was for kidnappers that everyone here believed in rumours of the fae stealing children.

Most of the customers had cleared out by a quarter to two in the afternoon, and Rosemary sat down for a cup of tea and a lamb, mint, and potato pasty.

"Finally," said Marjie. "I told you to go and take a break earlier."

"I know you did," said Rosemary. "But I didn't want to – especially when the whole place was full of all that nasty gossip."

"Oh, that crowd have nothing better to do with their lives than bicker about other people and make up vicious lies."

"That was my take, exactly," said Rosemary. "Poor Prue. It's bad enough that she's already suffering just about the worst thing imaginable, let alone having a bunch of gossips spreading fake rumours like that. I thought Myrtlewood was different from other places. I didn't realise that kind of mean behavior happened here."

Marjie sighed. "It happens everywhere, I'm afraid. Anyway, let's change the subject. How about we go and have a peek through the window of that empty shop two doors down and see how you like it."

"Oh yes?" said Rosemary, feeling herself perk up immediately. "That sounds like fun, umm, window shopping?"

"In a sense!" said Marjie. "Come on, get your coat."

Rosemary didn't initially think her coat would be warranted for a walk one third of the way down the block, but the biting wind made her grateful that Marjie had insisted on it. They walked past the hair salon next door and arrived outside an empty shop. Rosemary had never noticed it before, probably because there wasn't much to see.

A drab canvas awning extended above door and windowfront, covered in mildew. The shop's exterior had peeling paint in an unappealing slate grey, with speckles of a putrid green peeking through that

Rosemary recognised as a '90s 'avocado' design fad. The interior didn't look much better.

Rosemary held her hand up against the glass to cover the reflection of the glaring overcast sky above. She saw what looked like several broken chairs, and a big corner booth upholstered in torn yellowy-brown fake leather. Towards the back sat an old juke box and a big wooden-panelled bar.

"What was this place?" Rosemary asked. "A dive bar?"

"Something like that," said Marjie. "It was frequented by a rough crowd and served as both a watering hole and a barber shop."

"Multi-purpose," said Rosemary. "Do you really think I should be setting up shop somewhere with a sordid past?"

"The rent will be low enough to be worth it alone," said Marjie encouragingly. "Besides, this place needs someone like you to spruce it up and show it some love."

"It is a great location," said Rosemary, looking around at the other shops on the street. "Oh, except for..."

The door of the shop on their right opened and Liam walked out, his sandy hair ruffling in the wind, his blue-green eyes widening in surprise.

It's right next to Liam's bookshop.

Rosemary had never been into Liam's shop, largely because of that awkward incident where he'd asked her out on a date and she'd had to turn him down.

It wasn't personal. Liam was a genuinely good man, and he was rather good looking too, and a far more suitable match than a certain vampire would be. In fact, he and Rosemary had once had a sweet and fleeting fling when they were about sixteen while she was in Myrtlewood staying with Granny for the summer. But Rosemary had sworn off dating.

Liam didn't take rejection very well and had managed to avoid her since the uncomfortable incident, but now, standing three feet away from each other, he could no longer pretend she didn't exist.

"Uhh, Rosemary."

"Hi, Liam," said Rosemary with a friendly smile and a little wave.

"Marjie," he said with a nod.

"Good day, dear," said Marjie.

"Uhh...yes. Got to run!" Liam said and indeed began running in the opposite direction.

"What was all that about?" Marjie asked with raised eyebrows.

"It seems rather childish, doesn't it?" Rosemary said. "Liam asked me out and I said no. Surely we can be adults about it."

"It must have hurt his pride, dear," said Marjie. "Either that, or he's madly in love with you and doesn't know how to face the fact that you don't feel the same way."

"Don't be ridiculous," said Rosemary. "He hardly knows me."

"Haven't you ever heard of love at first sight?" Marjie asked.

"I've heard of a lot of nonsense. It doesn't make it real. Anyway, enough about Liam. We're not here for him, we're here for this." She gestured towards the shop again.

"What do you think, then?" Marjie asked. "Do you want to be my almost-neighbour?"

"It's going to be a heck of a lot of work!" said Rosemary. "But I think it might just be perfect!"

LATER THAT DAY, Rosemary got out of the car to find the street near Fin's Creek was deserted, although she saw a few faces peep out of the windows of the houses nearby.

She wondered if they were afraid to go outside after the incident.

She walked through some long grass towards the creek. She'd managed to find the location using the map app on her phone, though she'd had to drive around several times because of her lack of sense of direction before getting to her destination.

The breeze through the trees was making whispering noises. The willows bent and boughed and the tall poplars creaked above. It would have been beautiful without the sinister feeling in the air.

It seemed strange to Rosemary that despite the child's disappearance there was no tape or any signs of a police search party. They must really be sure that Gretchen was gone from this world. Rosemary wasn't taking any chances. She couldn't bear to think how she'd feel if Athena disappeared.

The air felt oddly thick around her, and though she tried to breathe normally, it felt laboured.

"So, this is it," she said to herself. "This is where children go missing."

It was some comfort to know that they weren't presumed dead. That they were hopefully alive in some other world.

She wondered whether they missed their parents as much as their parents surely missed them or whether they would end up feeling okay about it, forgetting their families, and going on an adventure like the children in Peter Pan.

Rosemary paced the area, feeling as if she was being watched. There was nothing out of the ordinary that she could see. She walked down one side of the creek, crossing over some stepping stones to check the other side. Aside from the heaviness in the air and the uncomfortable feelings, it was just like anywhere else.

She walked back across the water and down the bank. Something caught her eye. A bright purple feather lay on the damp earth. It certainly hadn't been there before when she'd walked past. It did seem otherworldly. Rosemary reached forward to pick it up, but then she hesitated. It was possibly dangerous and certainly some kind of evidence. Instead, she pulled out her phone and took a photo that she could pass on to Detective Neve.

As she straightened up she had the sudden feeling she should leave as soon as possible and so, quickly, she did.

CHAPTER
TWENTY-ONE

The following day, the eerie experience at Fin's Creek was still playing on Rosemary's mind. Rosemary had texted Detective Neve the photo she'd taken of the feather and received a message back that it did look like something the fae would leave behind. She had thought about reporting her missing necklace too, though she decided to wait for a bit. The police obviously had enough on their hands with the missing child. The tea shop was still over-crowded and filled with spurious gossip. Hardly any of the customers were even there for food or beverages.

Rosemary decided to take a quick walk on her break, to take her mind off her numerous worries.

She peeped through the window of the empty shop, imagining what it would be like with a lovely bench and display cabinet filled with delicious chocolates. It still seemed like a pipe dream, though now, with her inheritance coming through, it was so close to her reach that she could almost taste the cocoa and vanilla.

She glanced next door towards Liam's Bookshop feeling a pang of regret.

I really should go in there and try to smooth things over with him.

It would be hard to avoid Liam if they became neighbours. Rosemary wasn't looking forward to talking to him, since he'd clearly been avoiding her. She gritted her teeth and rolled her shoulders back, then made her way through the door of the bookshop. A little bell rang but she could see no one inside. She looked up, over the stacks of books and shelves.

"Hello," she called.

A crashing sound startled her and she assumed Liam must have knocked something over, out the back.

She wasn't sure whether to just leave now before things got more awkward. Maybe this wasn't a good time, and he wouldn't be in the right mood to see her.

Then she heard the growl. A low deep sound like some kind of wild animal.

"Uhh, Liam?" she asked.

Rosemary felt her heart pounding in her chest. Something inside her was telling her to run. She began to turn around but movement caught her eye.

She froze.

A great hulking beast prowled slowly towards her. It was at least twice the size of a human and covered in fur like a dog.

"Uhh, hello? I'm going to hope that you're just a very large...and friendly shifter," Rosemary said.

The beast growled again.

"Maybe not so friendly," she muttered, slowly backing out towards the front door.

The beast sprung at her. She raised her arms, feeling her magic sizzling, but the beast was too quick. It flung her to the floor. Rosemary rolled and then ducked behind a shelf, hoping that her powers wouldn't fail her now when she actually needed them.

She blasted a bookshelf towards the beast, intending to knock it out. No such luck. It was already on its feet again, pacing slowly towards where she crouched.

I've got two options, Rosemary thought. I can stay very still and see if it leaves me alone or I can just hope my magic is going to do its job and protect me.

She cursed herself for not practicing her magic more in non-life-threatening situations. She slowly raised herself up, holding her arms out in front. This time she focused on aiming her magic more deliberately at the beast.

He growled again and sprung at her.

Rosemary braced herself, visualising her energy pulsing out towards the creature. She could feel it shooting down through her arms. It tingled in a slightly painful way, accelerating as amber light burst into the room, blindingly bright.

For a moment Rosemary couldn't see anything, and she wondered if she'd been knocked unconscious, but as the light faded she was still standing upright and perfectly fine.

The beast, however, had vanished. In its place was a very naked bookshop keeper.

"Liam! What the bloody hell was that?" Rosemary said as her childhood sweetheart opened his eyes and looked around the room blearily.

"Rosemary. What did you do?"

"What did *I* do? I just came in here to try and smooth things over with you. That is all I did! You, on the other hand, lunged at me in the form of a raging beast. What is it? A werewolf?"

"You got me," he said, raising his palms towards the ceiling. "It's not something I can help."

"So what, you just inhabit the shop sometimes in monster form and hope that nobody notices?"

Liam sighed heavily. "No. I'm usually shackled in a basement at this time of the month. The full moon caught me off guard. I was distracted thinking about...something else. I obviously didn't make it in time. I usually shut the shop, but I didn't even realise. What day of the week is it?"

"Thursday," Rosemary said.

"Thurs– Wait a minute," said Liam. He looked at her, puzzled. "How am I in human form?"

Rosemary shrugged. "Beats me."

"You did something," Liam said.

Rosemary glared at him. "You're accusing *me* of doing something after you attacked me?"

"No, it's not a bad thing. It's bloody brilliant!" said Liam. "What was it that you did?"

"It was just magic," said Rosemary. "I don't know."

"It's incredible. I've tried so many things over the years to stop the shift. But this...just happened. You did it without even trying."

"Fluke, I guess," said Rosemary, still shaking from adrenalin and not entirely ready to forgive Liam for the attack.

"I'm so sorry, Rosemary," he said, getting up.

Rosemary blushed and turned away.

"Oh, I better cover myself up," Liam said.

"I take it werewolves don't have the same convenient clothing magic as shifters, then," said Rosemary, recalling what Athena had told her about her school friend.

"I'm afraid not." Liam picked up a blanket that had been lying over a chair and wrapped it around his body to shield himself. "I'm still not quite in my right mind. But maybe...you've saved me somehow."

"That's great," said Rosemary. "Can we...can we just forget about this whole thing?"

"Yes, please do," said Liam. "Just don't tell anyone, okay?"

"Don't tell anyone that you turn into a raging beast at the full moon?"

"Exactly," said Liam with a gulp. "It's not exactly acceptable to be a werewolf in the magical community...to be infected. It's the disease, you see. There's a certain stigma. If people know they will stop coming to my store, or worse. I'd probably have to move."

A dark, brooding expression came over his face.

"I'm sorry," said Rosemary. "But you really expect me to not say anything after I was attacked?"

"I don't think it will happen again. Especially not if we can figure out how to harness your magic."

Rosemary felt as if a huge weight of expectation was suddenly being foisted upon her. She had no idea how she'd help Liam and she had far too much on her plate already.

"Even if I wanted to do that, we'd definitely need help," said Rosemary. "I barely know how to use it at all, and I'm not going to come over here and zap you once a month just so that you don't turn into the Big Bad Wolf."

"You're really not open to helping then?" Liam asked.

"I don't know," said Rosemary. "I just need to process, and I process by talking about things. And I talk to Athena even though she sometimes doesn't want to listen to me. But if I don't talk to anyone, then how can I figure out my position on all this?"

"You can talk to me," Liam said. "Look, take some time to process and come back later. Let's have a cup of tea."

"No," said Rosemary. "You just toddle on down to your dungeon or whatever and chain yourself up, because we don't know when this wolf mutation disease thing is going to come back on."

"You have a point," said Liam. "On Sunday, then? It'll be over by then."

"Right," said Rosemary sarcastically. "Because that's exactly how I want to spend my Sunday afternoon, being a magical counsellor to my ex-boyfriend with wolf issues."

"Okay," said Liam. "Take your time, but just..."

"Very well," said Rosemary. "I'll have a cup of tea with you at some stage, and I'll try to keep quiet until then."

"Thank you," Liam said, with unnervingly adorable puppy dog eyes totally dissimilar to the terrifying eyes of the beast he'd been just moments before.

Rosemary left the shop feeling at least seventeen times more confused than when she first went in. Not only had life in Myrtlewood just got a whole lot more complicated, but she had a new secret to keep, and she hated secrets. She had no idea what to think of werewolves and didn't understand why the townsfolk seemed so prejudiced about them, but her instinct told her that the mild-mannered bookshop keeper wasn't in any way evil. But even if he meant no harm, that didn't mean he wasn't dangerous.

So much for Liam being a nice normal bloke.

CHAPTER
TWENTY-TWO

Rosemary arrived at work on Friday feeling flustered, as she was late. Athena had been mucking around and didn't think it was her problem if Rosemary wasn't on time, since school didn't start until mid-morning.

"I tried my best," Marjie said, flinging her arms around Rosemary. "But alas, even my most powerful finding charm came to naught. I've no idea where your necklace is. Whoever took it must have been clever at covering their tracks."

"I don't get it," said Rosemary. "If magic can be used to disguise something like a necklace, why couldn't it be used to cover up the abduction of a child?"

"Excuse me, dear?" said Marjie. "I don't understand."

"Maybe Gretchen hasn't been taken to some other realm after all. Maybe someone kidnapped her and covered their tracks, just like whoever took my necklace. It could have even been the same person."

"Like who?"

Rosemary wrung her hands, wondering if she should let Marjie in on her suspicions. It wasn't that she didn't trust her dear family friend, it was possible that one of the customers innocently nibbling their cakes and scones was listening in. Besides, Rosemary was worried about coming across as paranoid. Even so, Marjie knew the town better than most people. It was worth the risk.

"Someone involved in the Bloodstone Society, probably," said Rosemary quietly. "I couldn't see who most of them were when they attacked the house. All those stupid dark cloaks got in the way. It could be anyone around town, maybe even the mayor. He's acting very suspiciously."

"Now don't go thinking like that," said Marjie. "You'll get your knickers in a twist with all that worry and it won't do you any good."

Rosemary sighed. Maybe she *was* just being paranoid, after all. She smiled apologetically at Marjie. "Thanks anyway for the finding charm. It was worth a try. I suppose I may never get the necklace back."

"Are you certain someone broke in and stole it?" Marjie asked. "Any ideas who it might be?"

Rosemary sipped the cup of tea that Marjie passed her. "A lot of people commented on it the other day," she said. "Mr June went a bit strange over it, remember?"

"Is that why you're worried about him?" said Marjie with a chuckle. "I do recall he made you feel uncomfortable. But I cannot imagine him like a common burglar, climbing in through a window or anything. He's much to pompous for that."

Rosemary smiled. "Good point." But she wasn't entirely convinced. Maybe Mr June had paid someone else to steal it, or used some pompous type of magic.

"Was anyone else at your house around the time?" Marjie asked.

"Only Sherry," said Rosemary. "And I can't imagine her doing anything nefarious."

"You're right," said Marjie. "Sherry is a sweet lass. I've never known her to be dishonest, though you could ask her if she saw anything suspicious."

"I could. I've been meaning to talk to her anyway," said Rosemary, picking at her fingernail. "I want to know what it was like when she was...you know..."

"Taken by the fae as a child?" Marjie prompted.

"Yes, and how it was that she got back."

"Tread carefully, there," Marjie warned. "You need to be aware that not everyone can talk about such things. In fact, it's a rare thing to hear more than a peep. Fae have powerful binding magic. I always wonder if it's to hide their dark secrets."

Rosemary shuddered. "That doesn't sound good. Who would have thought faeries would have dark secrets. I always thought of them as sparkly and fun."

"Well, they are strange folk," said Marjie. "I'm not meaning those with a bit of fae or nymph heritage, but the fully fledged high fae. They are bound to rules and etiquette."

"What does that mean?" Rosemary asked.

"Well, for one thing, they cannot lie, you see, and so they must bind themselves and others against revealing their secrets."

"*Why* do they need to be so secretive, though?" Rosemary asked.

"That's what I've always wondered. Probably just to protect themselves against vampires," said Marjie. "Speaking of vampires, look, it's your favourite lawyer."

"Where?" Rosemary asked, glancing around the shop.

"Just coming in from the underground entrance," said Marjie.

ROSEMARY TURNED BACK to the kitchen to see that Burk had indeed emerged from the trap door at the back and was brushing down his expensive-looking suit jacket.

He turned towards Rosemary and smiled, causing her to feel like a deer trapped in headlights.

"Rosemary," he said. "Marjie. Good day to you both."

"I suppose it is," said Rosemary.

"Listen, do you have time for a coffee?" he asked Rosemary.

"I'm a tea drinker," said Rosemary, "and I already have a cup of tea. Besides, I only just started work and I haven't done anything yet, other than stand behind the counter, chatting to Marjie."

"Nonsense!" said Marjie. "Off you go. Have a nice chat. It's a slow morning anyway and I've got no catering to do until tomorrow." She shepherded them both out from behind the counter with a cheeky wink and sat them down at a table.

"Will you be having the usual?" she asked Burk.

He nodded, returning Marjie's warm smile.

Marjie disappeared back to the kitchen and returned a moment later with black coffee in a floral tea cup.

Rosemary eyed it warily, wondering if it was blood-enchanted and what it might taste like.

"It's just coffee, Rosemary," Burk said.

"Oh, I didn't..."

"We can consume liquids fairly easily," said Burk. "But solid food makes us violently ill, as you've probably been told. Blood-enchanted food actually makes the food a lot like liquid, while maintaining its appearance of structure. It gives food some nutritional value we can actually absorb and a pleasant bloody taste."

Rosemary grimaced.

"My apologies," said Burk. "I forget that to most non-vampiric people, blood is hardly palatable."

"Don't get me wrong," said Rosemary. "I love a good black pudding. I just...umm...does it taste like human blood?"

"Mammalian blood tastes fairly similar, regardless of where it's from," said Burk. "Human blood is a lot like pigs' blood, which makes up the majority of what we eat."

Rosemary couldn't help but grimace again.

Burk gave her a quizzical look. "I'm just being upfront with you."

"Err, thank you, I guess," said Rosemary.

Burk shook his head dismissively. "Let's talk about something else."

"Okay," said Rosemary. "What do you have in mind? Surely you didn't just want to imbibe a hot beverage with me to tell me about your dietary habits, or is this a key part of educating a new worker at your local café?"

"No," said Burk, smiling. "I had something else in mind."

"Which is?"

"I intended to ask for your company for...an evening."

"What?" Rosemary was feeling dazed, her mind still miles away with thoughts of Gretchen and the necklace and the dodgy mayor.

"Would you do me the honour of your presence?"

"My presence where?"

"I suppose it could be anywhere."

"Wait a minute," said Rosemary. "Is this some obscure old-fashioned way of asking me out on a date?"

Burk seemed to pale a little. Then he cleared his throat. "You could put it like that."

"Oh!" said Rosemary, at first relieved that she'd worked out the mystery and then anxious about the entire situation. "Oh...well, you see, you're kind of my lawyer and also my grandmother's lawyer and that surely is multiple conflicts of interest right there, and also, I don't mean to be blunt but you are possibly about a million years old and the age gap is a little creepy. I mean, what am I supposed to tell Athena? I'm dating someone that could be my great, great, great, great, great, great grandfather? And also, I don't date."

Burk eyed her warily.

It took him a moment to reply. "I'm not that old," he said finally. "Well, I'm not a million. That's ridiculous."

Rosemary shrugged. "Close enough. It's not like you've told me anything specific about your age or what time in history you come from."

"It's a long story, and one I don't often share," Burk said. "I don't think you require my legal services anymore, which is why I've waited until now to ask."

"The answer would still be no," Rosemary said apologetically. "I really don't date."

"Why is that?" Burk asked. He was infuriatingly handsome at that moment, leaning back in his chair and stroking his chin with his index finger.

"Largely because I have literally the worst track record with men – notably one man – notably Athena's father."

"I see. So one bad apple has spoiled your appetite for the rest," said Burk.

"I suppose so. Also, my life is complicated enough with Athena, and discovering magic, and lurking looming dangers that seem to come at me every single week, and also, I'm setting up a business, so I have plenty of other stuff to think about and no time at all for romance."

"That's understandable," said Burk.

Rosemary felt a twinge of disappointment.

"Wait a minute," he said. "You're setting up a business? This is new."

"It is," said Rosemary.

"Anything you want to tell me about? Perhaps seek legal advice over?"

"You're not my lawyer anymore, apparently," said Rosemary. "And anyway, I don't feel ready to talk about it just yet. I want to let it bubble away and allow the energy to build up first."

"That sounds wise," Burk said.

"Thank you," said Rosemary. "People don't usually call me wise."

Burk smiled at her.

She was surprised that their previous date-related conversation hadn't seemingly made things awkward between them, unlike the situation with Liam. Perhaps having a few hundred years to overcome one's sense of personal rejection made all the difference.

"There you are!" said a hoarse voice from behind them. Rosemary turned to see Ferg in a fire-truck red three-piece suit. His arms were loaded up with baskets filled with little potted plants and eggs.

"Oh, hi Ferg," said Rosemary. "We were kind of in the middle of a conversation here."

Ferg looked from Rosemary to Burk.

"Don't mind me," said Burk. "I better get back to the office, anyway." He got up and walked towards the back of the tea shop, leaving Rosemary nursing her mild disappointment.

"What is it, Ferg?" she asked flatly.

"I've been meaning to check in with you about Ostara," said Ferg, panting.

"Ost...what? Oh that's right, the Easter thing that's actually the Spring Equinox with disappointingly non-chocolate eggs. Do you think you could make them chocolate, just this time?"

"No."

"For the children?" Rosemary asked.

"No. This is for you." He handed her a basket of little plants.

"Erm..."

"You've got a conservatory at your house," said Ferg. "I've seen it. Plus, you can use a bit of magic to speed up the growing process so that these tulips can flower. Old Galdie always helped us out a bit with that, leading up to the Spring Equinox."

"Ferg, I'd love to help, really, I would..."

"Excellent," said Ferg and turned to walk away.

"But!" said Rosemary. "There's just too much going on at the moment. I don't have any headspace to spare on gardening, or clearing out the old conservatory, which is in a right state. I'm too worried about that missing girl and trying to protect Athena. Besides, I don't even know how to use my magic to get things to grow, so I'm afraid you'll have to ask someone else."

Ferg gave her a stern look. "Rosemary, listen to me. If you really care about that little girl, you'll do what you can to help make this ritual work."

"Oh really?" Rosemary asked. "Why on earth...?"

"The equinoxes are when the veil between human and fae worlds is the thinnest," said Ferg. "If we have any chance of getting her back soon, it's through the ritual. Having a powerful witch like you involved will make all the difference."

"I told you I don't know how to."

"It doesn't matter if you don't have a full grasp of your powers yet," said Ferg. "The power is there, with you and Athena both. Besides, it will give you a chance to practice your growing magic on the plants."

Rosemary sighed. "Really?"

"Yes, really," said Ferg.

"What is he doing?" Marjie muttered, coming over towards the table.

"Ferg, are you bullying Rosemary into volunteering again?"

"I'm doing nothing of the sort!" said Ferg. "I'm simply informing her of how useful her magic will be for the equinox, which is also our greatest chance of getting little Gretel back."

"Gretchen," said Marjie and Rosemary simultaneously.

"Whatever," said Ferg.

"I suppose you do have a point there," said Marjie. "That was how we got wee Sherry back, after all, though it had been a whole year by that point."

"Sherry was gone for a year?!" Rosemary asked, in shock. "How awful for her family."

"It was a terrible time," said Marjie. "Little Liam could barely stop crying, at least at first. They were very close as similar-aged cousins, but after Sherry came back she was different. It has taken them years to form a solid friendship again."

"That's strange," said Rosemary. "I wonder if Sherry can give us any tips for how we could help Gretchen."

"She may not be able to speak of it," said Marjie. "But if you can summon an audience with your Granny's ghost, she might just be able to tell you how she helped Sherry cross back over."

"Granny did?" Rosemary asked.

"That's the story I heard," said Ferg. "And that's exactly why we need your help – we need the Thorn magic."

"I hate to say it, but he does have a point," said Marjie.

"I can try," said Rosemary. "But don't get your hopes up. Right now, my magic is utterly useless unless you're wanting an avalanche of blankets."

"Not right now, thank you," said Ferg with a deadly serious tone. "I will let you know if I get chilly though."

"Ahh, alright," said Rosemary.

"I'm certain that helping to grow these tulips will be a good opportunity for you to practice focusing your magic," said Ferg.

"I suppose, if I don't kill them all," Rosemary replied.

"Great. So it's settled then. You will help with the equinox."

"I suppose so," said Rosemary grudgingly. "But I'm not crossing over into faery land. I'm staying firmly on this side of reality."

"Excellent," said Ferg. "I'll bring around the trailer with the rest of the plants later on."

He turned on his heels and strode out of the tea shop before Rosemary could say anything else. She sat down, her mouth gaping, staring after him.

"Trailer load...?" she said weakly.

"Ferg doesn't do things by halves," said Marjie.

"That's for certain," said Rosemary. "That man is...something else."

Later, when Rosemary picked Athena up from school, the teen looked thoroughly embarrassed.

"What's all that crap in the back of the car?" Athena asked, gesturing to the baskets on the back seat.

"I was actually hoping you could help me with that," said Rosemary. "I've...uhh...volunteered to help Ferg with the equinox. Those are plants that I'm going to try to grow. I thought you be of some assistance."

"What?!"

"It's a long story. Basically, he convinced me that having the Thorn family magic involved would make the ritual more powerful and therefore make it more likely to get Gretchen back."

"And you believed that weirdo?"

"We aren't allowed to use the "w" word in a derogatory way anymore, remember what Granny said."

"Who died and made her queen?" Athena asked.

"She did, I suppose," said Rosemary. "Anyway, I don't want to go around offending people's religion or spiritual beliefs or anything, so I'm just trying to get out of the habit."

"Honestly, I don't care anymore," Athena said. "From now on, I'm just focussing on my school work and my friends. You can deal with everything else."

"I'm glad to hear it," said Rosemary with a grin, though deep down she was sure life was just on the brink of getting far too complicated for both of them.

CHAPTER
TWENTY-THREE

I t was a cold, frosty morning. Rosemary's breath formed clouds around her in the air as she drove along the narrow twisting road leading up a hill to a large mansion.

She had spent all night going around in circles in her mind, thinking about both the disappearances of her necklace and the little girl. It seemed too much of a co-incidence.

If the finding spells didn't work for either, surely the same person could be responsible. The mayor seemed likely as a suspect. He was acting suspiciously and had a drive for immortality. Maybe he was using the excuse of the equinox to steal a child in order to use magic...somehow. Rosemary wasn't sure of the details, but she knew it would sound mad to most people, even Detective Neve.

There were so many ridiculous rumours floating around the village that Rosemary was sure no one would take her suspicions seriously. Instead of calling the authorities, she decided to take matters into her own hands in an attempt to get some solid evidence first.

She'd asked Marjie for directions to the Mayor's house. Her concerns had grown after everything she'd heard about the Mayor, Mr June, in recent days. Besides, he had taken such an interest in the emerald necklace when she saw him that she was sure he must be the culprit.

Rosemary even wondered whether he'd used the dinner party she'd thrown a few weeks before as an excuse to scope out the house for valuables or to plant some kind of magical assistance that might help him to rob her later on.

She approached the big black door and knocked on the shiny brass knocker, shaped like a goblin face.

An attractive man answered, tall with dark skin and piercing amber coloured eyes. He was wearing a purple satin dressing gown.

"Sorry to bother you," said Rosemary.

"Are you here for Don?" the man asked. "I'm his husband, Zade."

"Yes. Don, as in Don June. Mr June, the Mayor," Rosemary rambled.

"Come in," he said. "If you'll excuse me, I'll go and change."

"No, don't trouble yourself," said Rosemary.

"Don't worry," said Zade, with a warm smile, "I need to change anyway. I've been lounging around for too long already. Just make yourself at home. Don will be right down." He ushered Rosemary in and disappeared off upstairs.

Rosemary stood in the hallway wondering how such a nice man had hooked up with the greasy and pompous mayor. She glanced around at what she could see of the house. Everything looked expensive, if a little gauche for her tastes.

"Ah, Rosemary," said Mr June, coming down the stairs. "What can I do to help you? As you know, I'm always here to listen to the concerns of my citizens."

"Well," Rosemary began, but Mr June cut her off.

"Actually, it's very fortunate to you came," he continued. "I have some business that I want to discuss with you regarding certain magical artifacts."

"Oh yes?" said Rosemary, surprised.

"Yes," said Mr June. "I do believe the late Madam Thorn had quite a few special treasures that I might want to purchase if you would deign to sell them to me."

Rosemary looked at the mayor suspiciously. Why would he want to bargain with her if he had just robbed her? She wasn't sure if he was genuine, or whether this was some kind of red herring to throw her off the scent.

"Look," she said.

"Oh, my," Mr June said, cutting her off again. "Where are my manners? Please come into the parlour, make yourself at home, and of course, I must offer you a beverage. What would you like? Tea? Coffee? An early morning pick me up?"

"Tea will be fine, thank you," said Rosemary, relieved when the rather overbearing man stalked off to the kitchen, leaving her in peace.

Rosemary paced the parlour, keeping an eye out for anything that looked suspicious. A polished wooden side table with a drawer caught her eye. She listened out for footsteps, but the house seemed silent enough. She knew she shouldn't, but her curiosity got the best of her. She crossed the room towards the drawer and pulled it open. The inside seemed to be largely filled with papers, but Rosemary rummaged through just in case there was anything incriminating.

"Excuse me," said a voice. Rosemary jumped.

Zade stood in the doorway.

"Sorry!" she said. "I was just admiring this table. What wood is this?"

"Mahogany," he replied dryly.

"Here you are!" said Mr June, re-entering the room brandishing a cup of tea. Rosemary took it and tried to hide her embarrassment.

"Ah, there you are, darling," Mr June said to Zade, who gave him a peck on the cheek and then walked past him towards wherever the kitchen must be, leaving Rosemary feeling relieved.

Mr June looked at Rosemary with a rather jolly smile. "Now, Ms Thorn! How can I help you?"

"I noticed you admired my necklace the other day," said Rosemary.

"Indeed, I did. I apologise for the misunderstanding. Are you willing to part with it?" he asked. "I do believe that item would be a wonderful addition to my collection."

"Yes, well, it's missing," said Rosemary.

"How unfortunate," said the mayor, though he didn't seem all that surprised.

"I'm not sure what happened," said Rosemary, watching Mr June carefully.

"Would you like me to try a locator spell for you?" Mr June asked.

"Marjie has already tried that," said Rosemary. "In fact, I must confess, that's the reason I've come here."

The mayor raised his eyebrows.

"Suspicions have been raised that maybe...you took it," she said quite frankly.

"My dear girl! How dare you come to my house and accuse me of petty theft!"

"That's the thing," said Rosemary. "It wouldn't be petty thief if it's a valuable magical item."

"That's even worse," said the mayor. "I will not stand for this! I'm outraged!"

"What's the matter, dear?" said Zade, standing in the doorway.

"This woman has the audacity to come to my house and accuse me of stealing!"

Both men looked at Rosemary. She felt distinctly uncomfortable. "Look, it's just...I heard some things. I thought maybe...maybe you knew something."

"That's not what you just said," said Mr June. "I think you should be going now."

"I caught her rummaging around in your drawer earlier," said Zade.

"Really? How outrageous! Why didn't you say anything?"

"She said she was admiring the woodwork, and I gave her the benefit of the doubt."

"I thought Madam Thorn would have taught you better than to invade somebody's personal property!" said Mr June.

"I'm sorry," said Rosemary. "You must understand that the necklace is very important to me."

"I understand enough," said the mayor.

"You'd better get out of here," said Zade.

Rosemary's heart began to race as she realised the trouble she'd gotten herself into, but it was for a higher purpose. She had to figure out what was going on.

"Just wait a minute," said Rosemary. "What about the missing girl?"

"Excuse me?" said Mr June.

"Gretchen. She disappeared around the same time as my necklace and finding charms don't work on either situation and...and..." Rosemary suddenly became aware how foolish she sounded. "If it wasn't you, then why aren't you out there looking for her? Surely, as the mayor you should be doing something about this!"

Mr June just stared at her, gobsmacked.

"Now you're accusing my husband of kidnapping?" Zade said, appalled. "Is this some kind of witch hunt? Are you prejudiced against us because—"

"No! Nothing like that," said Rosemary, even more alarmed. "I'm... okay, I'll admit it. I'm grasping at straws here. Are you sure there's nothing you can tell me? If it's not you, then who else would have an interest in my necklace?"

"A great many people, I dare say," said the mayor. "How awful that you've jumped to conclusions like this. I might not be the most popular person in town, but I'm a public figure and I deserve your respect."

"Okay. I'll just be going then," said Rosemary, anxiously backing out of the room.

"Not so fast," said the mayor.

"What? I thought you wanted me to leave."

"Not before I hand you over to the authorities," said Mr June. "I was just stalling. I've tripped the switch and the police will be here any minute."

"The police!?" said Rosemary, her panic quickly turning into dread. "But I didn't do anything."

"You came into my house under false pretences and proceeded to go through my personal things. That's breaking and entering."

"Oh, it was not," said Rosemary. "You let me in yourself."

"That was before I knew about your uncouth behaviour."

There was a knock at the door.

"Come in!" the mayor called out, and Constable Perkins entered the room followed by Detective Neve.

"Miss Thorn!" Constable Perkins bellowed, his cheeks red. "What kind of trouble are you getting into now?"

"This woman came into my house and accosted me – accused me of stealing, and kidnapping! She invaded my house and rummaged through my things. It's unacceptable, criminal behaviour."

"Rosemary?" Detective Neve's voice rose in pitch and Rosemary mourned for the potential friendship that was quickly slipping away due to her own reckless behaviour.

"Well, I suppose that's all true." Rosemary conceded. "But criminal? That's going a bit far."

Neve's expression was clearly unimpressed.

"Look, the only reason I came here is because I think he might have stolen my necklace."

"Why didn't you just tell us about your suspicions?" said Neve.

"I didn't have any evidence," Rosemary admitted. "And I didn't want to look foolish." She blushed, feeling much more foolish now.

"Of course there was no evidence," said the mayor. "Because I've done no such thing. Now arrest her, immediately."

Constable Perkins took a step forward, but Detective Neve held him back. "Arrest her for what exactly?"

"Yes, what exactly?" said Rosemary, crossing her arms and feeling relieved that Neve seemed to be taking her side.

"Invasion of private property!" said Mr June.

"Didn't you let her in?" Neve asked.

"That's beside the point," he replied.

"Look. I'm sorry," said Rosemary. "I just really need to get my necklace back. I feel all strange without it and maybe that's caused me to be a bit irrational and jump to conclusions." She looked at the mayor, deciding that now was not the time to repeat her suspicions. "You're right. I didn't have any evidence. It was just a hunch."

"She didn't really do anything wrong," said Zade.

"Aren't you on my side?" Mr June folded his arms.

"Of course I am. It's just...well, she was just having a nosy around. It's not like she damaged anything."

"Look," said Detective Neve. "I think this time the situation just calls for a warning. Rosemary, please don't break into anyone's house again."

"I didn't break in," Rosemary insisted. "We just went over this. He let me in."

"Still..." Neve shook her head and began to gently lead Rosemary to the door.

"I'm sorry," said Rosemary again as she walked out of the house with Neve. "I promise I'll go to the police next time something goes wrong or I have a suspicion about anything."

"Thank you," said Detective Neve, sounding like a harassed kindergarten teacher.

"It's just..." Rosemary stammered, as she made her way towards her car.

"I hate to say this because I think you're a great person. But can't you *do* anything?"

Neve's posture deflated.

"Sorry," Rosemary repeated.

"Thanks for triggering my impostor syndrome," said the Detective with a sad smile. "As one of the few non-magical people in this town, I went into law enforcement because I wanted the power to help. Only, it turns out I'm totally helpless at times like this."

"Oh," said Rosemary. "I didn't know."

"I'm doing everything I can – by the book. Plus a lot more. I'm leaning on my own personal connections to try to figure out how to get that little girl back, but it's a brick wall at every turn. Do you want us to look into your necklace as well?"

"No. You clearly have enough on your plate," said Rosemary. "Maybe we can work together. Only, I suppose I'd only cause you more trouble. The present situation is a prime example of that."

"Thanks for trying to help," said Neve. "Let me know what you find out, or if anything else goes wrong, and who knows, maybe we can work together at some point."

CHAPTER

TWENTY-FOUR

Athena walked across the road towards the town square feeling nervous. She'd never met up with friends outside of school before. In fact, she'd never really *properly* had friends, considering they moved around so much and she didn't fit in with most other kids her age.

That was, until recently. Elise and Sam had started to become pretty good friends at school, even if they did hang out with some ridiculous hooligans, like Felix in particular. Deron was okay and so was Ashwagandha, who sometimes joined in, sitting with their group at lunch time.

She recognised Elise's hair from across the square, easily spotting her standing next to Sam. They waved to Athena as she made her way over.

"Hi," Athena said, hoping she didn't sound stupid.

"You've made it!" said Elise.

"Yeah, Mum let me out of the house for a change," said Athena. "She reasoned that in the middle of the day with all the people around here I'd be safe enough."

"Your mother is a tad over-protective, isn't she?" said Sam.

"Tell me about it," said Athena. "I can barely do anything without her breathing down my neck these days."

"We're going to meet Felix and Deron later," said Elise. "Is that okay?"

"Sure." Athena shrugged. "I don't mind."

She hoped that her new friends weren't just interested in her for the novelty value or because they'd heard about her family's power. They seemed nice, and genuine enough. It would be awful if they got bored with her or were terribly disappointed when they figured out that she didn't really have any aptitude for magic.

"So what are we going to do?" Athena asked. "You said something about ice cream. Is it from the grocery store?"

"Oh no," said Elise. "We have to go to Mervyn's."

"Mervyn's?" Athena asked.

"Yes," said Sam. "Mervyn's ice cream parlour."

"I didn't realise we had an ice cream parlour in Myrtlewood," said Athena.

"Mervyn's is the best!" said Elise. "It closes up over winter, but at this time of year, it reopens again. And there are always a few extra surprises."

"That sounds amazing," said Athena. "Lead the way!" Then she wished she hadn't said that.

Athena tensed at her choice of words. They came out overly cheesy, as if she was on some sort of children's television show. She bit her tongue to try and stop herself from saying too much more. But fortunately, Elise and Sam didn't seem to notice, and Athena allowed herself to relax a little.

She followed them to a shop with pastel blue-and-pink-striped awnings out front. Inside it looked like an old fashioned ice cream shop through the window.

"This does look awesome," said Athena. "I love the little booths."

The booths were striped in various shades of pastel as well, like something out of a 1950s television show.

"Shall we go in?" said Sam.

"After you," said Elise.

Athena pushed the door open and a little bell tinkled above her. She cautiously approached the counter. A man stood behind it. He had long hair tied up in a bun and was wearing a pastel striped apron with a huge smile on his face.

"Welcome!" he said. "You're my first customers of the season. Ice creams are on the house to celebrate!"

"Oh wow!" said Sam. "Excellent. I won't have to use up all my pocket money.

"That's great," said Elise. "How sweet of you, Mervyn. How are you, anyway? Did you have a good time at sea?"

A faraway look came over Mervyn's face. "Yes, it's always marvellous."

"How long were you away?" Sam asked.

"Two or three months, I think," he said. "That's the only time I can get away and be with my people."

"Your family live at sea?" Athena asked.

Mervyn gave her a wink. "You're new around here, aren't you?"

"I'm afraid so," said Athena.

"I'm Mervyn Wade, your humble local town Merrow."

"Merrow?" Athena asked.

"That's the old Irish word," said Elise. "It means—"

"Mermaid Man...err Merman," said Mervyn. "You know, I'm trying to use the human terminology. It always confuses me. What's the difference anyway? Genders are much the same."

"You can say that again," said Sam with a giggle.

"You're a Mer er...person?" Athena said, stuttering over the words.

"Of course," said Mervyn. "Not many of us live on land, but the ones who do still need to spend a decent amount of time at sea. Otherwise, we get land sick."

"Land sick, like seasick?" Athena asked.

"You catch on quickly," said Mervyn with another wink. "Now what would you like?"

Athena surveyed the array of ice cream spread out before her. There were some regular flavours like chocolate and strawberry ripple, among other more unusual flavours like blackberry and thyme, boysenberry and sage, and frankincense and dark chocolate.

"Wow, so much to choose from," said Athena.

"I'll have the usual," said Elise.

"Blueberry coconut cream," said Mervyn. "With a half scoop of blackberry and thyme."

"That's the one," said Elise.

"That sounds good," said Athena, baffled by the choice. "I think maybe I'll just have the same."

Mervyn got to work scooping their two cones.

"It's so hard to choose, isn't it?" said Sam. "I think I'll just have regular old chocolate. Can't go past the classics."

Athena smiled at them, now wondering whether she should have chosen a simpler flavour.

They took the ice cream and sat down in one of the booths.

It was still fairly early in the day and so there weren't too many people around. Athena tasted her ice cream to find it was absolutely delicious and complex. The flavour was almost dizzyingly good.

"So how's it going?" Elise asked. "Are you settling into Myrtlewood okay?"

Athena was too absorbed in her ice cream to answer straight away. Eventually, she looked up and cleared her throat.

"I guess so," said Athena. "Mum is still a little bit frazzled. She's paranoid that I'll go missing like that little girl. Also, some special necklace of hers has disappeared, which hasn't helped things. She's super anxious. She probably just lost it behind the couch."

Sam and Elise both laughed, putting Athena at ease.

"Is your dad around?" Elise asked.

"No," said Athena. "At least it's better when he's not."

"Mine either," said Elise. "My father wasn't magical. He freaked when he figured out what Mum was. I don't really know him. Sometimes I wish I did, though, especially when Mum's being a pain. I wish there was somewhere else I could go to escape her new moon cleaning sprees."

Sam laughed. "Your mum is such a character, Elise."

"My dad has sort of been in and out of our lives," said Athena. "I think he's missing at the moment, but really that's nothing unusual."

She didn't want to say too much at first. After all, she hardly knew Elise and Sam. She often found herself bursting with rage at her father and hardly ever had anyone to talk to about it since Rosemary made excuses for him that just made her angrier. It was nice to have other people to talk to, and Athena couldn't help but express a few resentful sentiments about how Dain had never been helpful, how he'd taken their money and gambled it away.

"That sounds awful," said Elise. "Maybe I'm better off not knowing my dad after all, if he's anything like that."

"Don't you ever want to forgive him though?" asked Sam. "People say forgiveness is a good thing."

"No, he hasn't done anything to deserve my forgiveness or my trust."

"I wouldn't forgive him," said Elise. "Just because he donated his DNA to your cause, doesn't mean you owe him anything."

Athena laughed at Elise's way of putting it.

"I'm serious," said Elise.

"But he's family," said Sam.

"Just because somebody's family, it doesn't mean that they should be in your life," said Elise. "If someone is really toxic like that, it's better to cut them out altogether."

"True. Sometimes I wish I could cut off various limbs of my family," said Sam. "As accepting as the village is of my identity, my brothers are pests. No matter what I say or do they still won't respect that I'm non binary. They keep calling me by a very gendered version of my name. It just really upsets me. It's like they're taunting me with it deliberately. They're trying to show that they have the power in the situation and they're not going to respect me and my identity."

"That's awful!" said Athena.

Sam shrugged. "It sucks but I guess I'm used to it. I just hope they stop being such pests at some point."

"One can only hope," said Elise with a strange look on her face.

"Speaking of pests, Felix just texted to say that he's not going to be in town after all. He's got some other family thing."

"Is there's something going on between you and Felix?" Athena asked Elise before she could stop herself from blurting out the invasive question. There was a moment of silence in which Athena blushed and then added, "You're not together or anything?"

"Oh no," said Elise. "No, we've known each other for too long. In fact, I think he likes you."

Athena practically spat out her ice cream, but she didn't want to waste any of it as it was so good.

"That's an incredibly awkward thing to say," said Athena. "I mean, I know my question was awkward too. Sorry."

"*I'm* sorry," said Elise. "I shouldn't have mentioned it."

"Is there someone else you like, then?" Sam asked.

Athena blushed.

"There is!" said Elise. "Are you going to tell us?"

"I don't know," said Athena. "It's...it's a bit personal."

Elise shrugged.

"No pressure," said Sam.

Athena really wasn't used to sharing confidences with anyone. In fact, she was mostly used to trying to hide any personal details from her mother's prying eyes. But it was nice to be able to share with her new friends. And so, she offered a little bit of an explanation.

"There is this one guy," said Athena.

"Ooh!" said Elise. "Anyone we know?"

"I don't think so," said Athena, thinking of Finnigan's picture up in the school. "He's not really from around here."

It wasn't entirely true, but it was the closest Athena could get to the truth, without going into an explanation that she didn't understand how to clear up, seeing as the whole situation with Finnigan was shrouded in mystery.

"I hope it works out for you," said Elise.

Athena smiled. "What about you, is there anyone you like?" she asked.

"Not really," said Elise, with a blush.

"Me neither," said Sam. "Which is just as well because I don't think there'd be anyone who'd like me back."

"Don't be so defeatist," said Elise. "You're a wonderful and very cool person and you have lots of excellent qualities."

"Now I feel foolish," said Athena. "I told you about my crush and neither of you have one."

"There's nothing to feel foolish about at all," said Elise. "We won't tell anyone and I promise I'll tell you the next time I like someone." She smiled at Athena.

Suddenly, the embarrassment of the situation lifted and Athena didn't feel so awkward or self-conscious anymore. It was nice having friends.

CHAPTER
TWENTY-FIVE

Rosemary was relieved to find that Athena returned from her outing, not only safely, but in a good mood. They spent the rest of the day watching old movies and reading books. In the evening the house felt rather chilly, so they both decided to go upstairs and put on warmer clothing.

Athena paused on the upstairs landing and stood silently, looking ahead.

"What is it?" Rosemary asked.

"It's...the door!" said Athena. "The one you told me about."

Rosemary tilted her head to see around her daughter. It was indeed the door, the mahogany door gilded in roses, the magically-appearing-then-vanishing door that led to the tower.

"Do you...do you think *she* wants to talk to us?" Athena asked.

"Who? Granny?"

"Yes. Isn't that how you had that chat with her last time?"

"I suppose it could mean that," said Rosemary. "Or it could just be the house."

"Do you think we should go up?" Athena asked.

"I suppose so," said Rosemary.

They approached the door cautiously, unsure whether any sudden movements might make it disappear again.

Rosemary rummaged in her pocket for the key, but the door had other ideas. It sprang open without so much as a push, causing Rosemary and Athena to scramble back in surprise.

"Is it safe?" Athena asked.

"Of course it is," said Rosemary, though her tone was far from certain.

She took a tentative step towards the open doorway. Nothing seemed amiss, so she proceeded up the stairwell with Athena following close behind.

"This is amazing!" Athena said as she looked around the enormous tower room, which Rosemary could have sworn was even bigger than when she'd first discovered it.

"It is, isn't it?" said Rosemary. "I guess this was where Granny did most of her magical workings. At least that would explain all the equipment on the table."

"And the giant cauldron," said Athena.

"Yes, and that."

"Hello, dears!"

Rosemary and Athena both jumped and then turned in the direction of the mirror to see Granny standing there, clad in bright purple, her wild white hair tied back in a red scarf, hands firmly on her hips.

"Granny!" Rosemary cried, happy to see her favourite elderly relation, despite the circumstance.

"Who else would it be? The ghost of Christmas past?" Granny asked.

"Umm, hi," Athena said.

Granny grinned at her. "My, how you've grown," she cooed.

"It has only been a week or something since we last saw you," said Athena.

"I didn't mean grown in size," said Granny. "I mean in power."

"I wish!" said Athena. "Mum's the only one with real powers. I just hear inconvenient noises in my head."

Granny tutted as if she knew much better.

"Granny Thorn," said Athena. "Can you help me learn proper magic? Is there anything up here – maybe a book – that can help?"

"You don't need a spell book to give you powers," said Granny. "You, my dear, are twice blessed."

"What does that mean?" Rosemary asked.

"It's like I told you before, if you ever bothered listening," Granny said. "She has other magic on her father's side. Of quite a different variety."

Rosemary's jaw dropped. "You did *not* tell me that. What are you saying about Dain?"

"Athena's father? Oh yes. He's definitely one of them."

"Them?" said Rosemary. "You don't mean–"

"The fae," said Granny.

"And you didn't think to tell me that?!" Rosemary asked.

"I thought you must have known, deep down, dear," said Granny. "Athena has always had that otherworldly nature about her."

"Fae magic?" Athena asked, not sounding surprised at all, just curious.

"You *knew*?!" Rosemary asked her daughter, before turning back to the mirror. "And you! You're telling me you knew that my daughter is a faery?" Rosemary asked.

"That's part of her heritage, of course. I really thought you would have worked it out by now."

Rosemary sighed. "What else have you been keeping from me, I wonder?"

"Plenty of things, no doubt," said Granny, winking. "I'm an open book for the most part though, so feel free to ask if you think of anything."

Rosemary sighed. "Sure, you're chatty as all Hermes when you don't have anything useful to say."

"Try me," said Granny, crossing her arms.

"Children are going missing," said Rosemary. "And that reminds me – I don't know how this keeps slipping my mind, but Athena's father is missing too, isn't he? That's what you told me last time."

"Away with the faeries," said Athena.

"What?" Rosemary asked.

"I've been reading about it in the school library. Fae have the power to make you forget," Athena said. "That's why you keep forgetting about Dad. In fact, I'm willing to bet that it's also why you keep forgetting things in general. You spent so much time with Dad – more than anyone should considering what a deadbeat he is – and it must have messed with your memory."

"You mean on top of what Granny's spell to hide our magic already did to me?" Rosemary asked, glaring at her grandmother.

Athena shrugged. "Maybe."

"Wait a minute. So that's why you hear voices? Fae can read minds?" Rosemary clasped her hand over her mouth in surprise. "Oh no! You're saying Dain could read my mind all these years? No wonder he always found my money stash no matter how hard I tried to hide it."

Athena sighed.

"And you!" said Rosemary. "How did you know about this?"

Athena shot her a slightly guilty look. "Finnigan told me a little."

"Finnigan!" Rosemary cried, feeling her blood beginning to metaphorically boil. "That boy! He's to blame for all this!"

"What on earth are you talking about?" Athena asked.

"Well, he's fae, isn't he? That explains it. And fae took that little girl – and he's always trying to get you to disappear off with him, like at the pub that first time."

"Mum, you're sounding quite mad."

"I don't care!" Rosemary shouted. "I don't want you seeing him."

"Calm your britches!" Granny's voice boomed, as if over loud speakers.

Rosemary visibly deflated, like a small child being scolded.

"What's this about a child disappearing?" Granny asked. "Give me details."

Rosemary explained about the situation with the little girl who'd gone missing, and the suspected abduction by faeries, or perhaps something more sinister.

Granny tutted again. "First Dain, now this. They really should have learnt by now not to meddle."

"What does this have to do with Dad?" Athena asked.

Granny scratched her chin. "The specifics evade me. Has anything else happened that seemed suspicious?"

"My necklace seems to be missing as well," Rosemary said. "I left it on the bathroom bench by the sink and Athena swears she didn't take it."

"Oh, I know about that," said Granny.

"You do?" Rosemary and Athena both asked.

"Yes, I have certain abilities to detect the goings on in my house," said Granny.

"So what happened?" Rosemary asked. "Who took it?"

"That remains a mystery," said Granny. "Whoever took it knows how to magically cover their tracks, so to speak."

Rosemary felt a creeping discomfort.

"You're saying someone came into the house and stole it?" said Athena. "I was sure Mum just lost it behind the couch or something."

"Quite probably," said Granny. "Or they found some other way to get it out of here, but that is less likely. The house is well-protected."

"So you think the missing necklace might be connected to the missing girl? Or Dad?" Athena asked.

Granny shrugged. "Beats me. But the fae folk are known for taking shiny things, and that boy of yours sure was a shiny one."

Rosemary glared at her grandmother. "He's not mine, and he's not a boy. Apparently he's not even human!"

Rosemary pulled out her phone and began dialling.

"What are you doing?" Athena asked.

"I need to file a missing person's report regarding Dain, before I forget again."

"You think the authorities are going to believe it when you say he was captured by faeries? Who are also his own kind?" Athena asked.

"Fortunately, we're in Myrtlewood," said Rosemary. "So yes. I'm calling Detective Neve."

Athena and Granny waited while Rosemary called the detective, saying she needed to report a missing person, and gave some brief details about Dain. Neve said she'd be right over.

"Come on," said Rosemary, feeling grumpy that her grandmother hadn't thought to tell her any of this before. "Let's go downstairs and wait for her."

"Suit yourselves," said Granny.

"But how do we get up here again, Granny Thorn?" Athena asked. "How can we get to this awesome tower room when the door keeps disappearing?"

"It's *my* room and I'll let you in when I feel like it," said Granny Thorn firmly.

"What happened to 'the dead shall have no claim over the living'?" Rosemary asked. Granny was beginning to fade out, and as grumpy as she was, she had a pang of regret that Granny would soon disappear again.

"I'm not claiming you living folk, just my special room. You have the whole rest of the house, which you can care for as you see fit. Besides, I don't see why you're sleeping in that tiny room when you can have my old bedroom and get rid of all the junk that's in there."

"I thought it was out of respect, actually," said Rosemary. "Really, Granny? You just want me to throw out all your stuff and move into your room and deck out the house as I see fit?"

"I left it to you, didn't I?" Granny said, her voice becoming quieter.

"All except the tower, apparently," said Athena. "What's the point in living in a big old house if I don't get to sleep in the tower?"

Granny grinned at her. "I like her. A girl after my own heart!"

"Wait," said Rosemary. "If the fae magic doesn't affect Athena because she's fae, why did she forget about Dain and about the car?"

It was too late for a response from Granny, who had disappeared, leaving the mirror looking perfectly ordinary.

Athena shrugged. "Maybe I just didn't care enough to remember, or I blocked it out because I can't stand Dad. Or maybe it was a different spell that time, on purpose. Oh, I know, the fae might have human witches working for them and they used a special kind of magic because they wanted me to forget..."

ATHENA CONTINUED to hypothesise as they made their way back downstairs to wait for the detective, but she stopped on the landing, in front of Rosemary. "What's that creaking?"

Rosemary groaned. "Not more surprises!"

The sound was coming from Granny's old room.

Rosemary tentatively peeked in through the open door to see Granny's possessions had vanished. The old rickety bed had been replaced by a larger four poster that looked to be carved out of cherry wood. Rosemary watched in delight as it made itself with a plum-coloured quilt, lavender sheets, and far more pillows than anyone could reasonably use.

"I guess this room is mine now," said Rosemary. "If Granny insists."

She checked the closet to find her clothes had already been magically transported there, and noted her other belongings were tidily arranged around the room.

"Finally!" said Athena. "I thought you'd never move out of that kid's room. I suspected it was some kind of childhood regression thing."

Rosemary shrugged. "Maybe it was. But don't we all need to regress once in a while? Curl up in the foetal position, that sort of thing."

"I guess you have gone through a lot of change lately."

"We both have, love," said Rosemary.

"Now you have a much cooler bed than me," Athena grumbled and looked out the windows to the darkening sky.

They continued on downstairs. "I suppose I should rustle up some dinner," Rosemary muttered. "Beans on toast?"

"Fine," said Athena, glancing at her mother. "What? What are you frowning about?"

Rosemary was indeed frowning. "Don't think I've forgotten that you knew all this stuff about fae and didn't tell me."

"Actually, I was hoping you *would* forget about that," Athena said.

"It's not a joke, Athena. This situation is dangerous. I can't have you holding things back from me like that."

"I'm still coming to terms with it, okay?" Athena said. "How would *you* feel if you found out your whole life had been a lie?"

"Kind of terrible, actually," said Rosemary. "Remember, it happened about a week ago."

"No one told *me* my father was some kind of mythical being."

"That's not my fault," said Rosemary. "No one told me, either."

"It's clearly *his* fault," said Athena. "And you never even get mad at him, which I assume is to do with his fae magic too. I've been mad at him for years and now I don't even know what to think."

"You still should have told me," said Rosemary sternly. "I'm your mother. I need to know things."

"And I need my privacy!" Athena shot back.

A knock at the door interrupted their argument. Detective Neve had arrived. She was dressed in somewhat more casual clothing than Rosemary had seen her in before, jeans and a knitted woollen navy jumper.

"Tell me what you know," Neve said. "When was the last time you saw Dain?"

"The thing is," said Rosemary, "I didn't exactly see him. I texted him and he appeared to have arrived with the boxes of our stuff from Burkenswood. Our old car was even here, but he had disappeared."

Neve nodded. "No sign of him since?"

"Nothing," said Rosemary. "The car seemed to disappear too. I'm not even sure when. I didn't remember. Actually, I keep forgetting everything about it."

"It does sound a lot like fae magic," said Neve.

"We think Dad is fae, too," Athena said. "At least, that explains all the noises in my head."

Neve gave her a quizzical look. "You're saying your father is high fae and was living in the human world?"

Athena nodded. "That's what we think. Not that he was any good at the human world stuff. He was totally useless, as a matter of fact."

"It's very rare," said Neve. "Those with both fae and human heritage can get on alright here, for the most part, but fae without any human DNA to ground them... Well, they tend to stick to their realm and only cause trouble here occasionally. For one to be living here for years is almost unheard of."

A tingle of fear ran down Rosemary's spine that she couldn't quite explain. "Do you think this has anything to do with the little girl who went missing?" she asked.

"It's hard to say," said Neve. "Children have gone missing before. Usually it happens around the equinox."

"Marjie mentioned that. It's just awful!" said Rosemary. "Why would anyone live here when such a thing happens?"

"Actually," said Neve, "some families with young children choose not to live here for that reason. You won't see many babies around, because fae have a long-standing habit of trying to swap them for their own kind."

"Changelings," said Athena.

"That's right. They cause havoc. But with older children, disappearances are rarer. Besides, they can happen anywhere. It's only a little more common in places like Myrtlewood where the magical energy is so strong. It thins the veil between the worlds even further."

"What happens to the kids that disappear?" Athena asked.

"They sometimes do come back," said Detective Neve. "Though people say they are different. They won't have aged as much as they should have because time works differently on other planes."

"It happened to Sherry, didn't it?" Rosemary asked.

"I can't talk about personal details unrelated to your reported case," said Neve with a tired smile. "You should ask her about it if you want to know more."

"I just keep thinking about that woman – Prue," said Rosemary. "The expression on her face..."

"I see a lot of things in my line of work," said Neve. "But when children are involved, it's always heart-wrenching. We are going to be busy down at the station, so don't be surprised if I have to delay our dinner invite for a while."

"I completely understand," said Rosemary. "Dinner is a low priority."

Her stomach chose that exact moment to protest such a statement with a loud growl, making them all laugh, though given the circumstances, it came out as half-hearted chuckles.

"The other thing," said Neve, "is that I'm going to have to go out of town again. I won't be on duty, but feel free to call me. Leave a message if I don't answer."

Athena and Rosemary shot each other worried glances.

"A work emergency?" Athena asked.

"I'm afraid not," said Neve. "This is a personal matter. It's my aunt, you see. She was totally fine until just recently, but now she's talking about missing children and babbling."

"Missing children, like Gretchen?" Athena asked.

"No," said Neve. "Someone else who never existed, I'm afraid. We think it might be dementia."

"I hope it all works out," said Rosemary, though in her mind she was wondering whether this could be another wild goose chase taking the only competent law enforcement out of town at a critical moment. Neve had been away during their last enormous crisis, leaving them to deal with Constable Perkins who caused more harm than good.

"Thanks," said Neve. "Take care, and I'll update you when I find out anything else about Dain and the circumstances of his disappearance."

"Thank you," Rosemary said, seeing Neve out.

As soon as the door was closed she rounded on Athena.

"I still cannot believe you didn't tell me about you being a faerie. Or about Dain!"

"Settle down, Mum. I told you, I'm still processing."

"You can process when we're out of danger."

"I'm not a baby. Why do you think we're in any kind of danger?"

"What if they come for you?" Rosemary asked.

"That's ridiculous," said Athena. "Why would they?"

"They came for Dain, didn't they? Isn't that what Granny implied?"

"He probably owed them money!"

Rosemary sighed. "You're not taking this seriously."

"I'm still grappling with the fact that we are in a situation warranting taking faeries seriously!"

"Athena!"

"What?"

Rosemary looked at her daughter's defiant expression and it only fuelled her rage. "You're grounded until further notice."

"Don't be ridiculous. I didn't do anything wrong."

"You didn't tell me something which was very important," said Rosemary. "And I am going to take this seriously even if you are determined not to. The danger is very real."

"You've never grounded me before. This is stupid!"

"I've never needed to," said Rosemary.

Athena crossed her arms and scowled. "Fine. I don't care. Take away all my human rights and imprison me for all I care."

"And you're forbidden from seeing that faerie boy – Finnigan – too," said Rosemary.

"What?"

"It's too dangerous!"

Athena gave her mother a disgusted look, then turned on her heels and stormed upstairs.

CHAPTER
TWENTY-SIX

Athena paced her room. She didn't feel hungry. Well, she did, a little, but she didn't want to take her mother's peace offering of beans on toast, left outside the door, because that felt like admitting defeat or conceding on something important.

Rosemary was clearly out of line. Just because fae might be responsible for one disappearing human child and for claiming back one of their own kind, it didn't mean all fae were bad. Besides, there was no conclusive proof that the fae were behind any of this. For all they knew, it could just be spurious rumours or someone making it seem like the fae so that they could get away with it. Whatever *it* was.

Athena was sure that Rosemary was jumping to conclusions, and worse, she was being fae-phobic or species-ist or perhaps something else that hadn't been adequately named by humans because almost the entire population wasn't aware any of this existed.

It wasn't fair to discriminate against Finnigan, who had done nothing wrong, just because Rosemary was scared of the fae.

On top of that, Athena was furious that her mother was being insanely over-protective. I can look after myself! I might not have Mum's Buffy-strength or vampire-slaying powers, or anything that resembles useful magical defences, but I'm not a baby!

She badly wanted to call Finnigan and talk to him about all this, but she didn't dare. Though she knew she could talk to Elise at school and maybe even Sam or Ash, it wasn't quite the same as talking to Finnigan.

He understands me in a way that others don't, but he's so damn evasive.

Athena felt a pang of longing and wanted to call out to him, but she knew now that Granny would be watching. And, mad as she was with Rosemary's controlling behaviour, she also didn't want to make things worse for herself by revealing how simple it would be for her to call out to the fae boy, how easily she could slip away into the night and never have to deal with her mother's annoying over-protectiveness ever again.

Instead, she patted the little kitten on the end of her bed with a resigned sigh.

"At some point, Mum is going to have to let go of control," she muttered to the cat. "Or I'll have to take matters into my own hands."

CHAPTER
TWENTY-SEVEN

Rosemary opened her eyes, feeling awful. It was far too early to be awake and there was a banging sound that simply would not go away.

It took her a moment to realise the noise was somebody knocking at the door downstairs that continued into what seemed like endless drumming.

She groaned.

The sound continued, only punctuated occasionally by slight pauses, before it continued rat-a-tat-tat.

Who on earth would be knocking so persistently at this ungodly hour?

Rosemary moaned as she got up, covering herself in a dressing gown, and made her way downstairs.

Ferg was at the door.

"What are you doing here?" Rosemary asked.

"I'm here to deliver the plants, of course," said Ferg.

"Plants?" Rosemary asked as something familiar clicked in the back of her mind. "Oh, that's right. How did I sign up for this?"

"You wanted to help with the Spring Equinox," said Ferg. "And help you will!"

Rosemary groaned again. "Fine, I'll show you around to the greenhouse."

"Excellent," said Ferg. "The trailers are here and ready for unloading."

"Trailers, plural?" Rosemary peeked behind him to see two cars with large trailers laden with plant pots. "What have I done?"

"It's not what you've done. It's what you're doing for the goodness of the town. And we're very pleased. We appreciate it very much, Rosemary."

Rosemary gave a half-hearted wave to the eclectically dressed people standing by the trailers.

"Shall I introduce you?" Ferg asked.

"Don't bother," said Rosemary. "At this time of day I'm never going to remember anyone's name."

"Very well," said Ferg.

"The greenhouse is this way." Rosemary pulled a coat on top of her dressing gown. She stumbled outside, and around the side of the house.

The greenhouse, unlike the central part of the house, was in a dishevelled state just like the two wider wings of Thorn Manor.

"Oh no, this simply won't do," said Ferg. "Oh, no, no, no."

"What?" Rosemary asked, unimpressed.

"Tulips are beautiful divine blooms. They require a lovely environment. This is objectively un-lovely."

"Where are we going to put them?" Rosemary asked. "Outside?"

"At this time of year?" said Ferg, outraged. "No, they must go in the house."

"In the house? No way!" Rosemary protested.

"But they'll need your constant care and attention," said Ferg. "You'll need to work your magic on them."

"Constant?!" Rosemary asked.

"Well, not a lot of attention, perhaps not constant," said Ferg. "But regular."

Rosemary sighed. It was too early in the morning for her to properly process what was going on, let alone adequately fight Ferg, who seemed to have a will of steel.

"I guess I've got to pick my battles," Rosemary muttered. She stumbled back into the house. "You can just put them in there." She waved in the general direction of the living room. "I'm going back to bed."

"Very well," said Ferg with a cheerful smile. "I'll see you again soon, Rosemary. Thanks for all your help."

Rosemary waved weakly and wandered back upstairs feeling bamboozled. She had no idea how to magically grow plants, or even grow them the regular way. But it was far too much to think about at this time the day. She'd have to look at some possible options in Granny's books later. After all, she did still want to help get little Gretchen back. She didn't see any other way around it.

She fell back into bed with a thump, wondering how she'd ever gotten herself into such a mess.

CHAPTER

TWENTY-EIGHT

It should be easy, Rosemary told herself. She focused on the bucket of water sitting on the kitchen bench, willing it to rise.

Nothing happened.

She tried again, concentrating as hard as possible.

"What are you doing?" Athena asked.

"Concentrating," said Rosemary. The water slopped over the side of the bucket.

"Well, if you were trying to make a mess on the counter, congratulations I guess," Athena said.

"I'm *trying* to use my magic to make the freaking plants grow."

"Mum, have you lost your marbles?" said Athena. She wandered out of the room. "Ah! What happened to the lounge?"

"Ferg," said Rosemary, as if the single word was explanation enough.

Athena looked at her and then burst into hysterical laughter. "This is you helping with the ritual?" she asked, catching her breath before laughing some more.

Rosemary narrowed her eyes at her daughter. "I was trying to use my elemental magic, you know...master the element of water or something. Plants need water to grow."

"You might want to try moving a bit closer to the targets," said Athena.

"Fine." Rosemary picked up the bucket and placed it in the middle of the living room, which was now filled with hundreds of plant pots. "This is ridiculous. House – I hope you've got this covered." She tapped the wood of the wall nearest to her.

"Now who's ridiculous?" said Athena.

"I don't want everything getting soggy, okay?"

The house creaked. Rosemary chose to take that as a sign of agreement. "Here we go." She held her hands in front of her, focusing on the bucket, visualising the element of water, of emotions and connection, but all she connected with was her frustration and sense of overwhelm at being in far over her head.

"Nothing?" said Athena. "Maybe you're full of too much hot air to work with elemental water."

"Hey," said Rosemary. "That's a bit harsh."

"No," Athena said. "I mean, your elemental make up is more fire and air. You know, I've been learning about this in Cosmos and Astrology class. You're a Sagittarius with a Gemini rising, plus you've got a bunch of other fire and air in your chart."

"I thought star sign stuff was all nonsense," said Rosemary. "I've read my horoscopes in magazines. If I was a true Sagittarius I'd be out in nature, travelling and having big adventures, plus everyone would think I was wise."

"Yes, but because you have a Gemini ascendant people think you're shallow and ditzy, even if you've got a bit of depth underneath."

Rosemary frowned. "That's true, I suppose. And you're no typical Leo or you'd be off performing."

"Virgo ascendant," said Athena. "With a changeable Pisces moon. It's no wonder I burst into tears so easily as a child."

"What does all this have to do with growing these blasted plants?" said Rosemary.

"If you can't connect with water easily, maybe try it another way. Use your magic – use the air to carry the water."

"Oh," said Rosemary. "I see. That's not a bad idea. I'll give it a shot."

She closed her eyes again, imagining her magic shooting out into the water. The element of air came easily to her, like Athena said. It was light and quick, and clear. She pushed her hands out, as if directing a current of air towards the bucket. A gentle spray landed on her skin. She opened her eyes to find the water spraying out in delicate sprinkles, all over the plants, miraculously missing the living room furniture.

"Brilliant!" Rosemary exclaimed.

A slow clap sounded from Athena. "I'm impressed. You're finally learning how to use your magic intentionally when you aren't even in crisis."

Rosemary shrugged. "I figured this ridiculous plant situation is a good excuse to experiment."

"Aren't you supposed to be using magic to make them grow super-fast, not just to water them?"

"Yeah, don't remind me. I have no idea how to do that."

"There are plenty of books, Mum."

"You know I can't follow instructions. It's just like when I cook. I have to be intuitive."

"Alright, have it your way," said Athena. "I don't even know why you agreed to help with this anyway. What a sucker."

"Ferg convinced me that it's the best way to help get that little girl back."

"Well, you're going to have to try a little harder."

Rosemary looked around the room at the glistening plants. Her gaze drifted outside the window. "I have an idea," she said, closing her eyes.

The element of fire is new beginnings, she recalled. Passion, energy, instigation...

She connected with the fire within herself, with her strong will and drive, then she imagined the plants all growing, remembering a lush spring day in her childhood when she was visiting Granny, running across the lawn, picking daisies, helping to pot bulbs in the greenhouse.

"Wow! Mum!"

"Don't distract me."

"No seriously, look!"

Rosemary peeked to see bright green were springing up in every plant pot in the room.

"Amazing!" said Rosemary.

Athena beamed at her. "Very impressive. I bet you can get them to bloom in no time."

"That's a relief," said Rosemary. "Maybe I will be able to help get that girl back after all."

"Hey, you're not going to the fae realm, are you?"

"There's no way in Cerridwen's Cauldron," said Rosemary. "It's too dangerous. I don't even know if humans can go in there."

Athena shrugged and looked out the window.

"You want to go there, don't you?" Rosemary said. "We all want to find out what happened to Dain, but Athena, it's not safe."

"I told you I don't want anything to do with Dad."

"That's probably just as well," said Rosemary. "Because I absolutely forbid you to go to the fae realm."

"You know you can't protect me forever," said Athena. "I mean you can barely protect me as it is. I can look after myself. I don't belong to you."

Rosemary was bereft. Never, in all the years since she'd had Athena, had she felt so alone.

"Athena, you're all I have," she said.

An expression of guilt crossed Athena's face. "I can't be everything to you, Mum, I need to have my own life. And I'm not all you have. You've got a whole big house. You've got tons of money. You've got Marjie and your job. You've got your business to set up. You've got everything, and what do I have?"

"I thought you liked it here," Rosemary said.

"I do," Athena replied. "I just...I don't have cool powers like you and I'm still trying to figure everything out. Let me figure it out on my own. You can't do everything for me."

Rosemary sighed and raised her arms, walking towards her daughter to hug her. "I know you're good at looking after yourself. Just understand. I can't bear the thought of anything bad happening to you."

"I'm not a kid anymore." Athena gently pushed Rosemary away. "I just need some space." She stomped out of the room and upstairs.

Rosemary's feeling of triumph at using her magic to water the plants quickly evaporated.

"Time for some tea, I think," she said to herself.

CHAPTER
TWENTY-NINE

Athena was clearly in a foul mood when Rosemary picked her up after school on Monday.

"I shouldn't have to wait half an hour for you to finish work," she said as she got into the car. "I'm perfectly safe walking around in broad daylight."

"That little girl disappeared in the middle of the day," said Rosemary, steering Granny's lovely old Rolls Royce out into the street.

"I'm not a bloody five-year-old!"

"You sound hangry," said Rosemary.

"I'm just plain old angry."

"Not hungry at all?"

"No."

"Well, that's too bad, because I thought we could go to the pub for an early dinner."

"Fine," said Athena. "Do whatever you want, just like you usually do."

"I thought it would be a nice thing to do," said Rosemary. "Friday night at the pub, fish n' chips for dinner."

Athena sighed. "Whatever."

"Aren't you glad the week is over?"

"No," said Athena. "That just means I have more time imprisoned with *you*."

"Oh, don't be so dramatic," said Rosemary. "There's your Leo side showing."

They spent the rest of their drive in silence.

Athena's mood didn't lighten, even after they arrived into the warm, cosy atmosphere of the pub.

Rosemary looked around for Sherry, who didn't appear to be behind the bar. She had called the pub earlier to try to arrange a catch up after she'd heard about Sherry's involvement with the fae, but no one had answered. Rosemary reasoned that surely if Sherry had disappeared into the other world and come back, she might have some useful information that could help to bring Gretchen back, provide some clue about Dain's whereabouts, and protect other children in Myrtlewood.

There were no staff in sight, and as it was so early, only a few customers were present, clustered around some of the tables. Rosemary didn't recognise any of them in particular, though they seemed to give her a look that said they knew who she was.

It was a strange thing to be known and revered, purely for her family's reputation. Rosemary gave a polite nod and led Athena to what had already become their usual table.

She grabbed the menus that were propped up by the salt and pepper and handed one to Athena who gave her a glum look.

"Oh, come on!" said Rosemary. "This arrangement isn't forever, just until it's safe."

"And what if it's never safe?" Athena asked. "Are you going to try and keep me locked up until I'm thirty?"

"Of course not," said Rosemary. "But I'm currently legally responsible for you, and as you keep saying, you don't have any clear magical powers that can defend you yet."

"Actually, I do," said Athena, pulling a small arsenal of charms out of both of her pockets and dumping them on the table.

"Put those away before Constable Perkins shows up and tries to arrest us," said Rosemary. "I mean, it's good you've got all that but... Wait, when did you even have time to make them?"

"It's not like I have much else to do these days," said Athena. "I set up a little production stand in my room just so I have something to do at night. Maybe I can start a business of my own selling exploding charms and make enough money so I can afford to move far away from *you*!"

"Don't be ridiculous," said Rosemary. "I'm not that bad."

"You are," said Athena. "I don't even want to talk to you at the moment." She looked away from Rosemary and around the room instead.

"You're looking for *him*, aren't you?" Rosemary asked. "You're in a terrible grump with me because I told you that you're not to see Finnigan."

Athena chose not to respond and the silence was deafening.

"What will it be then?" a tired-sounding woman's voice said.

Rosemary looked up to see Sherry, looking very pale.

"Oh, it's you two," Sherry said with a wan smile. "Sorry I haven't returned your call from the other day, I've just been so exhausted lately."

"Is everything alright?" Rosemary asked. "You don't look very well."

"It's this time of year," said Sherry. "It always gets me. The thinning veil does strange things to my constitution, ever since...Anyway, what will you be having? Dinner is it?"

"Fish 'n chips, please," said Rosemary.

"Same, thank you," said Athena, giving Sherry a bright smile and then returning to glare at Rosemary.

"Lovely," said Sherry. "And I'll bring you some mulled mead, on the house!"

Sherry's voice sounded as if she was trying for enthusiasm, but it didn't carry through to her expression.

Rosemary tried to give Athena a meaningful look, but the teen was staring at the table. Clearly, there were no young fae men around to distract her from the fascinating wood grain. The food arrived a few moments later, as prompt as usual.

Rosemary eyed the crispy golden battered fish and fried potatoes with mouth-watering anticipation. She tasted it, only to be utterly disappointed.

It was bland and somehow bitter, even though none of the ingredients should have been bitter to begin with.

"Maybe the oil has gone bad," Rosemary said.

Athena didn't respond. She ate her food in silence, as if trying to punish her mother by withholding her verbal participation.

Rosemary took a sip of mulled mead. It, too, tasted bland, and for a moment she wondered whether there was something wrong with her sense of taste, and then she remembered Sherry's tired and pale demeanour.

"Stay here," said Rosemary.

She got up from the table and made her way towards the bar where Sherry was polishing glasses.

"It's terrible, isn't it," said Sherry as Rosemary approached.

"The food? It's...not quite as good as usual," Rosemary admitted.

"I'm sorry. My magic has gone all weak and our usual chef is on leave tonight."

"It's fine," said Rosemary. "I'm more worried about you, actually."

"I'll be right as rain in no time," said Sherry. "Once the equinox passes, that is."

"There's still a couple weeks to go," said Rosemary.

"Don't remind me."

"Is there anything I can do to help?"

"Nothing as far as I'm aware, unless you have some kind of antidote to the pull of the fae."

"Is that what's going on?" Rosemary asked. "What is the pull of the fae?"

"You probably know already that I was one of the children who was taken. The whole town has been talking about it, what with poor Gretchen going missing," said Sherry.

Rosemary nodded.

"Well, that place," Sherry continued. "It does things to you. It's almost as if a part of me was left behind there. I've never felt whole since."

"I was meaning to ask you about that," said Rosemary. "I wondered if there was anything you could tell me about how you got back. Anything that would help us get Gretchen back."

Sherry shook her head.

"It's awful," she said as tears visibly welled in her eyes.

"I'm sorry," said Rosemary. "I didn't realise. Was it traumatic – your experience over there?"

"No, quite the opposite," said Sherry. "But it's awful that I can't talk about it. All these thoughts spiral around in my head, but their magic is so powerful. I can't say anything. It kind of...drives me mad."

"Marjie said the fae have strong magic that stops people revealing too much information about them," Rosemary said. "It must be strange to have all that going on in your head and never be able to communicate about it."

"People said I came back changed," said Sherry. "But it was mostly just...so much in my head. A whole other world, that I can't even speak of at all. Though, even if I could, I don't know how I could even begin to explain."

"And it gets worse at this time of year?"

"Yes, I can almost forget about it at other times, but right now I feel like that little lost girl all over again. The memories come back. It's almost as if I can taste it. The other world is so close, and my spirit longs to cross back over."

Sherry clamped her hand over her mouth as if to stop herself from saying anymore. She looked surprised at what she'd revealed.

"It's okay," said Rosemary. "Let me know if there's anything I can do to make you feel better. We have a lot of books at the house and apparently a lot of magic even if we don't know how to use it properly yet."

Sherry shook her head. "It's no use. I'll just tough it out, as usual. Fae magic is far too strong."

Rosemary patted her friend on the shoulder reassuringly.

"It will be okay," she said, even though she was in a position to make no such promises.

THIRTY

As Rosemary made her way back to the table she noticed some familiar faces sitting across the way. She double checked to make sure Athena was accounted for and then headed towards Agatha and Covvey, the two eccentric townsfolk who had invited themselves to her dinner party not so long ago.

"Good evening, Rosemary," said Agatha. "Pull up a pew and join us."

"I won't trouble you for long," Rosemary said. "I hope you're both having a lovely evening."

"As good as any," said Covvey gruffly.

"I'm trying to find out about something," said Rosemary. "And I just remembered that you're a famous historian."

"How did you know?" Agatha asked suspiciously.

"Marjie told me, and apparently one of Athena's teachers is related to you."

"That little minx," said Agatha.

Rosemary wasn't sure if she was referring to Marjie or the teacher, but it seemed irrelevant. "But it's true, isn't it?" She smiled at Agatha.

"I might know a thing or two about magical history," Agatha conceded.

"Well, if you wouldn't mind, I'd quite like to know a bit about the fae realm and how all of that stuff works. I imagine a local historian would have some information."

"You don't want to go messing about with that stuff," Covvey growled. "Keep well away. You don't know what you're getting into."

Agatha sighed. "Since that little girl went missing the other day, people keep asking me as if I know blimin' everything. And you will find bits of information scattered around in *The History of Myrtlewood* and various other publications of mine, but I'm afraid there's not a lot to say."

"What is it with this place?" Rosemary asked, exasperated. "People aren't allowed to talk about who's a vampire. No one will tell me anything about fae, never mind the awful crap they do, and shifters are bound to attack at any moment."

"Watch your mouth," said Covvey, sounding hostile.

"I didn't mean to hit a nerve," Rosemary replied. "I just can't get my head around all these different magical creatures."

"Who are you calling a creature?" Covvey said aggressively.

"No one in particular," said Rosemary.

"Now listen young lady," Covvey continued. "Your Granny knew a thing or two about how to behave in polite company, and it would serve you well not to go around talking smack about things you don't understand."

Rosemary raised her hands in innocence. "I didn't mean to say anything offensive."

"Don't mind him," said Agatha. "Something's got his goat tonight and he's always a little bit sensitive when people talk badly about shifters. You know he's a wolf shifter."

Rosemary's eyes widened.

"Why'd you have to go and tell her?" Covvey said. "She's obviously prejudiced."

"Don't be silly," said Agatha. "You're not sensitive like vampires. You don't care who knows as long as they're magical."

Covvey folded his arms and looked down at the table with a stony expression.

"A wolf shifter?" Rosemary said, remembering the incident with Liam and how he'd been so sensitive about his otherness. "Like a werewolf?"

A vein bulged in Covvey's temple. He looked up at her with fire in his eyes. "How dare you! I'm no bloody werewolf! I'm a natural-born shifter, not infected by some heinous virus."

Rosemary felt her cheeks redden in embarrassment. Liam wasn't exaggerating when he talked about the prejudice against his kind. "I'm sorry. It looks like I stepped on your toes too many times this evening already. I'll just excuse myself."

She quickly nipped back to the table where Athena sat, staring at her phone.

"Let's get out of here," said Rosemary. "I feel like I've offended half the town without even meaning to."

Athena blew out a puff of air. "Fine. It's not like you care when you only offend me."

As they left the pub, Rosemary noticed Burk sitting across the room. She raised her hand to wave to him, but then noticed he was seated at a table next to a rather attractive woman with slick, wavy brown hair and a glamorous outfit.

Rosemary felt a bitter taste in her mouth and pang of emotion that she didn't want to call jealousy.

"What is it?" Athena asked, following her gaze. "Oh, so now will you admit you like him?"

"Don't start," Rosemary said.

Rosemary and Athena didn't talk on the drive home, but as they pulled into the driveway a strange light began to filter through the trees.

Rosemary's heart began to accelerate as they drew closer and it became patently obvious that something was very wrong.

Alarming bright yellow and red lit up the way ahead of them.

The car drew close and Rosemary's jaw dropped.

"No," said Athena.

"What on earth?" Rosemary cried, slowing the car. "Thorn Manor! It's on fire!"

Athena was silent in shock as the full realisation hit both of them.

"Not just part of it," said Rosemary. "Not just a small fire. The entire thing is in flames!"

Even the tower was covered in a vibrant blaze.

"I can see that," said Athena, her voice croaky.

"Not good," said Rosemary.

"Is that all you can say?" Athena asked. "Not good!?"

"My words aren't working properly," Rosemary mumbled.

"Who do we call?" Athena asked. "Is there even a fire department out here?"

Rosemary had been in so much shock she hadn't even thought of that. "Good question. Maybe the police will know?" Rosemary fumbled for her phone.

"It's probably too late. We've lost everything," Athena said, her face ashen. "Everything we own is in that house."

The loss began to sink in for Rosemary. It was more than mere possessions. It was the only place she'd felt at home and had huge sentimental value. Never mind that it had been in the family for generations. And what did this mean for Granny's ghost?

Rosemary could barely breathe. She finally found her phone and started looking up the Detective Neve's number.

"It's going to be too late," Athena said. "By the time the fire truck gets here, it'll all be gone."

Rosemary couldn't respond. Athena was surely right. The flames were huge, and yet, from where they were in the car Rosemary could feel no heat and see no smoke.

"Wait a minute." She got out of the car.

"Mum! What are you doing?" Athena asked.

"Just checking something."

Rosemary stared at the flaming house, noticing that the flames made no sound, either. Not a crackling. Not the sound of the wood beams bowing in the heat. In fact, the fire didn't seem to be doing much at all.

"What's going on?" Athena got out of her own side of the car to join her mother.

"I wish I knew," Rosemary said. "It's not...real."

Athena took a step closer.

"Wait," said Rosemary, holding back as Athena raised her hand. A ripple formed in the air, as if she'd touched upon some kind of membrane surrounding the house.

The fire flickered for a moment, like a dying light bulb, then they brightened.

"Wow!" said Athena as the flames burst into leaves and flowers in vibrant green and pink. "Are we tripping?" she asked Rosemary.

"I don't think the food at the pub was *that* bad."

Rosemary stepped forward, ready to try to channel her magic and protect them from whatever attack this surely must be.

The flowers and leaves grew to cover the entire house. Athena tapped against the membrane again and the foliage transformed into violet butterflies.

There was a moment of stillness followed by a gust of wind.

They all took flight, glowing in the air as they formed the words STAY AWAY, before vanishing completely.

"What – on – earth?" Rosemary stammered.

"It's the fae," Athena said in an eerily certain tone. "You've been asking too many questions and they know it."

"Hasn't everyone?" Rosemary asked. "The whole town is wondering about the missing girl."

"I think that was a warning for us, in particular," Athena said. "The fae don't want anyone to know about them."

"Well, if they don't want anyone to know about them, they shouldn't go around taking children. Should they?" said Rosemary. "We can't just leave poor Gretchen in their realm. What do you know about all this, anyway? Why are they so secretive?"

"Something to do with vampires, I think," said Athena. "Like, they've been at war for thousands of years. Fae taste delicious, apparently. The vampires hunted them to near extinction or something."

"I've heard mutterings about this," said Rosemary. "But how does it all connect?"

"I don't know. The fae have got a whole lot of binding magic so you can't talk about them, and it hurts the people who do know stuff if they say anything. I tried to find out and that's pretty much all I've got."

"Vampires," Rosemary said, feeling a cold discomfort in the pit of stomach as she thought of seeing Burk at dinner with another woman earlier.

"They, that's a good point," said Athena. "You should ask Burk. Didn't you say he's a million years old or something? He might have even been around when the war started."

Rosemary gave her daughter an exasperated look. "I don't think so."

"Mum," said Athena. "You want to get to the bottom of this, don't you?"

Rosemary nodded grimly.

"And I want you to stop being so freaking over-protective and leave me alone, which you did swear to do, once this whole fae thing is resolved."

"I'll think about it," Rosemary said. "Wait a minute. If this is really true, then aren't all the vampires after you?"

"The fae have powerful magic. Don't you think they would have thought about that and put protections in place?" Athena said in frustration. "No one can even see what I look like." She explained about the drawing situation with Sam.

"But that's ridiculous. How? And why would no one have noticed it before?" Rosemary asked.

"I think it must be in my genetics," said Athena. "There's something that obfuscates me somehow, so people don't my face for too long. Sam had to because it was part of the class. I don't recall anyone ever trying to draw me before."

"I know what you look like," said Rosemary.

"I've been thinking about that," said Athena. "You stare at me far too much. Maybe the genetic link overrides the fae magic. And other fae folk can see me too, I think."

"Why didn't you tell me any of this before?" Rosemary asked.

"I would feel more comfortable telling you about my life if you weren't so invasive and over-protective," Athena said.

And with that, they both went into Thorn Manor, to find it all exactly as they'd left it. The fire illusion had changed nothing.

CHAPTER
THIRTY-ONE

Athena paced her room. It was now or never. She'd been holding off on leaving, but every day that went by made her more desperate to know the truth about herself, just as time passing made her miss Finnigan more.

It was an ache in her heart that felt more like a drug addiction than anything she could imagine.

He'd told her to call when she was ready to go to the fae realm.

She needed to understand her heritage, to understand her powers and where half of her DNA apparently came from.

The closer they came to the equinox the harder it was getting to leave unnoticed. Rosemary barely let Athena out of her sight. Unfairly grounded as she was, she wasn't allowed to go out alone. The only privacy Athena had was in her bedroom.

She smiled to herself. If only Mum knew that this is the most dangerous place.

She looked around her room with its magically created balcony, that Rosemary thankfully hadn't yet noticed. She knew it wouldn't take much effort to climb from the edge of the balcony, down the side of the house, and head towards the forest. Granny might be watching her every move, but once Athena was gone there would be nothing either her mother or Granny's ghost could do about it.

Athena had done some research into the fae, although the internet was probably not the most reliable source of information. She'd scoured all the books she could find on the subject too.

In light of everything she'd learned, she packed her bag with useful supplies: Jaffa Cakes, a bar of chocolate, and two small packets of crisps in case she needed sustenance. She'd read that eating in the fae realm could be dangerous.

She wasn't sure if the charms and potions she knew how to make would work in a different realm, but she'd prepared and packed a whole bunch just in case, along with some shiny trinkets from her jewellery box, crystals and glass pebbles, and a vial of salt. She'd read that the fae were partial to cream, and so included a couple of little bottles of it in case they proved useful.

Athena popped downstairs to make herself a thermos of tea after Rosemary had gone to bed. *Tea is important.* She might be going into another world, but it was important that she had her priorities straight.

Packing everything tightly into her backpack with a couple of small spell books, Athena tried to put on the bag but found it awkwardly heavy. She remembered a quick charm for lightening the load and quickly brewed up the relevant magical powder.

She dusted it over her bag and discovered, to her delight, that it was as light a feather, "at least in this world," she muttered to herself.

She put it on over her warm coat and patted the little black kitten one more time.

"Goodbye Serpentine, or Fuzzball, or whatever your name is. I'll see you again soon...I hope."

She was dressed for travel with her sensible leather boots and jeans. She paced the length of her room again, several times, building up the courage, and then, without thinking too much, she braced herself against her fear.

Athena slipped out to the balcony to find it quickly morphing to include a trailing staircase all the way down to the lawn below.

"Thank you, house," she said softly. "Look after my mother for me. Will you?"

She stepped quietly down to the lawn and then ran to the edge of the forest.

"Finnigan," she called out. "I'm ready."

This was where he'd told her to meet him when she'd talked to him through her mind earlier. In an instant he was there beside her, his pale skin glinting in the moonlight.

"Athena, you came," he said, his expression gleeful like a small child at Christmas.

A thrill rolled through Athena and she couldn't help but smile.

"Are you afraid?" he asked.

"I'm terrified," Athena replied. "Quickly, let's go before I lose my nerve."

He took both her hands in his. A pale green light emerged from between their palms and then shone out ahead of them, shifting into a dotted line through the forest.

"Now what?" Athena asked.

"We follow," he said.

He let go of her right hand, keeping hold of her left, and they walked through the trees following the lighted path.

"What should I be expecting?" Athena asked.

"You'll see," Finnigan replied.

As they reached the end of the sparks of illumination, the flecks of light gathered together again like a shimmer of fireflies, then dispersed and reformed, creating an archway in front of them.

"Fairy lights," Athena said. Finnigan gave her a curious look. "Never mind."

"We go through," he said. "Keep hold of my hand."

Athena took a deep breath, and, grateful for the warmth Finnigan's hand, she stepped with him through the archway and into another world.

CHAPTER

THIRTY-TWO

A sudden burst of light shocked Rosemary out of her slumber. She ran to the window to see a bright flare of blue and white in the forest.

"Oh no. No, no!" Rosemary cried. "Athena! They're back – the Bloodstones."

She ran towards Athena's room, only to find it empty.

"No, no, no, no...Athena!" Rosemary called out. She ran quickly to search the rest of the house, her heart hammering in her chest, breath catching in her throat. Her daughter was nowhere in sight.

The world seemed as if it was blurring. Time slowed. Rosemary struggled against the riptide in her mind that was trying to pull her under.

The door to Granny's secret room was nowhere to be seen. Rosemary hammered on the wall, just in case, but nothing happened.

Cold, cold anguish and panic took over, immobilising Rosemary.

She stood on the landing, unable to function, barely able to breathe.

Athena's gone...Athena's gone, she thought, over and over in her head. She had to do something, anything.

A thought flashed through her mind. She ran back to her bedroom to find her phone and called Detective Neve. There was no answer. Rose-mary left a frantic message. Then she called Marjie. She didn't know what else to do and this, if anything, seemed like a good excuse to disturb somebody's peace.

Marjie answered on the second ring. "What time is it?" she asked groggily.

"Athena. She's gone. They've taken her," said Rosemary.

"Who's taken her, dear? Do you think she's run off with her friends or something?"

"No," said Rosemary. "I'm sure it's the fae."

"Take a few deep breaths in and out," said Marjie.

Rosemary tried to do as she was told. Her breath shuddered in her chest, disobedient.

"Now, where was she when you last saw her?" Marjie asked.

"She went to bed," said Rosemary. "At least, she was in her room."

"Is there anything unusual about how she left it?" Marjie asked. "Any sign of struggle?"

Rosemary checked. "The bed's still made. They must have gotten her before she even went to sleep. I can't believe I let this happen," said Rose-mary as her eyes fell on a small blue envelope lying on Athena's pillow with the word 'Mum' written on it. "I think there's a note."

"What does it say?"

"What if it's not safe to touch?"

"Do you want me to come over there and check?"

"No, it's fine." Rosemary picked up the note and nothing happened. Her heart sank when she recognised Athena's handwriting. "Do you think they made her write it?"

"I don't know, dear," said Marjie. "Have you read it yet?"

Rosemary tried to hold her shaking hand still and concentrate as she read.

I'm sorry I have to leave so abruptly, but it's the only way. I need to find out for myself about my heritage. This is not about Dad and it's not about you. It's about me. I need to do this for myself. I know you'd never let me go, so I only hope you forgive me.

"I CAN'T BELIEVE IT," Rosemary said after she'd read the note to Marjie. "Athena wouldn't do this without someone leading her astray. It's that boy!"

"That might be so," said Marjie. "But right now you have to deal with the fact your daughter's gone to the fae realm."

"How do I get her back?" Rosemary asked. It was her single-minded focus and she was absolutely determined to do it.

"Now that might be a little more complicated."

CHAPTER
THIRTY-THREE

"Granny!" she yelled, but no answer came. "Granny! I need you!"
Silence.

Rosemary walked slowly down the stairs. She could barely see through the dark feelings of anguish clouding her mind. At a normal time of crisis she would automatically put the kettle on in pursuit of the soothing power of tea, but this was not a normal time.

She could not think. She could barely breathe.

She walked without awareness of her body or of what she was doing. One foot automatically placed itself in front of the other, her mind scrambling to tell her this was an anomaly, a delusion, a dream, and that surely she would wake up any minute.

Rosemary found herself in the living room, surrounded by tulips. The tulips she had helped to grow with her magic. She'd managed to make them bloom, but that seemed like a lifetime ago. The flowers were out of place. They taunted her with their bright tones of red, yellow, and purple, when surely given the present situation the entire world must have lost all hope of joy or colour.

This can't be real.

Rosemary pinched herself, trying in vain to wake up.

It's not a dream.

Athena is gone. From this world, at least.

She opened her mouth and an unearthly wail escaped, along with it, a great rush of dark grey energy.

"Nooooo!" she bellowed.

The energy expanded out from her and then dispersed, leaving a trail of destruction in its wake.

As the cloud cleared, Rosemary looked around in shock to find that every last tulip had withered and died back into the soil.

A darkness inside her preened in satisfaction. If Athena is gone, then surely nothing bright and beautiful belongs here.

The dark energy that had escaped left Rosemary feeling limp and haggard. She collapsed there, on the living room floor, unable to bear any more of the present reality.

ROSEMARY OPENED her eyes and looked around. She was in bed, in her room. Her lovely new room with the carved wooden bed and plum décor. Everything should have been normal, but it wasn't. She felt as if she'd been run over by a truck and then backed over again several times.

She was burdened by the lead weight of emotion from what must have surely been a nightmare.

She breathed a sigh of relief and then was startled by a knock on her bedroom door.

"Athena?" Rosemary mumbled.

"Don't mind me," Marjie said, bustling in with a tea tray. "I'm just here to help."

"What?" Rosemary asked, confused.

"I came as quick as I could and found you collapsed on the floor surrounded by dead plants. I told that silly Ferg your magic wasn't ready to help with the plants."

"No, no, no," said Rosemary. "She's really gone."

Marjie gave her a sympathetic look.

"It wasn't a dream?" Rosemary asked.

"I'm afraid not," said Marjie.

Rosemary lay in bed, unmoving, a deep grief washing over her.

"Now, now," said Marjie. "Sit up. Here. Drink your tea."

Rosemary allowed Marjie to prop her up in bed with a stack of pillows because it seemed easier than trying to refuse. She took a sip of Marjie's special tea and immediately felt a warmth spreading through her, though it wasn't nearly enough to lift the burden of grief.

"Thank you," Rosemary said. "I feel a little better. I'm no use to anyone if I can't move."

"Oh love, now you must take it easy. What did you do to the plants, then?" Marjie teased gently.

"I actually...made them grow," Rosemary said. "Then, after I found out Athena was missing, something happened, and they all died at once. Anyway, we've got more important things to think about than plants."

"You might say that," said Marjie. "But remember we need the blooming spring bulbs for the equinox ritual – to pay tribute to the Goddess. If that doesn't go to plan, then who knows how we're going to get Athena or little Gretchen back."

"Do you think it will work for Athena too?" Rosemary asked hopefully.

"There's nothing sure about it," said Marjie. "None of us knows what Galdie did to retrieve Sherry from the fae realm, or whether it was pure luck. And I suppose it also depends on whether your girl is ready to return."

"What do you mean?" asked Rosemary, narrowing her eyes.

Marjie sighed. "You think she went with that boy?"

"Either that or she was taken by somebody else."

"The situation with Athena could be quite a different circumstance from the situation with Gretchen," said Marjie. "We know that young children have disappeared to the fae realm multiple times, but I've never seen a fully-fledged teenager wandering in there of her own accord. It should be impossible, but I suppose one with her heritage..."

"Don't tell me you knew about that as well!" Rosemary said.

"I'm sorry, dear. I forget you were living in the mundane world almost completely until just recently. You *so* belong here that it's hard to imagine you anywhere else."

"That's a nice thing to say," said Rosemary. "But how did you know about Dain?"

"Galdie told me the minute she met him that her granddaughter was involved with a fae boy. I thought she meant a dryad or a nymph, but she was quite sure he was the real deal."

"And you didn't think to tell me?"

"I thought you knew, dear. It was rather obvious to your grand-mother. I've never met any of the true high fae myself, so I wouldn't know, but I trust Galdie. They're said to be quite clever at disguising themselves, but I was sure Athena had that otherworldly look."

Rosemary grimaced. "High fae? Is that a rank thing or are they just smoking magic pixie weed?"

"I suspect it's more like a species."

"Well, I had no freaking idea that all those years I was involved with a mythical creature."

Marjie gave her polite smile. "Would you like some more of my special tonic?"

"Make it a triple," said Rosemary. "I don't know how I'm going to get through the day. I need all the help I can get."

"I'll give you the maximum dose," said Marjie. "Anymore and you'll feel all squishy."

"Thank you," said Rosemary. "And thanks for coming to look after me. I don't know what to do with myself."

"It's no trouble at all," said Marjie. "I'm here to help."

"What about the shop?"

"Herb will look after it for the day," said Marjie. "He made a fuss, but I told him where to shove his little trains."

Rosemary gave an involuntary laugh, despite the fact that she wasn't feeling like amusement should exist in the same world as her other emotions right now.

She couldn't stay in bed. She had to get Athena back.

"I have to go," Rosemary said.

"You might want to get changed first," said Marjie. "It took a lot of effort to magically bring you up to bed, but I didn't go to the trouble of trying to change your clothes. You look like you might need to shower as well, before you go into town."

"No, I mean I need to go to the fae realm. I need to follow Athena and bring her back now."

"That will be tricky," said Marjie. "Children may have been known to slip across when the veil is thin, or be taken, but adults are another matter entirely. Athena may have been able to go through easily because of her heritage. I suppose she would have the DNA to unlock the gate."

"There's a gate?" Rosemary asked. "Where is it?"

"From what I understand, it can be summoned, but it doesn't belong in a fixed location in this world, although there are places where the veil is thin – all those stories of the fairy rings between mushrooms, and obviously Fin's Creek has been the location of many disappearances."

"There must be some kind of spell," said Rosemary. "Some kind of magic that can get me there."

"Fae magic is different from ours," said Marjie. "Not something witches can perform or even comprehend. They've protected themselves well, against the vampires of course."

"Will you help me?"

"Of course, dear," said Marjie. "Though our best bet is to prepare for the equinox."

"But that's not for two weeks!" said Rosemary. "I can't wait that long. Anything could happen to Athena in that amount of time."

"It's possible Athena will pop back by then," said Marjie. "I bet that girl is more powerful than even she realises."

"We can only hope." Rosemary took a big sip of tea, feeling Marjie's soothing uplifting magic at work. It did nothing to dispel her extreme dread, but it did calm her nerves a little.

Marjie excused herself and went downstairs to the kitchen. Rosemary was left alone for a moment before the little black kitten appeared, jumping onto her bed with a trill and prancing towards her.

"Hello, little Fuzzball," said Rosemary, raising her hand to pat the purring furry creature. "Or should I call you Serpentine? Athena would like that."

The kitten nuzzled at her palm.

"You miss her too, don't you," Rosemary continued. "Don't worry. We'll get her back."

The furry creature looked her in the eye with such knowing that Rosemary felt goosebumps prickle her arms.

This is no ordinary cat and the Thorns are no ordinary family.

She pulled together every ounce of strength she had, determined to retrieve her daughter, no matter what the cost.

CHAPTER

THIRTY-FOUR

Rosemary was vaguely aware that she looked dishevelled, but she didn't care. Her hair was a frizzy mess and her clothing was even more mismatched than on laundry day as she strode across the town square.

"Good morning, Rosemary," said Ferg. "How are those tulips growing?"

She was not in any state for small talk let alone having to explain what happened to the blasted flowers.

"Not now. I'm in a hurry," she said, brushing past him. At least that's what she intended to say. The words came out as more of a murmur.

She pushed her way through the doors of Burk's law office, feeling a twinge of embarrassment on top of everything else. She didn't really want to see the annoyingly attractive vampire after feeling jealous of seeing him at the pub with someone else. She smothered the emotion. She had more important things on her mind.

Rosemary had remembered, as she lay in bed trying to sleep the night before, that if vampires and fae had been at war for a long time, then surely vampires would know something. Athena had even suggested that before she went missing. But Rosemary had been too stubborn or too proud to listen.

Rosemary needed to find out what Burk knew, even if it was just what wouldn't work. Any information could save her time. The sleek silver-haired woman at the front desk eyed her suspiciously.

"I need to see Burk," Rosemary said.

"Mr Burk is not available right now." She flashed a false smile. "You can make an appointment."

"I need to see him now," said Rosemary, realising she sounded unhinged. "Look, I'll just call him."

"Don't trouble yourself," said Burk, emerging from the passageway. "Rosemary, come into my office." He held the door open for her.

Rosemary gave the receptionist a strange look. "She said you weren't here."

"Charlotte tries to protect me from interruptions," Burk explained dismissively as she followed him into his office. "Rosemary," he said, turning to her. "What's wrong? I've never seen you look so troubled."

"It's Athena," Rosemary said, not able to hold back the tears. It struck her that she hadn't cried. Not when she first discovered Athena was missing, not the next day, and not in the night when she was trying to sleep, but now being asked a simple, kindly worded question was all too much.

Burk disappeared from the room, jolting Rosemary, but he was back a moment later with a box of tissues. He held one up for her.

"Thank you," she said, taking a few more from the box. She dabbed at her eyes, trying to stem the stream of water that was now running down her face.

"Take your time," he said.

"Athena...she's gone missing."

"Where did she go?" Burk asked.

"It's the fae. They took her."

"That's impossible," said Burk. "She's too old to be abducted by those vile creatures."

Rosemary felt mildly offended on Athena's behalf, but she didn't let on. "I don't know the full story," she said, deliberately withholding Athena's fae heritage from the vampire who might very well not be able to control himself if he knew what she was. "I don't know how it happened. All I know is she's gone. I need to know how to get her back."

Burk crossed his arms and looked down to his desk. "If she had gone anywhere else I might have been able to help you."

"You must know something," said Rosemary desperately. "First that little girl went missing and now Athena." She burst into tears again.

Burk consoled her for a moment before another idea struck.

"Do you think this could have something to do with the Bloodstone Society?" Rosemary asked. "Are the fae involved with them?"

Burk shook his head. "The fae keep to themselves."

"Or maybe it's all a trick – the Bloodstones could be setting us up, making us believe it's the fae when really they are to blame."

"That's possible," said Burk. "But from what I understand the Bloodstones are still dispersed, just like their power. I suspect they'd have a hard time organising all this. Besides, it's not their style."

"Well, if you're sure. I need to know everything I can about them – *the fae* – anything at all that you can tell me."

"They are cold creatures."

"That's a bit rich coming from a vampire."

Burk frowned. "Is that what you think of me?"

"I'm sorry," said Rosemary.

"You should surely know that vampires tend to retain whatever values they had as mortals. Fae are...different. They have their own way of doing things, their own kind of code with very strict rules. They have never made any sense to me. During the war..."

"The war in which they were hunted by vampires?"

Burk gave her a pained look.

"What? Athena told me – your kind finds fae blood irresistible."

"That's true," said Burk. "But they weren't exactly helpless or blameless. There were attacks from both sides while the war lasted."

Rosemary looked at him sceptically. It sounded like Burk was making excuses for his kind, to make them not sound that bad. But this was hardly the time to argue with a vampire. "So the war ended. Then what happened?"

"A kind of cold war, I suppose," said Burk. "The fae keep building their protection. Over the last hundred years or so the borders have been closed. Young children can cross over sometimes, but adults can't, and I thought it would be impossible for a teenager."

"Well, it turns out they can take teenagers if they want to," said Rosemary, relieved she hadn't told him about Athena's heritage, especially after he'd just admitted that her blood was irresistible!

"Just tell me anything you think might be of help, so I can go to the fae realm and bring her back."

"I can't tell you how to get there," Burk said. "Although your best hope is probably the Spring Equinox."

"So everyone keeps telling me," said Rosemary. "But I can hardly wait that long. I've got to do something now."

"I think you're underestimating how hard it is to get to the fae realm," Burk said. "As far as I know, it has not been done by an adult human in over a hundred years, despite many seasoned witches trying."

Rosemary felt awash with hopelessness. "But Marjie said Granny helped get Sherry back... the Equinox?"

"Don't believe everything you hear," said Burk. "If the ritual is performed properly, the veil will lift for a moment, and you might have a chance. The only problem is you'd need to be in two places at once to actually get through."

"What do you mean?" Rosemary asked.

"The town square where the rituals are performed is a sacred space, designed to protect people from disappearing. The regular rituals honour the gods and goddesses so that they offer their protection. If the Goddess Eostre is satisfied at the Equinox she will bring good fortune to the town."

"For real?" Rosemary asked.

"You're saying you are willing to believe in vampires and fae but not goddesses?"

Rosemary hadn't thought about it a lot, but she did recall the appearance of cloud formations that could well have resembled the goddess Brigid around the time of Imbolc.

"Sure, fine, I'll go along with it," said Rosemary, furrowing her brow. "But at least I can *see* you in the flesh."

Burk gave her an odd look. "The point is, the ritual is performed in the town circle, but you won't be able to cross-over there."

"No, that can't be right," said Rosemary. "Ferg said they need me for the ritual to work. I have to be there."

"That makes sense," said Burk. "The more powerful the ritual, the more likely the veil is to lift enough to let someone through on either side."

"But you said I can't cross into the fae realm from there?"

"No. The centre of Myrtlewood is too well protected. There will be no entry point to the fae realm from the circle itself. If you're able to get from the town centre at the apex of the ritual to a weak point in the veil you might be able to cross over."

"Like Fin's Creek?" Rosemary asked. "That's where that child went missing."

"Yes, that's probably your best bet," said Burk.

"But how? I can't teleport. This isn't Space Trek or whatever."

"That is beyond me," said Burk. "I only wish I could move fast enough to carry you there in time."

"A noble sentiment," said Rosemary.

"The point is," said Burk, "I'm committed to helping however I can. I'll see what else I can find out. I have some sources who are very knowledgeable on magic."

"I appreciate it," said Rosemary.

As she got up to leave, Burk took her hand and gave it a little squeeze. She caught a look of vulnerability in his eyes. It was hard to believe that those same eyes belonged to someone capable of ruthless violence, of someone who found fae blood irresistible. She made a note to keep Athena well away from him when she came back, because Athena was going to return. Rosemary was absolutely determined about that.

"If you need anything – anything at all – don't hesitate to call me," said Burk.

OVER THE NEXT FEW DAYS, Rosemary kept herself busy, combing through Granny's books, looking for potential ways to enter the fae realm. She was surprised at how little information on the fae was contained in Granny's vast magical book collection.

She wondered multiple times if Dain, too, had been abducted by the fae and wished that he was still around so she could ask him to explain everything. *What could his own kind want with him? Maybe he owes them money! Do they even use money in the fae realm?*

She was almost totally clueless.

Much of the information she found online seemed like speculation and conspiracy theories, none of which was helpful.

Rosemary had managed to amass a sizeable collection of items said to be in some ways effective for warding off fae. In her desperation, she'd spent hours wandering through the forest around the house, hoping that whoever cast the illusion to make the house look as if it was in flames might return.

Based on something she'd read in a book, she set traps in the forest around Thorn Manor in an attempt to capture any faery creatures that might turn up, using saucers of cream as bait in the hopes of getting more information. So far she had caught one drunken dryad clad in nothing but leaves and a tiny blue pixie.

The only information she'd been able to divulge from threatening the dryad was that the politics in the fae realm was incredibly complicated. He rambled on about a missing prince and warring factions. Rosemary's eyes had glazed over. Surely none of this information was in any way useful to getting Athena back.

The pixie was even less useful and far more impolite, leading Rosemary to utter a string of expletives before setting it free.

She hadn't given up on Ostara as a last-ditch attempt to save Athena.

With help from Ferg and Marjie she'd managed to re-plant hundreds of pots with tulip bulbs and use her magic to regrow them, so at least they were prepared for the ritual.

Every day brought the Spring Equinox closer.

Rosemary felt the tension in her gut increasing. If everyone around town was correct, this was the one chance she had in the foreseeable future of getting Athena back. The risks were immense. All she could do was prepare as much as possible, to research and practice following instructions so that she could actually get her magic to work properly, at will. This proved no easy feat, but every day she was getting a little better and making fewer mistakes around the house. Water and Earth elements were still a challenge, but Rosemary had gotten quite proficient at air and fire elemental magic, and could create fireballs at will. She could even combine the two to create a purple lightening ball which not only looked impressive, it did a decent amount of damage when she hurled it at an old tree stump in the garden.

Athena would be proud, thought Rosemary. If only she were here to see it.

CHAPTER

THIRTY-FIVE

Athena held tight to Finnigan's hand as she stepped through what felt like many layers of silk except...it was all just energy...floating. As she entered the fae realm, it also entered right through her skin.

It passed through her entire being, every layer taking with it any doubt or fear she'd held about leaving her home behind, along with her exhaustion she'd been carrying for years.

In fact, it seemed to Athena that some knots had been released in her body, as if some old wounds, remnants of her former self, were being stripped away and lost forever. With that realisation came a sense of powerlessness. After all, she hadn't chosen to go through any particular internal change.

But even still, it didn't feel bad. In fact, Athena felt much better, more like her actual self. As they continued walking through many layers of subtly coloured mist, she began to see the outline of tall, oddly spindly lavender coloured trees, backlit against a deep violet sky.

Tiny lights dotted the air above them, which Athena quickly realised were many thousands of glowing butterflies.

"This way," Finnigan said, leading her towards a cobbled path that shone silver though there was no moon in the sky.

"Where are we going?" Athena asked.

"I'll take you to my home," he said. "But first, we need to get permission for you to be here."

"I don't know about that," said Athena, nervously pressing her fingernails into the palm of her hand.

"It's not my rule," said Finnigan. "If you're here without a proof of passage you're bound to be hunted."

Athena gulped.

"Fine," she said.

Being hunted by fae after the performance they put on at her house the other night did not sound like fun.

They passed enormous toadstools growing in purples and reds and greens. Athena longed to reach out for them, but Finnigan pulled her away.

"Don't touch anything unless I say it's okay," he said. "The fae realm might look like a beautiful fairy tale, but it's very dangerous here. There are plenty of risks that you won't recognise."

Athena nodded and continued on.

As they walked along the path, Athena noticed a large pond dotted with pastel coloured lily pads. She glanced towards the water to see an otherworldly creature there, which moved when she did. "It...it can't be," said Athena. "My reflection? Is it enchanted?"

"No," said Finnigan. "You look different here as well." That was when she noticed that Finnigan had also made some kind of transformation from entering the fae realm. His skin was glowing and his ears appeared more pointed. His hair had taken on a silver gleam, but she'd not noticed it before in the low light under which everything had looked vaguely more purple than usual.

His limbs appeared longer and more distinctly slender, though his clothes seemed to fit just the same.

"Am I taller?" Athena asked, examining her own long limbs.

"It's all a matter of perspective," he replied.

As they continued walking Athena had the distinct feeling of being watched. "Do you think someone's following us?" she asked Finnigan.

"Undoubtedly," he said. "All the gates are watched."

"Is that because you need to protect yourselves against the vampires?" Athena asked.

"Shush," said Finnigan. "Don't say that word around here. It will not go well."

"Okay, I get it. You don't like them," said Athena. "But they're not all bad."

Finnigan gave her a piercing look. "I don't think you should say that around beings who have been persecuted by them for thousands of years."

"Sorry," Athena said. "I guess I should have thought about that."

Finnigan ignored her and carried on. "When we go to the high office, just tell them that you have fae heritage and ask that they grant you refuge."

"Refuge?" Athena said. "I'm not in danger."

"Just say it," said Finnigan. "Otherwise, you might not be allowed to stay."

Athena's chest tingled in a silent alarm. "I just pretend that I'm in great danger? That I've been hunted by...err...things that I can't talk about."

"Exactly," said Finnigan.

"Is there anything else I should know before I make a complete fool of myself and become the target of half of the fae realm?"

"Just don't say anything," Finnigan said. "If you're not sure, I can help you. I can speak for you."

"Really?" Athena asked, raising her eyebrows.

"Come on," said Finnigan, pulling her faster along the forest path.

Athena was taken aback by Finnigan's gruffness, though she was too lost in wonderment at the stunning landscape around her to worry. The trees above glowed in all shades of purple. It was breathtakingly beautiful if only Athena had time to appreciate it as they hurried along.

"It does feel nice here," said Athena. "I thought it would feel strange and weird, but it feels..."

"Like home?" Finnigan asked with a smile.

"A little," said Athena. "Even my body feels more comfortable, like I'm not all weighed down."

"The atmosphere is different here," said Finnigan.

"Like a different gravity," said Athena. "Or whatever the magical equivalent of that is."

"Gravy tea?" said Finnigan.

"Never mind."

Athena realised how different they were, really. Finnigan may have visited the earth realm, but it seemed he'd never lived there. He hadn't been schooled there since he was very young, and that was in a whole different time in history, and yet, he was somehow more similar to her than almost anyone else she'd met.

The thought made her feel even more alone in all the worlds.

Up ahead she could see the spires of some kind of grand structure. "Is that where we're headed?" Athena asked.

"Sort of," said Finnigan.

"What do you mean, *sort of?*" Athena asked.

"You'll see soon enough." They approached the large structure, which Athena hesitated to assume was a building. It was shaped like an elaborate circus tent in varying shades of natural colours. It had towers that looked a lot like acorns. The entire structure seemed to be made entirely of leaves.

"It's so cute!" Athena said. "Please say that's where we're going."

"Over here," said Finnigan, leading Athena around the side. She felt disappointed, as she wanted to enter the odd building.

"Isn't this the office?" she asked.

"Technically yes," said Finnigan. "They don't really like to be indoors."

"Then why have buildings at all?"

He shrugged. "Maybe it's for keeping up appearances. Or maybe it's shelter. I don't know. They're always around the back, anyway."

They walked around the side of the building towards a clearing at the back. At the centre of the clearing was an enormous table made out of an old tree stump. Dotted around it were large mushrooms stools, and perched on the stools sat an assortment of bizarre looking creatures.

Their skin seemed to glow in the violet light. It almost looked translucent. Their limbs were long and their ears were sharply pointed. Their eyes gleamed with a preternatural light and they were clad in skeleton leaves that appeared to be pasted together with sap and other natural fibres to form elaborate ball gowns and suits with matching hats.

"Who dares interrupt us at this hour?" said a haughty voice. It came from a figure to the left of the table dressed in a white skeleton leaf ball-gown. She stood and strode over to them.

"Young Finnigan. Have you caught a prize?" She eyed Athena suspiciously.

"No, my lady," said Finnigan, bending into a low bow that seemed a little bit excessive to Athena, but she followed suit and gave a kind of half curtsey.

"Apologies for the interruption," Finnigan said. "In my scouting of the earth realm, I discovered one of our own. She seeks safe passage."

"Let her step forward," said a deeper voice, coming from the head of the table. Athena looked towards the figure, perched elegantly there, who wore a top hat made of green leaves and a dapper suit to match.

"Ismalia," Finnigan said with another bow. "Please meet my friend Athena Thorn. Athena, this is the high clerk of the Western Gate, Ismalia."

"A human?" Ismalia said, her eyes wide.

All eyes around the table watched Athena. She felt a sudden chill of danger.

"Tell them," Finnigan said, elbowing Athena.

"I think I need...to be a refugee...erm, safely. I need to run away. I'm in danger..." Athena rambled, feeling a lot like her mother.

Ismalia raised her eyebrows. "Come closer."

Athena stayed still until Finnigan pushed her forward.

"Let me have a look at you," said the fae, taking off her top hat. She raised her hand. The tip of her delicate long index finger glowed. She swirled it over Athena and her face lit up in a smile. "I think you do indeed have royal fae blood."

"Royal?" said Athena, before remembering to keep quiet.

Ismalia's green eyes lit up in a way that made Athena distinctly uncomfortable. "Very well," she said.

She let her finger glide down until it touched Athena's nose with a little ting.

Athena felt seasick.

"Don't worry, it'll pass," Ismalia said as the other fairies giggled.

Finnigan took Athena's hand and spoke to the unusual fae. "Many blessings upon you for your graciousness." He bowed. "We'll be going now."

"Do stay for some tea," said Ismalia.

"We're in a hurry," said Finnigan.

"Nonsense. You know you must stay, if we invite you to tea. Have you forgotten our Lore?"

Finnigan straightened his back, bowed, and sat down on one of the empty mushrooms. He pulled Athena towards the table on the other side.

"Tea?" Ismalia asked, brandishing a teapot that looked to be made out of a mushroom.

"I'm okay," said Athena. "I bought my own." She reached into her bag for her thermos.

"What are you doing?" Finnigan whispered.

"I read that I can't eat the food here."

"Don't worry about that," he said quietly. "You're fae."

"How adorable. She's overly cautious," said Ismalia. "It's alright, my dear. You can eat the food here."

"Err...Excuse me," said Athena. "How can I trust that what you say is true? I know nothing about this place."

Ismalia laughed. "Surely, as an earthly being you know that the fae cannot lie?"

Athena remained silent.

"You have safe passage here," Ismalia continued. "One such as your-self, with your heritage. Anyway..." She laughed again.

Athena shot Finnigan another sceptical look. He nodded reassuringly and she relaxed a little. After all, she was in dire need of a cup of tea.

"You know, as a child this would have been the highlight of my life," said Athena. "Having tea with fairies!" A silence fell around the table. "Oh no. I've done it again, haven't I? I've said something offensive."

"Never mind," said Ismalia, although there was a definite tension in her voice.

"We don't use that word," said Finnigan.

"Thanks for telling me," Athena hissed in a low whisper. "Can you please let me in on the other rules while you're at it?"

"For a start, don't ever say thank you to the fae," Finnigan whispered back. "It's considered incredibly rude."

"How odd," Athena muttered quietly. "I mean, I'm sure I read that online, but I didn't think it was true."

"We do have a rule about having to be polite," Finnigan continued, keeping his voice down.

"Really?" Athena rolled her eyes.

"Yes, really," said Finnigan. "Don't roll your eyes, whatever you do. It is not polite."

Athena sighed and raised her hands in surrender. "I apologise," she said, looking around the table. "I'm new to all of this."

"And you'll be forgiven. For a few more moments, at least," said Ismalia, grinning from ear-to-ear, clearly listening in on their conversa-tion. "After that, we will not to be so generous."

Athena felt a cold chill. She knew that these creatures might seem delicate and harmless, but she could tell they were really very deadly, much more frightening than vampires, at least the nice vampires that she had met.

Ismalia poured an indigo liquid into a cup that looked to be made of a tulip-like flower.

"Tha— I mean, I accept your gracious hospitality," said Athena, reaching forward to take the cup, which was soft and supple in her fingers, just like real petals. The saucer that came with it was a large round lily pad leaf.

"At any rate, we cannot tell you *all* the rules," said Ismalia. "That is also part of the Lore."

"That's...just great," said Athena taking a sip of the tea. It tasted exactly like perfectly ripe blueberries. She couldn't help but smile as her whole body lit up at the delightful flavour.

"See, now that wasn't so hard, was it?" said Ismalia.

"It's delicious!" Athena said, and then she remembered what Finnigan had said before about not speaking as much as possible. She made a note to stay as quiet as she could for the rest of the engagement.

CHAPTER

THIRTY-SIX

Rosemary stood at the kitchen table, practicing a spell. The house around her was chaotic, reflecting her inner state. She'd been experimenting with the elements and potions. She had no time for chocolate, and the various bunnies and eggs cropping up everywhere had only reminded her of what Athena was missing.

Getting her daughter back was consuming Rosemary's entire focus. She just needed a clue as to how. She'd gone to great lengths to read up on astrology, though reading the stars seemed far too complicated. She'd had a go at using Granny's tarot cards but kept getting scary looking outcomes, like The Tower, so she'd turned to tea leaves instead but could not make any sense of them.

In a fit of desperation, Rosemary had even gone to see Crystal Cassandra, the gossipy woman who called herself the town psychic, only to be told some nonsense about her aura being too foggy to read. Rosemary had been eager to leave. That woman gave her bad vibes.

Rosemary sprinkled the powder in front of her into the small copper bowl and muttered the incantation from the spell book. Nothing seemed to happen. She sighed.

She hadn't been to work in days. She was relieved that she didn't

need the money anymore. At least in the short term, she was fine finan-
cially. She didn't want to be any more of a burden on Marjie than she
already had been, but Marjie insisted she was fine at the shop and
continued to drop around meal parcels at every opportunity, making
sure that Rosemary and the kitten were both fed. She didn't even stop to
chat, obviously because she had gotten sick of Rosemary refusing her
delicious gifts.

There was a knock at the door.

Rosemary gave up on the spell, and assuming the knock came from
Marjie, she went to the front door. Marjie's car was disappearing down
the driveway.

Rosemary couldn't help but smile at her kind friend who felt more
like family at this point.

She went to retrieve the package from the front door step. She could
have sworn she had the feeling that something was watching her from
the trees around the house.

She looked up, trying to make out any unexpected movement from
the forest.

Just then there was a rush of air. A figure appeared. Rosemary
shouted and raised her arms. A blast of energy shot out.

"Hey!" Burk said, shielding his eyes.

The handsome vampire stood on her doorstep, looking ruffled.

"Oh! You scared me," said Rosemary.

"I'm sorry," he said, standing back. "Rosemary, I just came to..."

"What?" She looked at him curiously.

"To give you this book," he said, reaching into his pocket and
producing a tiny green fabric-bound volume.

"A book for miniature people?" Rosemary asked. "Sorry, I can't even
make a joke anymore. I just say whatever thoughts come into my mind
and most of them aren't that coherent."

"Understandable," said Burk.

"What is it?" Rosemary asked, reaching towards the book.

"It was over a hundred years ago that this book was made. It was
commissioned by the High Councillor of vampires."

"You guys have a council?" asked Rosemary. "I had no idea being undead could be so bureaucratic."

"Painfully so," said Burk. "How else do you think we keep young vampires in line?"

"What did they commission a little book for?" Rosemary asked. A small glimmer of hope began shining inside her mind. *Could this be the missing piece of the puzzle?*

The small book barely filled her palm. There was no title on the cover or spine.

"It's about fae," said Burk. "This book was written by the wisest magical scholars around. This was a way we could gather enough information to combat them, and their tricks."

"I thought vampires hunted fae to near extinction," said Rosemary suspiciously. "Why would you need a book like this?"

Burk laughed. "If only it was that simple." He took a small step towards Rosemary. "Be aware, Rosemary. Be wary of the fae. They can be cruel. They have a totally different sense of morality from humans or vampires. The war was predominantly between our kinds, but believe me when I say that many magical humans were in support of us."

"That seems strange," said Rosemary. "Given you drink human blood – at least traditionally."

Burk looked mildly offended and slightly amused. "We are not the hideous demons we're often made out to be in all the stories." There was a bitterness in his voice. "Fae sought out and destroyed most of the volumes of this book. It contains some information that will be of use, just remember that it was written a long time ago, before all the protections were in place. It won't get you through the veil."

"Then what use is it?" Rosemary said, feeling the fluttery hopes that had awakened by the book wither and die in her chest.

"It has more information on the fae than you'll find elsewhere," said Burk. "And if you do make it into the fae realm, I believe there are some recipes here that will help to fortify you, both on your entry and to ensure your safe return."

"You sound so formal when you talk like that," Rosemary said.

"Modern language is, as they say, 'a stretch' for me," said Burk. "I've been around a long while and most of that time the language structure was more formal, at least in my circles." He rubbed his fingers through his perfectly styled hair.

"You know, you sound like a bit of a snob when you say that," said Rosemary.

Burk chuckled.

"But thank you for the book," she continued. "It's very kind of you."

"I only hope it helps," said Burk. "I'll keep researching to see what more I can find. Our Council keep a close eye on any activity happening at the edge of the veil, including any disappearances. It all happens too intermittently to predict."

Rosemary nodded. "Thanks again," she said, taking the little book and slipping it into her pocket.

"Rosemary, I..." Burk's words faltered. "I want you to know that I'll do whatever I can to help and that I...I care for you."

Rosemary felt a strange tug in her gut, but it did not seem like the right time to be having any feelings. It was kind of Burk to give her the book, but the last thing she needed was to get involved with a vampire lawyer who probably had boundary issues. Also, she hadn't forgotten that she'd seen him having dinner with an attractive woman only a few nights before. If he really cared for her then would he be dating other women? Not that that was any of her business.

"As I said before, let me know if there's anything I can do." He reached out and took Rosemary's hand, lowering his head and planting a kiss on her knuckle.

Rosemary gave him a quizzical look.

"I'm sorry," Burk said. "I'm just realising how strange the gesture must have seemed. I'm an old-fashioned chap."

Rosemary pulled her hand away. "Uhh... thanks, I guess. Have a good night."

She turned away to pick up the package of food that Marjie had dropped off and heard the rushing sound behind her telling her that Burk had left. She had no time to think about the vampire and his strange antiquated manners and his handsome features and his gorgeous eyes. She had far more important things to do.

She went inside and placed the pie and salad that Marjie had left her onto a plate. It was blessedly still warm. She took it to the table with the little book and began to study its pages, careful not to spill any food since it was no doubt irreplaceable.

As Burk had said, there were indeed useful-sounding recipes for things such as miniature cakes and biscuits that, prepared correctly, would fortify human strength and protect against the dangers between the realms, and also for adjusting on the return to the human world.

None of the recipes seemed particularly useful for vampires, although the book did say that vampires, regardless of their strength or enchantments, could not easily pass into the fae realm and could not survive there long even if they did.

Perhaps they had been training human spies to go in there and sabotage the fae. Rosemary wondered whether she could trust Burk. He always seemed quite genuine, if a little arrogant. He had been kind to her and Athena. But there was no way she could risk him finding out what Athena was.

Rosemary sat at the table, reading the book, until she could barely keep her eyes open.

She couldn't help but feel that Burk was being deceptive, at least to make it sound as if his side – the vampires – weren't really that bad.

Rosemary must have nodded off because she woke with her head on the table and a crick in her neck, lines from the book creasing her face.

It was a noise that had woken her, the sound of frantic knocking.

Sherry was at the door.

"Goodness," Rosemary said, feeling groggy. "What time is it?"

"Time?" said Sherry, her voice rough and high-pitched. "Who has a care in the world for time?"

It was then that Rosemary noticed Sherry was not at all pale or tired looking like she had been the last time they'd seen each other. Her eyes seemed to be almost glowing and a maniacal smile curled her lips.

"Sherry, are you okay?" asked Rosemary.

"I am magnificent!" said Sherry. Then she lowered her eyes. "Except, I heard about Athena and I am very sorry to hear of your loss."

"Is there anything I can do to help you?" Rosemary asked, in a tone of genuine concern.

"Help me? Oh, no, I'm on top of the world or...at least I will be very soon." She shot Rosemary another cunning smile.

"I thought the equinox made you feel drained."

"Usually it does, but I found something that makes me feel much better. In fact, I think I can help you."

Rosemary's heart thudded in her chest as her mind raced with the realisation that Sherry might be on some kind of magical drug. Even still, she could not ignore the possibility that she might be able help get Athena back.

"How could you help?" Rosemary asked.

"Just make sure you bring the following ingredients to the equinox." She brandished a crumpled shopping list with a bunch of herbs and crystals scrawled on it. "We need to create a doorway to get into the fae realm."

"You want to go back there?" Rosemary asked, surprised.

"I have some unfinished business with the fae." A troubled look crossed Sherry's face. "They took something precious from me and now I can finally get her back."

"What are you talking about?" Rosemary asked, but it was too late. Sherry had turned towards the forest. Rosemary caught a familiar flash of gold around the woman's neck as she ran away into the trees. Rosemary wondered for a moment whether she should go looking for her, but decided against it, as the forest had been giving her the creeps for weeks. Instead, she called Detective Neve and left a message.

LATER THAT NIGHT, as Rosemary was lying in bed, her mind ran through the encounter with Sherry. The glimpse of gold around her neck was from a chain, Rosemary realised, and it was so familiar because it was part of the missing necklace.

Rosemary had only caught a brief glimpse but she was sure of it.

Sherry must have taken it when she was visiting the house.

Rosemary got out of bed. She needed to talk to Granny, but there was no secret door visible on the upstairs landing. She went to the part of the wall where the door had once been and knocked. There was no response.

Rosemary knocked again and then began hammering at the door.

She took a deep breath as sobs wracked her chest. She wiped away her tears with the back of her hand.

"Granny! I need to talk to you. Right now! I don't care if this isn't a good time for you. You're a freaking ghost. I'm sure you have all the time in the world."

There was no response, so Rosemary raised her palms to the door, calling for her magic. Light radiated behind her hands. Nothing happened for a moment and then slowly golden edging appeared, tracing the outline of the door.

"Thank you," Rosemary said to the house. She opened up the newly-formed door and climbed the stairwell at pace.

"Listen here, old woman," Rosemary said, storming into the tower room.

"Can't you tell I'm busy?" said Granny, materialising in the mirror.

"I don't care if you're busy," Rosemary shouted. "Your great grand-daughter has gone missing!"

"I'm quite aware of that," said Granny. "That's what I'm busy with."

Rosemary stepped back in surprise. "I didn't realise you keep such close tabs on us."

"Of course I do," said Granny. "The two of you are so dense sometimes. Somebody's got to watch out for you. But rest assured, Athena is fine."

"She is not fine!" Rosemary stormed. "She's been kidnapped!"

"Rubbish," said Granny. "It's just a romp, that's all."

"A romp!" Rosemary was appalled. "We might never get her back. You should know how hard it is to get through the veil."

"Well, the equinox..."

"I know!" said Rosemary, still fuming at her grandmother's flippant attitude. "That's what everyone keeps telling me. But how? Marjie seemed to think you'd know."

"I just follow my intuition as far as magic is concerned," said Granny, with a little wave of her hand. "There are no instructions for any of this, not since they closed the borders when I was a little lass. But don't worry, the girl will surely be having the time of her life."

Rosemary was livid. It took her a while to calm down enough to speak again. Clearly Granny was too disconnected from the earth to understand the gravity of the situation. There was no use in getting into a pointless argument when Granny might be able to help, whether she realised it or not. Instead of fighting over whether Athena was in danger or simply romping about, Rosemary gritted her teeth and changed the subject.

"That's not the only thing I need to tell you about," said Rosemary eventually. "I just realised that Sherry was the one who took the necklace."

"That girl." Granny shook her head. "I wonder why she would have done that."

"I suppose she was the obvious culprit," said Rosemary. "After all, she had visited the house around the time it went missing. I just didn't believe she could have done it." She was silent in contemplation for a moment, then asked. "Do you think the necklace would have a strange effect on her?"

"There is no doubt in my mind," said Granny. "It's a powerful relic. The Thorn family have held onto it for generations, partly because our magic makes us strong enough to wear it. I doubt there's anyone else in the town who could pull that off."

"Thanks for warning me," Rosemary said. "What if I'd lent it to a friend?"

"How dare you lend out priceless family heirlooms!" said Granny. "I thought even *you* had more sense than that."

"I wouldn't have," said Rosemary. "I didn't even let Athena wear it. Sherry was in a very odd state. I thought she was high."

"She probably is. That magic is powerful."

"But she's had the necklace for at least a week," said Rosemary, "and the last time I saw her she was nothing like that."

"Maybe she only just tried it on?" Granny suggested.

"She said something about helping me get Athena back."

"I wouldn't trust her as far as you could throw her, love," said Granny. "Not when she's under the influence."

"She seemed really serious about it though," said Rosemary. "Loads of people have offered to help me, but when Sherry did my intuition told me she was genuine, despite her state. She said something else too. She wants to get something back from the fae realm – something she lost there."

"Now," said Granny. "That sparks a memory. Did she say something or someone?"

"Why do you ask?"

Granny waved her arm and a large drawer rolled open from the big wooden desk at the side of the room. It was filled with old fashioned files. "Let's see, where is it?"

Papers shuffled around and then a manilla folder flicked up and landed on the desk. "Here," said Granny.

"What is it?" Rosemary asked, crossing the room towards the desk.

The file opened and papers flittered around, leaving one on top. It was an old newspaper clipping with pictures of two girls on the front. One was clearly a young Sherry. The other had darker hair and a serious expression.

"Mei Lee," Rosemary said, reading the name under the picture. "She went missing at the same time. Why didn't anyone say anything?"

"It's one of the problems with living where the veil is thin," said Granny. "Fae magic affects everyone's memory, especially where *they* are concerned. When Sherry came back, no one knew who she was."

"How awful," said Rosemary. "Not even her parents?"

"They recognised her eventually, but I understand it was quite traumatic for her at first, coming back and finding herself treated as a stranger in her own home."

"I bet," said Rosemary. "No one is going to make me forget Athena. Just please try to help get her back."

"Fine, fine," said Granny. "But you're the key here. Your magic, now that you are using it properly, should protect you somewhat from memory loss, but the fae are strong. That's why I keep a record of the goings on. You can never be too careful."

"I think there was a recipe to help with this actually," Rosemary said. "Burk gave me a little book with useful information on fae. There's a lemon tart that protects against their charm."

"That does indeed sound useful," said Granny, giving her a knowing look. "That handsome vampire really is going out of his way for you, isn't he? Oh, to be young again!"

"It's not like that," said Rosemary.

"Whatever you say," Granny said, grinning.

Rosemary ignored her and looked back at the newspaper cutting.

"Do you think everyone forgot about the other girl?" she asked.

"Possibly everyone, except for Sherry," Granny replied.

THIRTY-SEVEN

As Athena finished her tea cup she realised the sky above them was lightening.

"How long have we been here?" she asked Finnigan. She was feeling slightly odd, and she didn't know whether it was due to the beverage she'd just consumed or just to being in a different world. It felt as if she'd only been gone twenty minutes, and yet she knew time didn't follow the same patterns as in the earth realm.

The creatures around her laughed at her question.

"Not long," said Finnigan. She noted the anxious look in his eyes. "But we'd better be on our way. We appreciate your splendid generosity," he said, standing and bowing towards the fae.

Athena followed suit.

"Leaving so soon?" said Ismalia.

"I'm afraid so," said Finnigan.

"Do keep us informed of your activities," said the fae clerk, tipping her leafy top hat. Athena was sure there was a hint of threat in her voice.

A light snoring sound interrupted them. Athena glanced over to see that one of the elaborately dressed fae had fallen asleep at the other side of the table.

Ismalia gave the sleeping fae a sharp kick and then clapped her hands together. "The night shift has ended! Time for the day to take over."

Her voice travelled across the lawn of wildflowers as if magnified by a microphone, towards the leafy building. A trumpet sounded.

Finnigan pulled Athena away and they headed off towards a path in the forest. She couldn't help but turn around to see the commotion, as half a dozen smartly dressed fae in red coats left the house and made their way out towards the table, clearly in order to replace the night shift.

"I'm not even going to pretend to know what that was about," said Athena.

"What? You expect them to work all night and day?" Finnigan asked. "Even fae need rest."

"No, not that," said Athena. "The night and day shift makes perfect sense. It's all that stuff about manners that I don't understand, and the strange tea. I'm sure it made me feel funny. Look, you told me you'd bring me here to explain things and you have explained almost nothing of any use to me. I've got far more questions than answers."

Finnigan ran his hand through his hair. "What is it you want to know?" he asked as he continued to lead her along the cobblestone path that glowed pearlescent under the soft lilac early morning light.

"I want to know what is going on in my brain when I hear the voices inside people's heads. Wait a minute. I haven't heard them. I haven't heard any voices or any fuzz since I got here."

"I think you'll find that particular ability works with humans, not fae, unless they are very closely connected to each other," he said.

"But it works with you," said Athena, wondering how she could feel so close to someone from the instant they'd met.

"It does," said Finnigan. "I assume it's only because I have both human and fae heritage, like you, remember?"

"You're just assuming this?" Athena asked. "Shouldn't you *know*? Have you ever seen any humans in the fae world or fae in the human world?"

"That's not as common as you might think," said Finnigan, giving her a slightly strange look.

"And why couldn't you just tell me all this before?"

"I told you I could say very little," said Finnigan.

"So what's new?" Athena said, feeling frustrated.

"What else do you want to know?"

"You told me you'd help me to hone the power, but I can't even use it here."

"Being here will help you," he reassured her. "Don't you feel it? This place is the natural home for you, for your body."

Athena closed her eyes for a moment, standing still on the path. She did feel peaceful, much more than she ever had before. It helped that her mind was still. Not having to deal with voices was a nice change, but even before the telepathy power had come in, she'd never felt this deep sense of calm.

"See, you know yourself better here," said Finnigan. "Besides, there's someone else who can help you."

"Who is it?"

"The Countess of West Eloria."

"West Eloria?" Athena asked. "Where is that?"

"All around you," said Finnigan. "This part of the fae realm is West Eloria. It's ruled by the countess."

"Are the other parts much different?" Athena asked.

"I can't tell you that," said Finnigan. "I've never been into any of the other regions. I'm...I work here."

"Oh, okay," said Athena, catching a slightly strained tone in Finnigan's voice. "What's she like, the countess?"

"She's strong and beautiful," said Finnigan.

Athena felt a pang of jealousy and wondered how old this countess was.

They walked on in silence for a while, until something caught Athena's eye.

Up ahead, through the trees, some interesting characters were approaching. They looked to be wearing bright red tutus.

"Stay close," said Finnigan suddenly, grabbing Athena by the hand, sending delicate shivers through her limbs and torso. She wasn't sure if it was just the chemicals of infatuation or something more magical, but she was distracted from wondering about that by the seriousness in his tone.

"What is it?" she asked quietly.

"Tribute seekers," he said. "Do you have anything in your bag that might make a good tribute?"

"What kind of thing?"

"Something shiny," said Finnigan.

Athena mentally took stock at the contents of her backpack, feeling uneasy when she considered all the charms and potions she'd mixed up to use as protection or self defence against the fae. She recalled some of the other things she'd packed, too.

"Do you think they'd like gemstones?" she asked, remembering how she'd raided Granny Thorn's rather extensive collection of crystals before she left.

"As long as it's not lodestone or hematite," said Finnigan.

"Don't you think I know better than to take iron into the fae realm," she replied. "I might be mostly clueless, but I do know a thing or two about folklore."

"Fine, just find something quickly, can you?" said Finnigan, not looking particularly impressed by Athena's knowledge of fae-repellent minerals.

"Probably." Athena shrugged, then took off her backpack and rifled through one of the side pockets as the red-dressed creatures approach them. Unlike the other fae creatures they'd met, these ones were squat and almost bell-shaped. She wanted to ask if they were a different species, but it seemed highly probable that such a question would be rude considering the fae obsession with politeness. She pulled out a small piece of rose quartz. It clinked against a tiny bottle of cream as she took it out of the bag.

"Tribute! Tribute please! Tributes for our fair queen!" the strange creatures called out, holding up a large yellow pail which they jingled around.

"You can explain this later," Athena said to Finnigan.

"Will you choose to pay tribute to our fair queen?"

Athena looked down at the small piece of rose quartz, and all of a sudden it didn't seem to be quite enough. She put it back into the pocket of her bag and rummaged around, hoping to find something flashier.

The taller tribute seeker made a large exaggerated sniffing noise. "What is that?" it asked. "Could it be...? Could it be contraband?"

Finnigan shot Athena a warning glance. She produced a large chunk of agate and held it up to the creature to see its dazzling green eyes sparkling at the sight.

"Such generosity," said the smaller tribute seeker, reaching out for the crystal. It held the agate up and sniffed again. "Could it be?" The creature's eyes seemed to grow bigger and bigger. "Cream!"

The other creature joined in a high pitched squeak.

"Stay very still," said Finnigan.

"Turn out your pockets!" said the taller creature.

"This is not good," said Finnigan. *Tell me you didn't...* His voice sounded in her head.

So it turns out the telepathy does work here, Athena thought.

Athena! Finnigan's voice rang in her mind.

Athena thought of the charms and spells in her bag, wishing she knew whether their power would work in the fae realm. She hoped that the creatures didn't have the ability to read her mind too, but she had a feeling she was going to find out soon enough.

So what if I bought cream? she replied to Finnigan. What's the danger?

Cream is like heroin to the fae, he said. It's expressly forbidden. Our best hope now is that they take the cream and run off with it to use themselves.

And what's our worst hope? Athena asked.

If you're discovered with cream here, things are not going to look good for you. We'll be locked up in a dungeon and tried for high treason.

Thank you for warning me about this earlier!

I'll see if I can distract them, he said and turned back to the fae. "That's an awfully nice frock you're wearing."

That's your attempt at distraction? Athena said in her mind, grateful that the other creatures hadn't seemed to pick up on the telepathy.

What, they're prone to flattery. It's a major weakness.

Athena glared at him.

"How sweet of you to say," the bell-shaped demon said. "However, there are other more pressing matters at hand. Turn out your pockets and surrender to me whatever it is that smells like cream." A dozen spidery limbs emerged, protruding from both creatures' backs like wings as they reached towards Athena threateningly.

Fortunately, I've got a better distraction, Athena thought. She reached into the main pocket of her bag. *Get ready to run!*

Wait, Athena, what are you doing? Finnigan asked.

Athena removed a small bundle that looked remarkably like a bath bomb. She held it up in the air and the creatures' eyes followed her.

The creature stepped towards the bundle and Athena threw it hard at the ground, taking Finnigan's hand and running with him as a huge explosion rent the air.

It was as if a whole carton of fireworks had been set on fire, complete with colourful sparkles.

Finnigan and Athena were blown back several metres in the air, and Athena was grateful that the thickness of the fae realm atmosphere cushioned their fall.

"Thank the gods that charm worked," Athena said as they dashed away through the forest.

"What was *that*?" Finnigan asked.

"I don't know," said Athena. "I mean, it was a defence charm I made, but I didn't even know which one I grabbed or if it was going to work. I didn't know if earth magic worked here."

"Normal human magic might not work here," said Finnigan. "Or at least that's the rumour."

"Maybe it just doesn't work as expected," said Athena.

"And you brought an arsenal?!"

"It's something that I used when we were being attacked a few weeks ago by the Bloodstone society. But the charms didn't have anywhere near that effect in the earth realm."

"I suppose your magic must work differently here," said Finnigan,

"It's not really my magic," said Athena. "I just followed the instructions."

"Don't be silly," said Finnigan. "Following instructions doesn't automatically lead to magic."

They decided to pause for a rest in a glade by a stream, having judged the tribute seekers were now far away enough that there wasn't any present danger.

"My mother has magic. She doesn't need any potions or charms or even spells to utilise it. She just hasn't bothered learning how to use it yet. Typical."

"I think you might find you have even more power than her," said Finnigan. "Not only from your human side but from your fae side as well. It's no wonder she tried to keep you locked up in the earth realm rather than letting you come home."

"That's not what she was doing. You are way off base, though if I do have power it'd be nice if I could actually use it properly." Athena sighed. "I suppose there are no shortcuts. I'll have to figure out how to practice, how to harness it on my own, just like I do with this stupid telepathy thing."

"You're doing quite well, really," said Finnigan.

"What do you mean?"

"Well, just before you were channelling your thoughts straight to me. If you hadn't been protecting them against the tribute seekers, they would have heard everything we'd said to each other."

"Really?" Athena asked.

"It took me a long time to learn how to protect my own thoughts from the fae," said Finnigan darkly. "It's the downside of being human.

They can pick up a lot of what you think. It took me years to figure out how to conceal my thoughts and avoid being punished for being impolite or resisting orders in my mind."

"You're saying I'm using it properly?" said Athena. "But how?"

"You focussed your thoughts," said Finnigan. "You didn't want them to overhear you. And you didn't put too much energy into worrying about it either. If you'd done that it would have just made it worse. Magic is always about will."

"Do you think I can use magic like Mum can? I mean, will my magic to just appear without a spell or anything?"

"Why not give it a try and we can see." He raised his hand as though to reach for her, but held it poised in mid-air. Athena reached her fingers out towards his until they were almost touching, then she concentrated on her very fingertips. Nothing happened at first, and then light began to glow from her index finger. It was joined quickly by her other fingers.

"Making light," she said, smiling.

"Is that what you're trying to do?" Finnigan asked. "I thought you'd do something more impressive."

"Hey!" She laughed and swatted him with her hand, forcing the light to die out. "Baby steps. I don't want to blow your brains out by accident."

"That's just as well." He laughed and pushed back at her and they found their fingertips interlaced. Smiles spread across both their faces.

"Athena, I..."

"Shush," she said. "I just want to enjoy this."

"Enjoy what?" he asked.

"I told you to shut up," said Athena teasingly. "Enjoy the moment. You silly boy."

"It just feels so lovely."

Athena grinned. "Something like that." She took a deep breath and closed her eyes, wishing that life could always be so sweet and so simple as it was in this very moment.

But the moment was short lived. As questions and worries surfaced from what felt like a former life.

"What happens to the children who disappear from the earth

realm?" Athena asked.

"I'm here, aren't I?" Finnigan asked. "I survived."

"You're fae as well as human," said Athena. "What happens to the others?"

"I was collected, very deliberately, despite my father's attempts to ward them off." There was a bitterness in Finnigan's tone. He clearly resented having been kidnapped by the fae and Athena could understand why.

"A little girl went missing the other day, do you know about her?"

"It's not really my area of expertise."

"But you know something. You must," said Athena. "What would the fae even want with human children?"

"That's not something I'm privy too," he replied. "I suspect it's something to do with building a stronger species."

"What now?"

"The high fae are all terribly inbred, you see, like fancy dog breeds or royalty in the human world. I don't understand exactly how, but I suspect the young humans are being studied."

"How ghastly," said Athena. "Do you mean in a lab?"

"Not like that," he replied. "Just...observed, I suppose."

"Still, that seems wrong," said Athena.

"They seem perfectly healthy, though," said Finnigan. "I stumble across them from time to time. They're all so young and beady eyed."

"They don't grow up?"

"No, not here. They look happy enough, though."

"I guess that's some comfort," said Athena. "But it's still terrible."

"There's a different kind of morality down here."

"So I gather," said Athena. "I thought I was about to be executed for not showing proper manners earlier."

Finnigan shrugged. "That wouldn't have been out of the question."

"Really?! Well, you'll have to give me a lesson in how to behave properly before we get much further," said Athena, propping herself more upright.

"Never give your full name to the fae," said Finnigan. "And try not to accept any gifts because it might get you trapped into servitude."

"I know all that." said Athena with a wave of her hand. "Or at least, I read about it in books, so I wasn't going to fall into any of those ridiculous traps. I'm not a fool."

Finnigan looked offended at Athena's comment, though she couldn't quite fathom why.

After some refreshments, consisting of tea and Jaffa Cakes from Athena's bag, they left the glade and continued on.

"Where are you taking me next?" Athena asked.

"Hopefully to somebody who can answer more of your questions," said Finnigan.

"Still so cryptic."

As they walked along the forest path, occasionally creatures flitted through the trees. Most of them were small and waiflike.

"What are they?" Athena asked.

"Various types of fae creatures," said Finnigan. "You have many of them in your realm too. They're not usually visible, but you might find you can see them now you've been here. It was good you brought food with you. Human food will help to keep you grounded. It seems to have made you less pale at any rate."

Athena blushed, feeling decidedly less pale. "I've never heard of Jaffa Cakes being considered so healthy," she said.

Finnigan laughed.

"I do feel more grounded," she reflected. "And my arms and legs look a bit more normal. Hey, do you think, whoever it is you're taking me to will know what happened to the missing children?"

"More than me," said Finnigan.

"I wonder how long it's been since I left home," Athena said, stretching her arms in the air. "I wonder if Mum's discovered I'm missing yet."

"It's hard to tell. Perhaps a week or two," said Finnigan.

"What?!" Athena cried. "You're joking."

"I might be wrong," he said, though she couldn't shake the feeling he was trying to placate her obvious distress.

"I'm going to be in so much trouble!" said Athena. "Maybe if I can find those kids, Mum will forgive me. Where do you think they keep them?"

"Probably near the castle," said Finnigan. "So it's a good job that's where we're headed."

"I don't get it," said Athena. "If they need humans so badly that they're willing to steal children, why did they look down on me for being human?"

Finnigan laughed. "Have you met the fae? Have you seen how arrogant they are?"

Athena sighed. "I'm afraid so."

"The thing is, human and fae relationships... well they're not considered appropriate now," said Finnigan. "But I heard that a long time ago, the fae would cross over into the human realm as often as they liked and steal potential mates, kidnapping them, bringing them back here."

"That's awful," said Athena. "Are you saying they forced—"

"Not exactly. You know, they're so polite and can be quite charming. But I don't think the human world appreciated it so much. It's probably why they teamed up with the vamps, to stop the fae."

"Is *that* what happened?" Athena asked. "From what you said before, I thought the vampires were in the wrong."

"Well, you didn't hear it from me," said Finnigan. "Around here those bloodsuckers are always in the wrong, but, from spending time in the human world, I'd say both species are at fault in some way. Vamps are natural predators for us, but the fae have no real grounds to be sanctimonious. Don't tell anyone I said that."

"You're upset that they took you," she said.

Finnigan paled. "I never saw my father again. By the time my mother got bored with me and sent me back, he was gone. Decades had passed. There was nothing left of my old home."

"How awful," said Athena. "I'm sorry." She reached out and took his hand.

"It's not all bad," he said. "At least I got to live in this time and meet you."

CHAPTER
THIRTY-EIGHT

osemary stood at the kitchen bench, midway through a spell. Against her nature, she was trying her hardest to follow the instructions. She did her best to ignore the state of the house around her. In her single-minded determination, she'd turned much of the available space into a kind of lab – experimenting with potions and elements. She'd dragged equipment into the living area from Granny's tower room and other things she'd found in the dusty wings of the old house.

As she worked the spell, light began to shoot out from her fingertips like tiny lasers, entwining in front of her into a loose weave over the items she'd laid out – amethyst, sage, salt, and black pepper. This was one of the recipes from the book that Burk had given her, though Rosemary was unsure whether it had ever worked particularly well, let alone whether it would work now, given how outdated the information was.

She was interrupted by a knock at the door. The light disappeared from her hands. She sighed, thinking it was probably just Marjie, delivering her some lunch. She held up her hands to try again. But then she heard another knock. Not Marjie then. Not unless there was something she actually wanted to talk to Rosemary about in particular.

Marjie had been very good at respecting Rosemary's wishes to be left alone. She'd had few interruptions, though she continued to be well fed. She did wonder whether she was racking up such a huge tab of gratitude to her family friend and employer that she would never be able to repay her in a thousand years.

A more urgent knock sounded at the door.

"Fine," said Rosemary. "I'm coming."

She opened the door to see four young faces looking at her. Not smiling exactly, though there was something like excitement in their eyes. Was it fear?

"I'm Elise," said the girl with blue hair. "And this is Sam, Felix, and Deron."

Rosemary nodded. "Athena's school friends."

"Yes," the girl continued. "We're sorry to hear about Athena."

"How did you find out?" Rosemary asked in a guarded voice.

"News travels fast around here," said the boy with red hair and a cocky expression on his face who'd been introduced as Felix.

"So it does," said Rosemary. "How can I help you?"

"We're worried about Athena too," said Elise. "We want to know if there's any way we can help you."

"Thank you for the offer," said Rosemary. "But, as the most experienced magical beings in this town can't seem to help me, I'm not sure there's much use. I'm sorry."

"We want to go with you," said Sam, who matched the description Athena had given of her non-binary school friend.

"Go with me where?" Rosemary asked.

"You're going after her. Aren't you?" said Felix.

"It's hard enough for me to figure out how to get into the fae realm," said Rosemary sternly. "And I wouldn't want to take the risk of bringing other people's children there. It's too dangerous, so please stay as far away as possible."

"Elise has pixie heritage," said the other boy with dark hair.

"Shut up, Deron," said Elise. "I am not a pixie. You know that my mother is a naiad."

"I'm afraid I don't know what that is," said Rosemary. "I assume you're some sort of otherworldly creature."

"Something like that. I've never been to the fae realm," said Elise. "But my grandmother grew up there."

Rosemary leant forward in a conspiratorial manner and said, "Look, I mean it. I don't want to bring any of you into this. But if your people know anything that might help me, please let me know."

"The fae are good at keeping secrets, aren't they?" said Elise with an awkward smile. "Your best bet is the equinox, but I'm sure you already know that."

"That's what everyone keeps telling me," said Rosemary, pulling back and resuming her normal volume of speech. "The only problem is the ritual needs to be performed at the town square and I need to be there. Apparently, my powers are important to make it effective, to have a chance of bringing Gretchen back, or Athena..." Her voice trailed off as her breath caught in her throat, overwhelmed with grief.

"I might be able to help you there," said a high pitched voice coming from the side of the driveway. They all turned to see a girl with her hair held tightly in a bun.

"What are you doing here, Beryl?" Elise asked.

"I heard you talking in town. I knew that this was where you were going, and I followed you."

"Why? asked Felix.

"I don't have any particular affections for any of you, but as you know, I'm an accomplished witch, and my family...Well, my family knows a thing or two about magic, you might say."

Rosemary was getting distinct impressions that reminded her of her own nasty, snobbish cousin, Elamina. There was something quite snobby and snarky in Beryl's manner.

"So what are you doing here, then?" Rosemary asked. She eyed the girl warily.

"It's not good for the town that people go missing," Beryl said. Every word was laboured. "It creates a nuisance, and the fae need to be put in their place. My family – the Flarguans –helped to push them back a hundred years ago."

"So where are your parents? Do you think they could help?" Rosemary asked.

"They're out of town on business as usual, and no, I'm not sure whether they *would* help. They tend to be quite occupied with their own interests." Beryl's tone was icy, as if she was concealing pain.

Rosemary's voice softened. "Did you come here to help?" she asked Beryl.

The girl nodded curtly, as if she'd prefer not to be there at all. "There's a spell. It can help you move time and space, so that you can bring two points together. I've been thinking about this all week. It's no use to try to move the equinox ritual from where it's been performed for hundreds of years. That will only weaken its power. And the weakest point in the veil, as you probably know, is at Fin's Creek, where that little girl disappeared. It's a complicated spell, far more advanced than any of you could pull off, more advanced than anything I've ever done," she admitted glumly. "But it's worth a try."

"Where is it? Can you give it to me?" Rosemary asked.

"I can deliver you the instructions," said Beryl. "But it requires some unorthodox ingredients." She looked at Rosemary, clearly uncomfortable. "We have some of them around the house. But the key magical supplies are not accessible for me or my sisters. In fact, I don't even know if or where my parents keep things like that. If you happen to have contacts in high places with a lot of money, then this would be the time to call on them."

Contacts in high places with a lot of money...Rosemary's shoulders sagged even further as her cousins came to mind. "I could ask Elamina and Derse."

"Oh, you know the Bracewell family?" Beryl asked, raising an eyebrow.

"I have the misfortune of being related to them," said Rosemary.

Beryl gave her a curious look as if she'd misjudged her somehow. "Well, now would be a good time to call in any favours."

Rosemary laughed. "I don't think they would consider that they owe me any favours at all, despite the fact that I restored the family magic, but they did seem to take a liking to Athena. Maybe they will help," she said, although in the back of her mind, she wondered, *at what price?*

She pushed that worry away, knowing that any price would be worth it if it brought her daughter back safely.

"Alright," said Beryl. "I'll bring you the spell and a few of the ingredients. I'm not going to help you cast it."

"And I don't want you to, either," said Rosemary. "Children should stay away from this, Beryl." All the other teens on her doorstep looked offended. "Look, I don't mean this as an insult. It's just too dangerous."

"Oh yeah?" said Felix. "And what exactly do you plan on doing to find Athena once you get to the fae realm?"

"Excuse me?" said Rosemary.

"What's your plan?" he asked, leaning against the doorframe. "You're just going to wander there and start calling out for her?"

"I've been doing what I can to prepare," Rosemary said.

"Well, you keep doing that," said Felix. "But bear in mind that you might just need us."

CHAPTER

THIRTY-NINE

As soon as Beryl had arrived the next day with the instructions for the spatial relocating spell, Rosemary quickly fired off an email to her cousin Elamina asking for help. She'd found the email address among Granny's contacts and hoped that it was still a current one. She also hoped that her irritating cousins would actually turn out to be useful for a change.

With no time to waste, Rosemary set to work, gathering the spell ingredients that she knew were the simple ones to find. To her surprise, later that day a silver Rolls Royce pulled up the driveway.

Rosemary went out to meet it to see that there were no passengers, just a driver. Rosemary recognised him from her cousins' previous visit.

"The mistress wanted me to deliver this parcel to you," he said in a slightly disapproving tone. He held out a square-shaped package wrapped in inconspicuous brown paper and tied with twine.

"Not Elamina's usual style at all," said Rosemary.

"There's a note," he said as Rosemary took the package.

He handed over a rather elaborate gold and purple envelope.

"That's more like it," she muttered, wondering whether the brown paper of the package was supposed to be a clever disguise to make it look less conspicuous.

"Thank you," Rosemary said the to the driver. He nodded and drove away.

Rosemary went back into the house. She closed the door behind her and leant against it, feeling her heart beating in her chest. She was one step closer, hopefully, to finding her daughter.

"What's all the fuss about, then?" said Granny, appearing in the mirror on the wall across from where Rosemary stood.

"Your other granddaughter is helping me get Athena back," said Rosemary.

"You must have been desperate to call in a favour from her," said Granny.

"Of course I'm desperate," said Rosemary. "Didn't you say you were trying to help us?"

"I was at first, but then I thought about it."

Rosemary stared daggers at her grandmother's ghost. "You thought what exactly?"

"That as she went willingly, it wasn't really my place."

"How can you say that?" Rosemary asked. "She's been gone for a week!"

"You don't think she'll just wander back in at any moment?" Granny asked. "Like I said, she's just gone for a romp with a boy."

"Stop calling it a romp! She's far too young to be doing that!" said Rosemary.

"I wasn't implying any explicit details," said Granny. "But surely, if she can get to the fae realm because of her heritage, she should be able to get out again."

"We don't know that Athena can get back by herself," said Rosemary. "Tell me, how did you help to get Sherry back all those years ago?"

"Is that what you've heard?" Granny said. "The funny thing is, all I did was perform the ritual properly at the equinox. Sherry showed up at Fin's Creek. She must have done something herself at the same time in order to get out, only she'd never tell me what. I don't think she could."

Rosemary was appalled. She'd been hoping Granny could shed more light on what had worked in the past. "You're infuriatingly unhelpful!" she said.

"I still think you're overreacting," said Granny. "When I was her age I ran off with a rather handsome wolf shifter and didn't come back for a month!"

"Spare me the details!"

"All I'm saying is things have a way of working themselves out."

"I admire your optimism," said Rosemary, "but I'm not taking any chances." She opened the envelope from Elamina.

My dear tragic cousin, read the refined loopy handwriting. I have gone to quite some trouble to source the ingredients that you seek. Unfortunately there was one item that is exceedingly rare and highly illegal in the magical world due to its danger, but you should find everything else in this box. Best of luck in figuring out what to do with all these items. I take it the spell is rather complex, and well beyond your abilities. I'm afraid it won't work at all unless you can source the remaining item. However, since I have gone to great trouble, you surely must agree that you're now indebted to us, and please believe me when I tell you that we intend very much to recall the favour.

Rosemary gulped. "What a fancy way of saying, you owe me one," she said to herself.

"Well, I'm just glad that you're finally practicing your magic," said Granny. "I forgot to mention, I was quite impressed with that plant growing trick."

"And you were no help at all," said Rosemary.

"Well, what do you expect? I'm dead!" said Granny, raising her arms. "And have far better things to do, but I'm glad you have everything under control here." And with a little pop, she was gone.

Rosemary sighed. Being dead sure seemed to have the effect of making Granny less concerned with the perils of the mortal world.

She took the package to the dining room table and opened it up, finding that it did indeed contain the ingredients she'd asked her cousin for. They were packaged elegantly in glass vials and little wooden boxes.

She checked them against the list. All the items were accounted for except for werewolf blood.

"And it just so happens that I know where to get some of that," she said to herself.

Rosemary hadn't seen Liam since she'd barged into his shop and been attacked, nor had she returned the two phone calls he'd made to her, as she'd had other things on her mind. This seemed like as good a time as any to pay him a visit. The full moon had passed, so she felt comfortable that he would be in human form.

She pulled up in the car outside his shop. The lights were on, and there didn't seem to be any customers milling about.

Perfect.

She got out and made her way inside.

The doorbell tinkled and Liam came out from the back room to stand behind the counter. "Rosemary!" he said. "What a surprise. I...thank you for coming. Have you had a chance to consider my offer?"

"Your offer for me to help you with your...situation?" Rosemary asked. "It just so happens I have a proposition for you."

"Okay, good!" Liam interlaced his fingers nervously. "What is it?"

"I need your blood," she said.

"My...my blood?" Liam asked. "Rosemary, it's not a good idea to try to turn yourself, or anyone else for that matter, into a werewolf."

"No. That is not what I mean," said Rosemary. "You might have heard Athena has gone missing."

"I heard a rumour," said Liam. "I didn't realise it was true."

"She's gone to the fae realm and the only way that I can figure out to get across there to fetch her back involves very specific timing and a very specific spell with very, very specific ingredients."

"You have a spell that requires *my* blood?" Liam asked.

"Werewolf blood," said Rosemary. "It's not specific to a particular werewolf, or to you. The spell is old, and it requires a whole lot of weird ingredients like ground narwal horn and roasted newt, hair from a dryad...odd things from a bunch of magical creatures."

"You're calling me a creature now?"

"Well, I don't know what to call you. But apparently everything we say is wrong and offensive, so maybe I'll just carry on talking all day and upset everyone else in the town while I'm at it," said Rosemary.

"I'm afraid it's impossible," said Liam.

"Oh no, I really could ramble on all day, just watch," said Rosemary.

"Not that. Getting my blood is impossible," Liam explained. "And not only is it expressly prohibited in the magical world, it's extremely dangerous. I've had to use a number of protections on myself so that I don't accidentally infect anyone if I get a paper cut."

"So it's your blood that causes the magical disease to spread?"

Liam shrugged. "It's a virus that can be spread through a number of different means. The most common is a bite."

Rosemary gave him a peculiar look. "Do you protect your teeth as well, then?"

"Of course," Liam said. "I've employed every magical protection that I could work up on my own. I haven't told anyone else. Not even Sherry, though she does look at me curiously, when I'm sick so often."

"There are obviously a lot of prejudices out there in the community," said Rosemary. "I want you to know that I don't have any of those myself, being quite frankly too naive to this entire world to know the difference between a werewolf, or shifter, or dryad, or anything else."

"That's actually somewhat reassuring, believe it or not," said Liam.

"Let me continue," said Rosemary. "I need to do whatever I can to get to the fae realm on the off-chance that I can get my daughter back. There are lots of risks and I might fail completely, but I have to try. I have to exhaust every possible option."

"Look, I get it," said Liam.

They stood for a moment in silence. Rosemary looked down at her feet, wondering what she could do or say to convince him.

Finally, Liam spoke. "I can...I can help you."

"Thank you so much," said Rosemary.

"On one condition."

"Name it."

"I need you to help me figure out how to get this...condition...under control."

Rosemary started to protest. She didn't have the time for this.

"Not right now," he said. "I mean, your focus is on your daughter. I get it, but please, at some point, fairly soon, I would really like for you to figure out if you can use your powers to stop this nightmare or at least keep it under control."

"Liam, I'll do what I can."

"You didn't sound like you would the other day."

"I was in shock," said Rosemary defensively. "What do you expect? You'd just attacked me as a great big wolfy beast."

"Okay. I get it," said Liam. "But I have your word?"

"Fine, anything," said Rosemary. "If I survive this, I'll help you."

Liam eyed her cautiously.

"Okay," he said. He closed his eyes as if mentally preparing himself, then he waved the palm of his right hand over his left. Rosemary watched as a pattern of shadows flowed out over the area. He took a letter opener that looked like a miniature sword from the drawer in front of him and raised it.

"Wait a minute," said Rosemary. "You're going to bleed all over the place if you stab yourself like that. Let me get something."

She reached into her handbag where she'd had the foresight to bring some of Granny's glass vials and corks to fit them.

"Here." She passed him a wide-lipped vessel.

"Thank you," Liam said, placing it down on the desk in front of him. He leaned over and pierced the skin on his palm. Oddly thick dark red blood oozed into the glass.

"Be very careful with this," he said, finishing up and handing the vial to Rosemary.

"I will," she reassured him.

She turned to go. Then, remembering her manners, she glanced back. "Liam. Thank you," she said.

"And thank *you*," Liam replied. "Not just for what you've promised and bargained for, but for keeping my secret."

"It's not mine to tell," she said.

She made her way back to the car with a lightness in her chest for the first time since Athena had disappeared. She hadn't solved the entire puzzle yet, but she had all the ingredients to help her get into the world her daughter had been taken to. There was nothing in her way. At least nothing that wouldn't move with a good hard metaphorical kick.

CHAPTER
FORTY

I t was finally that time of year. The air seemed to thicken in
anticipation, though the weather was fine. The morning of the
equinox dawned crystal clear skies.

Rosemary arrived at the Ostara ritual an hour early to find that Ferg
had already set up the hundreds of tulips she'd helped to grow. He'd
collected them from her house with a group of his eccentric volunteers
earlier that day before Rosemary had gone to Fin's Creek to place especially enchanted crystals in a circle there for the spell.

She'd dressed for travel, with her sturdy leather boots and warm
fleece-lined coat. She was even wearing the bundle around her neck that
Athena had insisted she make a few weeks earlier to protect her from
Dain's influence. It was a long shot, but she was hoping the protection
might extend not just to her ex's fae magic, but also to fae, more generally. She also carried a number of other hopefully-useful-items.

She had everything she needed in her large handbag, or at least
everything she could think of. A backpack would have been more practical, but a handbag seemed less conspicuous. The ingredients for Beryl's
spell, once prepared, amounted to only a small volume and didn't take
up much space. She also had a few other items that she'd prepared to

help her get in and out of the fae realm from the recipes in the book that Burk had given her.

"You're dressed awfully casually for a ritual," said Ferg. He was wearing a pale blue-and-pink-striped cloak with midnight blue robes underneath.

"And you're looking very formal," said Rosemary, trying to make polite small talk while her mind was clearly in another place entirely.

"I am," said Ferg proudly.

"I've been doing some research." Rosemary tried to sound casual. "In Granny's library, I found some useful additions for the equinox ritual." It was true that she'd scoured Granny's books, but she'd only found a few useful tips for dealing with fae.

"Oh yes," said Ferg, sounding interested.

"Well, you said you wanted me to lend my family's magic for the equinox ritual, and I did my research, so I'm just going to place these crystals over here in a little circle right in the middle. And these small bundles go on the outside."

"This is very unorthodox," said Ferg. "Your grandmother never did any of this."

"Well, you know, I don't want to take my chances."

"And how exactly do you think it will help convey our blessings to the Goddess and the guardians of all the other worlds, and especially to the fae realm, in the hopes that they grant us their good favour?"

It sounded a bit flaky to Rosemary. "I'm sure it will," she said.

She continued preparing in accordance with Beryl's family's spell on the off-chance that Ferg's grand notions of the Goddess conveying her favour wasn't enough to get her daughter back.

By the time she'd finished setting up, a bunch of people, many of them dressed in robes, had started to arrive. They milled around the circle.

Rosemary recognised a number of familiar faces, including the teenagers who'd visited her house. *Don't get any ideas*, she thought, giving them a suspicious look.

The beginning of the equinox ritual seemed quite similar to the last one that Rosemary had witnessed, though she hardly paid attention. The quarters were called and the circle was cast. A woman with long wavy blonde hair stood in the centre, and said some beautifully crafted words about the Goddess Eostre. Rosemary registered that it was lovely and poetic, but her main concentration remained focused on what she needed to do next.

As part of the ritual, a group of young children walked around with baskets of dyed eggs, handing them out to the circle participants. Rosemary smiled as she took the pink and blue painted item, finding that it was heavier than she expected. It was indeed a hardboiled egg rather than a hollow shell. She tucked it into her pocket because she knew she'd need her hands free.

For the next part of the ritual Ferg nodded to her. It was her turn.

"Now, if everyone will close their eyes," Rosemary said, "and chant with me: *the earth, the air, the fire, the water*."

The circle around her did as they were told, except the young children among them who looked on with curiosity as Rosemary stepped into the centre between her carefully laid crystals. She held out her hands and focused her energy, muttering the memorised chant, from the spell, which was drowned out by the chanting around her.

This had been part of her plan to distract everyone from the sneaky magic she had to do. But at the same time, she could feel the energy from the chanting contributing to her own power, emanating out into the centre of the circle and weaving around the light that began to shine from her fingertips. It lit up an intricate network between the crystals on the ground. Rosemary stepped into the centre and raised her arms.

She said the final words of the spell, commanding the magic to life.

Silence fell around her, though she could tell the circle of people were still chanting.

Rosemary waited with bated breath as the light between the crystals shone brighter.

A ring of dark blue swept up around in the air in front of her. It formed a portal with gaseous flame-like patterns around its outside. Ripples swam across its inky black surface.

She could see the willow trees surrounding the portal, transparent, just as she could see the circle behind of the townsfolk who were still chanting.

"This is it," she said to herself.

She'd done it. She'd created the spatial warp needed, connecting Fin's Creek and the centre of the town. Both were now temporarily in the same place.

She took a deep breath and stepped through, glancing back, only to see that others were following her.

"No!" Rosemary cried out.

It was too late. Sherry tumbled through, giving Rosemary a push, followed by Athena's school friends.

"No..." Rosemary tried to push them back into the earth realm.

It was too late.

The portal closed, but they weren't in Fin's Creek or the town centre. They all looked around, finding themselves surrounded by an eerie violet light.

"So this is the fae realm," said Felix, looking around.

"Why did you follow me?" Rosemary asked. "I told you to stay away. It's too dangerous."

"We needed to help Athena," said Elise.

"And we're not convinced that you know what you're doing," Felix added.

"Thanks very much for the vote of confidence." Rosemary turned away from the teens in exasperation. One teenager was more than enough, and now she had four on her hands, though right now there were bigger problems.

"Sherry," Rosemary said, taking hold of the woman's shoulders.

Sherry still had the otherworldly gleam in her eye.

"Sherry, did you take my necklace?"

"It was the only way," she said. "I'm sorry, Rosemary, I needed to come through. I'm not a powerful witch like you or a young one like these teens. I wouldn't have been able to follow without it."

"But why?" Rosemary asked. "I thought you hated this place."

"I needed to come back for her. I promised."

"Your friend?" Rosemary said.

"You know about Mei?" said Sherry in shock. "Everyone forgot her. Even her family. It was like how no one remembered me when I came back. Like I didn't exist. But I remembered everything. I could never forget my friend."

"My granny found a newspaper clipping just recently," said Rosemary. "The little girl, she disappeared when you did."

"I promised her I'd come back," said Sherry. "And now that I have, I'm not going to leave without her."

CHAPTER
FORTY-ONE

Everything was different – the sounds, the scents, the creatures. As they continued their journey through the fae realm, Athena marvelled at the physical terrain that unfolded around them. The shimmering plants and fungus seemed larger than life and came in all different colours. Enchanting mists swirled around them in spiralling patterns.

"Can you feel it?" Finnigan said.

"Feel what?" Athena asked.

"You belong here."

Athena winced, feeling the truth in his words but also recalling her mother and everyone she cared about back in the earth realm. Her old life seemed like a distant memory.

"How long have we been away?" she asked again.

Finnigan shrugged. "Not long."

"I think I should get back," said Athena. "It feels like it's all slipping away from me. Everything human, everything that I knew."

"If you need some grounding just eat some more of the human food you brought with you."

Athena reached into her bag for her Jaffa Cakes, only to find them crumble into dust in her hand. "What happened?" she asked. "I can't imagine them being so stale. Surely I only opened the pack a few hours ago. It shouldn't have changed that much."

"Things work differently here," said Finnigan. "Maybe it reacted to the air."

Athena opened a bag of crisps to find them in the usual condition. She ate the entire bag just in case, offering some to Finnigan, though he declined.

"You don't need to eat human food?"

"I spend most of my time here," Finnigan said. "I don't belong in the human world. Not anymore." A sad look crossed his face and Athena felt sorry for him, but he didn't seem to want to talk about it, so they continued walking on in silence.

"Okay. I really think I should turn back," she said again as mist grew thicker around them. "I need to go home."

"There's something you need to see first," said Finnigan, his voice sounding a little anxious.

"Alright," said Athena. "Then we'll go home. You promise?"

He nodded. "I intend to return to the earth realm as quickly as possible. I just need to show you something first."

Athena had an uneasy feeling, but she chose to follow him, not knowing how to navigate alone through the thick mist. A structure came into view ahead of them that looked like it was composed of dozens of enormous mushrooms.

"What is this?" Athena asked.

"The castle of West Eloria," said Finnigan.

"Is that what you wanted to show me?"

"Yes, I just have to introduce you to someone. It'll make everything clearer."

Athena hesitated.

"You'll love this. And besides," Finnigan coaxed, "the missing girl is probably here."

Athena's intuition was flaring. Something wasn't right, but what choice did she have? She didn't know how to navigate the fae realm alone, and besides, finding Gretchen and returning her to Myrtlewood would do a lot to appease her mother, who was going to be dreadfully mad.

Athena followed Finnigan uneasily towards the strange building.

The large doorway ahead looked to be made of silvery tree bark.

"You wanted to see what it was like inside a fae building," Finnigan said mischievously.

"I did, didn't I?" said Athena, marvelling at the odd organic architecture. "I didn't realise that we'd go to an actual castle."

"Here." He took her hand and pressed his other hand to the door. It opened, leading to grand hall. Athena walked in, holding Finnigan's hand.

The door closed behind them, jolting Athena.

At the other end of the building stood an enormous, glimmering throne set high up. It was surrounded by numerous other chairs and elaborate ornaments of fae creatures. As they neared, Athena could make out a figure on the throne with tumbling silver hair and a crown of flowers and leaves. Her dress too looked as if it were made entirely of rosebuds and spring blossoms.

"She's beautiful," Athena whispered as they walked closer.

When they got to be a few metres away, Finnigan bowed and Athena followed suit.

"Finnigan," said the woman who, Athena guessed, was none other than the Countess of West Eloria Finnigan had mentioned earlier.

"*What* have you brought me?"

"A halfling," said Finnigan.

Halfling? Athena shivered, feeling uncomfortable at the way he'd referred to her, noting that many of the other chairs on both sides of the throne were filled with powerful looking fae and flanked by guards.

"A halfling, yes," said the countess with scorn in her voice. Athena immediately disliked her.

"Not just any halfling," said Finnigan. "I do believe that her father is none other than the Queen's son, Prince Dain."

Prince! Dain! Athena was stunned. My deadbeat dad is not only fae, but he's also a prince?!

A tiny gasp escaped the countess's mouth and she clapped in excitement, causing a flurry of butterflies to fly up from her hands. Her eyes flared with a preternatural glow as she looked at Athena.

"You're telling me," said the countess, "that the prince got up to mischief on his little earth realm escapade? Oh my! You have done well, Finnigan. She's a pretty creature, even if she is only half fae."

Athena grimaced. Finnigan had told her it was rude to refer to people as half fae, but that obviously didn't apply to the countess. The way they were talking made her progressively more anxious. All she knew about fae politics was that it was complex, and the fact that her father was missing did not bode well with the news he was some kind of royalty.

"Finnigan, what is all this about?" Athena asked.

"Athena is special," said Finnigan. "She's not just half fae. Her mother is from a powerful witching family."

"Oh, indeed, this is a worthy prize!" The countess shrieked and stood up from her throne.

Athena turned to the boy she thought she knew.

There was a roaring in her head that eclipsed everything else as the realisation sunk in.

"You!" She looked at Finnigan. "You set me up. All along you *were* just a filthy spy. You captured me and played me for a fool. I'm some kind of prize to you? So you'll be rewarded by the fae? Is that it?"

Finnigan raised his arms as if to protest. "Athena..."

"How could you do this?!" Athena yelled.

Finnigan's face was clouded with unreadable emotion. "I had to. I was bound by the countess. Indentured...to carry out her will."

Athena sensed all previous feelings she'd had for the boy wither into bitterness and disgust. "And I suppose you had no free will of your own? Wait a minute, you planned this the whole time, didn't you? All of it. You cast that illusion on our house. So that Mum would know it was fae who were after me. This is all part of a bigger plot."

A smile crept across his face. "I was rather clever, wasn't I?"

Athena gasped. "It was you!" she glared at Finnigan. "You kidnapped my father!"

"I think of it more as 'guiding him back home'," said Finnigan. "He had been missing for a long time..."

"Don't tell me you also stole our old car?"

Finnigan shrugged. "I might have."

"You deceived us. But fae can't lie!"

The countess threw her head back and crowed with laughter. "Oh, that's such a good one," she said. "I absolutely love how humans still believe that rubbish. Of course we can lie!"

The dread was setting in, along with a cloudy feeling. Athena rubbed her eyes as if trying to wake up from a bad dream. "I don't understand," she said. "I need the truth. Tell me what's really going on here. Tell me what it is you're trying to do."

"Now, why would he go and do a silly thing like that?" said the countess. "You already know far too much. You cannot ever return to the human realm. We will keep you right here."

"No!" Athena cried as guards crashed forward, surrounding her. "You will not take me. You will *not* capture me!"

The fae guards were bulky and dressed in the red uniforms Athena recognised from the day shift at the clerk's office. They were armed with spears and bows. She closed her eyes, determined that everything she had would go into this fight.

She could feel them drawing nearer, her hope of escape diminishing, but her determination burning strong. Her sense of betrayal, anxiety, fear, and rage was bottling up inside. There was a roaring in her ears as the pressure became too much.

Just as a hand reached out for her, she released the tension she'd been holding.

A surprising spurt of bright light shot from Athena's fingertips, bursting out to fill the room.

All the creatures froze still, like statues, except Finnigan and the countess herself.

"No! Grab her!" the countess cried.

"No freaking way," said Athena, and she ran towards the nearest door, at the side of the throne room.

She busted through to find long winding passages. Wishing she'd had the foresight to run back outside instead, now she found herself trapped in the countess's castle, and it was only a matter of time before more guards or soldiers, or worse, came to attack her.

Footsteps sounded after Athena as she ran down the passageway. She had no idea of what she'd done before to freeze the guards. It had been some kind of automatic self-defence, but at least it was magic. *Real magic.*

Still, her energy seem to be flagging. She worried she'd have nothing left to fight off another attack.

She opened the door to what looked like a storeroom filled with boxes. Her heart thudded in her chest as she closed the door behind her quietly, then snuck in and hid behind a large stack. It would only be a matter of time before they found her.

She closed her eyes, wondering whether there was anyone who could help her now. She recalled what Finnigan had said about how she could communicate telepathically in a controlled way, getting herself to only be heard by people she wanted to communicate with.

It was a stab in the dark, but she'd run out of other options. There was nothing else she could think of. She had to try, even though she had no idea whether there were any friendly forces in the entire realm, or whether it was possible to talk to anyone back in the human world...her *own* world.

My real home.

Athena focused her mind outwards, calling out to anyone who genuinely had her best interests at heart, an ally, anyone who she could consider friendly.

To her astonishment, a voice called back.

I'll help you, if you can help me.

Who are you? Athena asked, wondering whether it was possible her communication had been intercepted by some fae servant of the countess, trying to draw her out.

I'm locked in the northern tower.

How do I know I can trust you? Athena asked.

Athena, it's Dad.

Dad? Athena responded in surprise. What are you doing here?

The cogs started to turn in her mind. Of course he was here. Finnigan had captured him and brought him here. The countess had imprisoned her father in much the same way she intended to imprison Athena.

I've been stuck here for weeks, possibly months, Dain replied. The countess has held me hostage.

You probably deserve it, said Athena drily. Her father always brought trouble.

I might do. I don't know the difference anymore. I just...I want to help you, even if it means risking my life. I owe you this.

You're right. You owe me this, said Athena. *Mum might forget how terrible you are and forgive you, but I don't.*

Fair enough, said her father. Come and find me. I'll send a signal.

Athena felt a low pulse like sonar through her chest, pulling her in a particular direction.

Her father was the last person she wanted to seek help from. In this situation, he might also be the only person who could help. Sure, she had been let down by him for years, but it was nothing compared to the fresh sting of very deliberate and wilful betrayal from the boy she'd thought she could trust.

Mum was right, Athena thought to herself. We do have bad taste in men in this family.

Hey, I heard that, said her father in her mind.

Athena's lips curled into a smile. There was something totally absurd about the situation, though it shouldn't be at all funny.

She followed the pulse, carefully darting along passageways, avoiding the scurrying fae who would no doubt be searching for her. They probably thought she was trying to escape, not running to one of the tallest towers, so at least she had that to her advantage.

After a while of scurrying around the castle, Athena found the door to the mushroom tower only to see that it was bolted with a heavy padlock.

Athena knocked softly on the door. "Dad, I'm here. It's locked."

"You can get through the lock, Athena. You're powerful. Use your fae magic," said Dain.

"I don't know how," Athena said.

"Just close your eyes and imagine the lock turning and...uhhh... twiddle your fingers around."

"Do I have to do that part?" Athena asked.

"No, but it'll help you to concentrate."

Athena did as instructed, and to her surprise, she heard a subtle click. The door sprung open, and for the first time in many months Athena laid eyes on her father.

He looked far paler and skinnier than usual. And she wasn't sure if that was just because he'd been in the fae realm for some time or whether his captors had also been starving him.

"Why are you locked up like this?" Athena asked, observing the shackles around Dain's wrists and ankles. "What did you do?"

"I didn't do anything," he replied defensively. "They kidnapped me. Look, Athena I know I haven't been a good father. You probably realise this by now...but I'm fae."

"You don't say," said Athena, observing her father in his fully fae form for the first time in her life. "I never would have guessed, despite your slender limbs and pointy ears."

"I know I haven't done anything to deserve your trust. But there's nothing more that I want right now than to help you."

"And what about Mum?"

"Is she here too?" he asked, surprised.

"No, forget it," said Athena. "We can talk about Mum later. Can you help me get out of here?"

"I can," said Dain. "At least, I can help a little. I don't know how to get back through to the earth realm alone."

"Seriously?!"

"There are a lot of protections put up against the fae," said Dain.

"Against the fae?" Athena asked. "I thought the protections were put up by the fae against the vampires."

"It's more complicated than that," said Dain. "The only way that I was able to escape this realm, many years ago, was because I followed a little girl back through on the equinox."

"But Finnigan could get through easily."

Dain scowled. "Yes, but Finnigan is part human like you. The little girl I followed was human. I helped her to tear a hole in the fae side of the veil, and it worked...with the help of her human magic. We needed both to get through. She helped me escape, though she never saw me. I'm thinking that, with your human side, we might be able to do the same."

"How do I get you out of the shackles?" Athena asked.

"It's complicated magic," said Dain. "I don't know. Do your best, or your worst."

She held up her hands, willing the shackles to open. Sparks flew in front of her and they clicked open immediately.

Dain looked astonished. "How did you do that?"

"I don't know!"

"That's your grandmother's magic!" said Dain. "That's the Thorn family magic. I thought it was hidden and bound."

"How do you know about all that?" Athena asked suspiciously. "Oh, never mind. Let's just get out of here."

She managed to break her father out of the rest of his shackles without too much magical effort.

"Thanks," said Dain. "Look, I'm not very strong right now. I haven't been fed properly."

"Can you eat human food?" Athena asked.

"Not right now. It would make me ill. I have to get used to it slowly."

"I can't really help you, then," said Athena.

"It's all right," said Dain. "I've got enough energy to do this and I can forage some berries on the way."

"Do what?" Athena asked.

"It's like teleportation."

"You can teleport!"

"Only in this realm. Quick. There's no more time for chit-chat. Take hold of my hands."

Footstep sounded in the corridor outside.

"Now!" he commanded.

Athena reached for her father's hands.

"Close your eyes," he said.

She did. It felt as if a wind whipped around them in that room, and when she opened her eyes again they were in the forest, surrounded by trees that glowed in the violet light.

CHAPTER

FORTY-TWO

"Are you okay?" Rosemary asked Sherry. She was looking peakish.

"I'll be fine," Sherry replied. "Let's just go. We need to find them."

"Can you give my necklace back first?" The brittleness in Rosemary's voice made Sherry stiffen.

"I would," said Sherry, "but I don't think I'll survive here for long without it giving me the magical boost."

"What about these children?" Rosemary asked. "Will they survive?"

"Everyone should eat one of these," said Sam, holding up some small pink cupcakes.

"What is it?" Felix asked.

"Maam made these cakes. She said they helped people go into the—"

"Wait a minute," said Rosemary, rummaging in her handbag and producing a small bag of baked goods. "Those look a lot like these ones that I made. How did your Mum get her hands on the books that the vampires had made about the fae?"

Sam laughed. "Where do you think the vampires got the information from? People always underestimate folk magic. Sometimes it's the simple things that work the best."

Rosemary opened her own bag, feeling slightly woozy herself. She took some cake and offered the rest around.

"No offense, lady," said Felix, "but I think Sam's ones look better. They're not all burnt."

Rosemary glared at him.

"We don't have time for bickering over baking," said Sherry. "How are we going to find them?"

"I have a locator spell," Rosemary replied. "It's supposed to track down humans, and I hope it works on Athena."

"Why wouldn't it?" Sherry asked.

"Never mind," said Elise, and Rosemary got the impression she knew more about Athena's heritage than Rosemary did. "We'll have to hope it works at all in the fae realm," Elise continued.

Rosemary brushed away her annoyance about being left in the dark. She tried to cast the spell by muttering the incantation and wiggling her fingers. There was a tiny poof but nothing else happened.

"Oh blast!"

She attempted it several more times to no avail.

"Let me try?" Elise suggested. Rosemary grudgingly handed over the crumpled piece of paper with the instructions on it. Elise and Sam looked it over, muttering to each other. Felix tried to weigh in, but his suggestions of adding more 'zazz' were declined.

Rosemary felt a little bit as she did with new technology, which young people seemed to always be so adept at.

"Okay, here goes," said Elise. She held out her hand and waved her fingers about in a complex pattern unlike Rosemary's attempts, saying the chant for the spell in a lower tone. A little glowing blue light appeared in front of her, shaped like a small diamond.

"I think it will help if we all concentrate on it, give it more energy."

They stood in silence, focusing.

The diamond began to glow brighter. It bopped in mid-air and then began to move through the trees.

"I think we're supposed to follow it," Sam said, taking off at a run.

Felix, quick as lightening, transformed into a fox and bolted ahead. *That's right,* Rosemary recalled. *Athena said he was a shifter.*

She and others followed through the forest.

The light was moving rather quickly.

As they continued, the terrain became more rugged. Huge mossy rocks dotted their path that seemed to glow in various shades of pastel.

"This one smells like lemon sherbet," said Sam. "I almost want to lick it."

"Don't!" Elise cried.

"I'm not that stupid."

A yelp sounded from Felix. Clearly, in his fox form, hadn't been able to resist the appetising scent. They gathered around him as he writhed on the ground, peach coloured bumps popping up all over his furry body.

"Get him to water!" Sam said decisively.

"Why?" Rosemary asked.

"Just folk knowledge," said Sam. "Maam always said, with otherworldly magic, water helps things flow through. I don't know if it will work..."

"It's worth a shot. I have water in my bag, here," said Rosemary, holding out her drink bottle.

"No, it has to be running water," said Sam.

"I don't know if such a thing exists around here," said Sherry, sounding rather dazed. "Or even exists at all. What exists? What does that word really mean?"

Rosemary ignored Sherry's deranged rambles. This was serious. They needed to act fast.

"If only he could talk," said Elise. "He'd have his fox hearing, but even if he can understand us I don't think he's in any state to move." She turned to Deron and gave him a meaningful look. "What do you think?"

"Worth a try," Deron replied.

"What is—?" Rosemary asked, but before she could continue what had built up to be a rampaging monologue of questions in her mind she gasped.

Deron was sprouting fur, all over his body.

"Not you too!" Rosemary said, turning to Elise. "Which thing did he lick?"

"Just wait," said Elise, placing a calming hand on Rosemary's forearm.

Rosemary watched in astonishment as Deron, who was already reasonably tall, puffed out and grew two feet.

"Oh, I see, another shifter," Rosemary muttered.

Standing in front of them was a black bear. He growled, making the hairs on Rosemary's arms stand up on end. Then, she watched as he picked up the writhing spotty fox in his arms and began to run.

"What about the diamond?" Sherry called out as they all followed. "Shiny, shiny diamond!"

"One thing at a time," said Rosemary.

Running in the fae realm felt a lot like moving through water, but at a faster pace. The effect gave her motion sickness.

Sure enough, up ahead a stream appeared. Deron was already there by the time they arrived, lowering Felix into the running water.

They watched with baited breath, not daring to express the possibility that fae realm water, with its otherworldly violet glow, might not have the desired effect, but might in fact do something even worse.

After a moment, Felix stopped writhing and became unnaturally still.

"Is the poor little dilly-dally going to be okay?" Sherry asked.

"Shush," said Rosemary, unsure if she was seeking silence or trying to soothe Sherry and indeed herself.

The spots were fading from Felix's body, and he'd transformed back into human form, but other than that, he remained still, carefully held by the friendly bear.

"Felix," Elise said gently. "Can you hear me?"

Rosemary's mind was racing with anxiety. What on earth was she going to tell the parents of these children whose lives she'd inadvertently endangered?

"Felix!" said Sam in a booming voice. "Time to wake up now!"

Felix coughed and spluttered and then grinned. "That was an adventure!" he said.

Elise looked daggers at him.

"Do not lick anything!" she said as they prepared to continue on. "Do not even touch anything unless I say so."

"Yes, ma'am," he said cheekily.

"It's not funny," said Sam. "We were worried, you could have—"

"Alright, I get it. I'm sorry for licking the peachy moss. I'll be more careful."

"Do you think he'll be able to return?" Rosemary asked. "I read that if you eat here you can't leave the realm."

"Who knows," said Sam. "Let's hope that only applies to food offered by the fae, not random moss. Or that it's just nonsense."

Rosemary crossed her fingers and muttered her own private spell, with the intention they'd all get out of the realm safely.

Fortunately, the shining diamond they'd summoned earlier had followed them. It hovered in the air patiently, waiting to lead them on.

Rosemary felt famished all of a sudden, only she didn't feel like the special shortbread that Sam was passing around to the others, or any of the baking she'd prepared either. She needed something more substantial. She reached into her pocket and found the egg from the ritual. *How convenient,* she thought, and ate it, glad for the protein boost.

They continued through the forest, careful to avoid any creatures coming their way, and definitely not licking anything.

After what felt like hours they stumbled across an enormous mushroom speckled with violet and lime green dots. It was as wide as a house, and seemed to be fitted with windows and doors.

The diamond hovered in the air above the arched front door.

They approached cautiously.

"It's locked," said Sam.

"How do we get in?" Rosemary asked.

"I think Felix will know how to handle this," said Elise, looking towards the mischievous boy who seemed to have recovered from his earlier mishap. "He always seems to know how to break into places he's not supposed to be."

"Stand back, ladies," said Felix.

"Fine, as long as you stop calling us that," said Rosemary. Sam gave her a grateful look, as did Deron.

Felix held out his hands. The lock cracked open, sending sparks flying.

Rosemary flinched as sparks hit her.

"I told you to stand back," said Felix.

The door swung open and inside, in the low light emitted from the crystal chandeliers above them, shone the faces of half a dozen young children.

CHAPTER
FORTY-THREE

The sky above them had darkened to deep purple, but the trees seemed to glow in a silvery light. Athena would have appreciated the effervescent beauty if it wasn't for the impending doom. "How do we get through the veil?" she asked her father.

"You'd know better than I do," said Dain.

"What do you mean? You said you could help me. Plus, you're a powerful fae."

"Sure," said Dain. "But like I said, the only way I could get through was to follow a human girl when she found her way back on the equinox, remember?"

"How did she do it?" Athena asked. "I'm still trying to get my head around the idea that the protections on the veil are cast from the other side."

"Of course they are," said Dain. "Humans have a lot of fear of the fae."

"And all this time, I thought they were protecting themselves from vampires," said Athena.

"Vampires are worthless bottom-feeders," said Dain. "I can't stand the bloodsuckers. But they're no big threat, especially now that they can't detect us anymore."

There was a whooshing sound, and bright light beamed through the trees.

"They've come after us," said Dain. "Quick. We've got to find some way to hide. If we're out in the open like this, they'll find us in no time."

"I know!" said Athena, remembering the leafy building she'd seen not long after first entering the fae realm. "Why don't we break into the clerk's office?"

"You're definitely my daughter," said Dain with a grin as he plucked a few berries from a nearby bush.

She pierced him with a glare. "Don't say that again."

"Sorry," he said as they ran quickly towards the familiar cobbled path which would lead them directly to the clerk's office.

"Can you go any faster?" asked Athena. "Or can you just teleport us or something?"

"Oh yeah," said Dain. "I've been out of the fae realm so long that I forget I can do that. Come on. Take hold of my hand."

Athena grabbed her father's hand and quickly found herself inside a strange room. The walls were made of leaves.

"That was an easy way of breaking and entering," said Athena. "Remind me to take you along next time I have to commit some petty theft."

"It really is unfortunate that it only works in the fae realm," said Dain. "But what did I just tell you?" Dain winked at her.

"Don't say it," said Athena. "You know, I'm not going to forgive you for the way you treated us."

The swagger and sparkle disappeared from Dain's demeanour. "I'm sorry. Really, I don't deserve your forgiveness. I was terrible at playing human, just like I was terrible at being a fae prince."

"I still can't believe you, of all people, are a prince, whatever that means here," said Athena.

"Please understand that I didn't know what I was doing."

There was a booming sound outside. "Err, that's great, Dad, but we kind of have bigger problems right now."

"No, please let me finish. Wait, you're calling me Dad again?"

"We don't have time for this," said Athena.

"But I owe you an explanation."

"Fine," said Athena, crossing her arms. "Tell me, why were you so terrible then? What's your excuse?"

Dain sighed and his shoulders slumped forward. "You need to understand how it all happened. When I was here I never cared for the pomp and ceremony. I especially couldn't stand the politics. It was awful."

"Uh huh," said Athena, tapping her foot.

"I found the earth realm relatively refreshing, in comparison," Dain continued. "Although I was so young when I went through the veil and I knew nothing of human customs. I guess that's why I was a target for the authorities. They picked me up and I ended up hopping from foster home to foster home."

"Oh?" Athena asked. She'd never heard anything much about her father's childhood before.

"Needless to say, I didn't exactly have the ideal upbringing. Some of the families I was placed in were kind, but I couldn't help it. I'd always get in trouble, run away or do something mischievous. And then I'd be moved. A lot of the time there was...violence. I won't go into the details. I just wanted you to know."

"Why did you never tell us this?" Athena asked.

"I was always the fun guy," Dain replied with a sad smile. "I didn't think anyone wanted to know my sob story."

"Well, all we saw was an irresponsible deadbeat messing with our lives, not to mention Mum's memory!"

Dain looked abashed. "I'm sorry about that. I never meant to do her any harm, either of you. The effects of fae magic are hard to predict on humans. Anyway, I'm not here to cry about my past. I was a terrible father. It didn't help that I had an addiction to cream, which led to a gambling problem among other things."

"We didn't know about any of that either. What is with the cream?"

Dain shrugged. "Haven't you always been partial to cream?"

"Sure," said Athena. "In a fairly ordinary way."

"Your human side must protect you," he said.

"What exactly is the effect that cream has on the fae?" Athena asked.

"Why? Do you have some?" Dain asked, looking back at her with a preternatural gleam in his eyes.

"Just explain it to me, Dad," Athena said, realising the renewed silence outside was even more worrying than the previous booming sound.

"It gives us quite a rush," said Dain. "Makes us lose all sense of rationality. That's the reason why I got kicked out of a lot of foster homes. I mean, it puts you in a wonderful mood at first. I would generously give away all of the money I had, even the shirt off my back. And then it would wear off and I'd feel awful."

"Interesting," said Athena. She felt her mind clicking away, calculating something.

"What do you have in that bag of yours?" Dain asked.

"Mostly explosives," said Athena. "Don't get any ideas."

Dain laughed, just as a loud bang rent the air.

"They're coming for us," said Dain, peeping out of the windows. "Quick. Let's find some way we can get a better view."

"They know we're here?" Athena asked, running through the leafy rooms. The building was quite a marvel. If only she'd had the time to admire the architecture.

"It looks like it," said Dain, peeping out of another window. "They're headed right this way.

Suddenly, the air began to swirl around them. An explosion of light cascaded through the building, reducing it to a great pile of leaves, sending them tumbling to the ground amid a writhing pile of foliage and the clerk's office staff.

"There you are," said the countess. "So careless of you to run from me. You know, there is no place you can hide in this corner of the realm."

Athena reached into her bag.

"Don't get any ideas," said the countess.

"What do I have to lose?" Athena asked.

"A riddle?" The countess looked puzzled and then she grinned. "Oh, I do love riddles."

The soldiers continued to advance towards them. Athena grabbed hold of a round shaped charm she'd prepared earlier and threw it out in front of her, towards them.

The explosion sent several of the fae guard flying back, but it wasn't enough.

Another guard lunged at Athena. Her survival instincts kicked in, along with her magical ones, and she reached out, grabbing the hefty guard with both hands, and flung him far and wide.

"I have the Buffy powers, too!" Athena exclaimed.

"What?" Dain asked.

"Never mind," she said as she punched and kicked and swept more fae guards away.

They kept coming.

Athena threw charm after charm, and hurled guard after guard, but eventually succumbed to the mass of uniformed fae, who pushed both her and her father's hands behind their backs.

"Athena!" a familiar voice called out.

"Mum?!" Athena turned, astonished to see not only her mother, but also her school friends, and Sherry from the pub, with a small group of young children in tow.

They were approaching the enormous pile of leaves which used to be the structure of the clerk's office.

"Leave my daughter alone," said Rosemary, light glowing from her hands.

"I would advise you not to try anything stupid," said the countess. "Otherwise, your daughter won't last much longer."

"She's bluffing," said Dain.

"Dain!" Rosemary said in shock, clearly only just realising he was present. "What are you doing? How did you get here?"

"It's a long story," said Dain.

A fox circled the clearing, growling, and Athena recognised him as

Felix. Seeing him gave her a warm mischievous feeling. Felix was always up to trouble, and he was full of ideas that would create the perfect disruption. Seeing him prowling around sparked something in Athena's mind, connecting the dots in the pieces of knowledge she had of the fae, weaving them into the perfect plot. It was a mad idea, but it just might work to get them out of there.

"Any last words?" asked the fae countess.

"Actually, yes," said Athena. "I would like to invite you to tea."

"Tea?" the countess asked. A hushed silence fell around them.

Rosemary looked at her daughter, gobsmacked.

"Yes, tea. I would like to invite you to tea right now," said Athena.

"Oh," said the countess, shocked. She seemed to be struggling, inwardly, with the request.

Athena smiled, knowing that the fae were tightly bound by the rules of etiquette.

It was more than just custom. It was the law, or perhaps the Lore. It was deep within them, compelling them to obey.

"This hardly seems to be the time," the countess said.

"Oh, but it's the perfect time," Athena said. "I've even brought the tea with me, all the way from the earth realm, in a show of gracious hospitality."

The countess paled. "But of course. How kind of you to offer. And... where is this tea party?" She struggled against her own words.

"Right here, of course," said Athena, waving her arms and gesturing towards the log table with the mushroom seating where the clerk had entertained her on her arrival.

The countess smiled, though it looked more to be a grimace. "How kind," she said coldly. "Though I wouldn't want to trouble you on such short notice."

"It is no trouble at all," said Athena. "But if you'd be so kind as to tell your guards to stand down—"

"Of course," said the countess. "Guards. Stand down. You may retreat to the outside of the clearing."

Athena smiled. This would at least buy them some time, and she had something else in mind. She knew there was still enough tea in her thermos for at least a few small cups. As soon as they'd sat down on the mushrooms stools, she picked up an empty vessel from the table that looked like a magnolia flower and poured out some rather tepid tea for the countess. Athena took care to hide what she was doing as she added a good dollop of cream from the little bottle in her bag.

"Tell me," the countess said suddenly, making Athena flinch. "What is that delightful smell?"

Athena glanced back to see a genuine smile spreading across the countess's face along with a gleam in her eye.

Dain looked at his daughter incredulously, knowing exactly what she was doing. He grimaced and grasped the table in front of him, as if visibly restraining himself from diving towards the cream.

"Here you go, your...err...highness," Athena said, handing her the cup. She then poured out the remainder of what was left in her thermos out into more cups, despite there only being a tiny amount to go around. She didn't add any cream to these, but handed them around the table to her mother, school friends, Sherry, and her father, who had all sat down for tea with the countess.

"What gracious hospitality," said the countess, half glaring maniacally and half smiling, equally maniacally. "It is actually quite delightful to find so many humans here. Surprisingly so. I see you discovered the children we took."

"Oh, umm..." said Rosemary, smiling at the children who stood nearby, all in a row, watching with curiosity.

Athena looked across at them. There was a red-haired boy who was taller than the others, a dark-haired girl who reminded Athena of someone she knew, two blonde girls who looked to be around four or five, and strawberry blonde twins who were young enough to be toddlers.

"Why did they stay so young?" Rosemary asked.

"That's something we're working on," said the countess. "We'd like for them to be a little older, so that they could breed."

"Breed?!" said Rosemary, clearly mortified.

"You, however." The countess pointed a finger around the table. "All of you might be of breeding age."

"We are most certainly not," said Rosemary. "Especially not the teenagers!"

"A pity. Our genetic variety is very low, you see," said the countess. "But don't tell anyone else I said that. In fact, remind me to put an enchantment on you so you'll all forget. We can't have anyone else knowing we'd even consider the possibility of cross-breeding with mere humans." She took another sip of tea, becoming sillier by the minute. "I do say, this is the most delightful beverage I ever drunk...drunken... drunkie dunk."

Athena noticed that the countess's cheeks had become rosy and her eyes glowed brighter and brighter.

"What delightful company you all are," the countess said, waving her hand. Sparks flew out from her fingertips and lit up the air like fireflies. "Oh, what an enchanted evening!" With another wave of her hand the sparks began darting about. The children laughed in glee and began chasing them around the clearing. The countess was clearly high on dairy fat and wouldn't be much of a threat, but the guards were unaffected, and there surely wasn't enough cream to go around them all. Athena considered how she might spray it everywhere with magic and create chaos in which they might escape, but then the countess spoke.

"This has been quite delightful." The countess drained her cup. "I feel so wonderful. How will I ever return your gracious hospitality?"

"Err, if you'd be so kind..." said Athena. She'd had an idea.

It was a longshot, but it was worth attempting, especially since the countess seemed to be in such a good mood. If Dad lost all sense of reason and became so generous he gave all our money away when he'd had cream, then surely there's a chance...

"To return our hospitality," Athena continued, "you could simply take down the fae side of the enchantments on the veil, so that we can get back to the human world."

The fae countess threw back her head and cackled hysterically.

Athena felt herself tense in preparation for battle, but then the countess pulled herself up straight, still smiling brightly. "But of course! It would be rude not to," she said and giggled gleefully. Then, with a wave of her hand, she sliced a crescent moon shape in the air above the table. It peeled back to form a door.

"What now?" Rosemary whispered.

"We have to get through the human magic on the other side," said Athena. "Okay, we're all going to have to work together on this one." She stood, taking her mother by the hand.

"What?" Rosemary asked.

"You've been practicing your magic, haven't you?" Athena said. "I could tell by the way your hands were glowing before."

Rosemary nodded. "Yes, but I don't know how to get through."

"The Thorn family magic is incredibly powerful," said Sherry. "This wall in front of us is powerful too, but mostly against fae magic."

"She's right, Mum," said Athena. "We can do this. It's nothing compared to what we're capable of. We just have to imagine the protections dissolving."

Rosemary and Athena both held out their hands towards the door, visualising the defences on the other side peeling right back like the fae side had moments before.

"It's working!" said Sherry.

Athena looked to see green trees visible through the hole in the veil.

"Oh, what clever little creatures you are," said the countess. "You want to get back? Here, off you go!" She raised both arms dramatically.

Ribbons of magic flew out, sweeping up all of the earth beings.

Athena instinctively reached out and grabbed Dain's wrist as they were all pushed through the portal.

Bright light shone out, and then faded.

Rosemary, Athena, Sherry, Dain, the other teenagers, and the children who had been lost, all found themselves standing in the middle of the town square.

The whole area was now deserted, except for Ferg who was sweeping up some petals nearby.

"Oh, it's you lot," he said flatly. "Don't make a mess. I've been cleaning up from the Equinox for at least half an hour."

Rosemary and Athena looked at each other and then both collapsed in exhaustion onto the soft earth realm grass, laughing and relieved beyond belief.

CHAPTER

FORTY-FOUR

"I 'm so sorry," said Detective Neve as they all sat around the police station. Rosemary had one of the six children on her lap, the little boy with bright red hair, who said his name was Harry.

"I have a feeling bad things happen when you get called out of town," Rosemary said to Neve. "Was it another trick to get you out of the way?"

"It really was a family emergency, like I told you," said Neve. "Just a coincidence this time."

"Is everything okay with your aunt?" Rosemary asked.

"Something's happened to her memory, as we feared. She seemed fine until a few weeks ago, but now I'm afraid she's got sudden-onset dementia. She keeps ranting about her little girl who went missing. It's unfortunate my auntie is so far away. My family moved out of Myrtle-wood years ago."

"Oh, how awful to lose a child," said Rosemary. "Think of what the parents of these children must have gone through."

"That's the thing," said the detective. "My aunt didn't have a child. Seems a strange thing to make up."

Rosemary shrugged. "Stranger things have happened around here."

"You bet," said Neve, looking around at the children. "So these are all the ones who disappeared over to the fae realm."

"All the ones we could find," said Rosemary. "They were all kind of clustered together in a giant mushroom."

"The mind boggles," said the detective.

"It doesn't make much sense to me either," said Rosemary. "Even though I was there to witness it."

Just then, Prue burst through the doors of the police station. "Gretchen!" she cried. The little blonde child ran into her arms.

"It's just as well the mother remembered," said Sherry. "It wouldn't have been long before she would have forgotten all about her, just like I was forgotten about." She cradled a little dark-haired girl on her lap who looked to be about seven years old. "Mei and I went missing at the same time."

A strange shiver ran down Rosemary's spine. She turned back to Detective Neve, recognising some familiar features.

"Your aunt used to live in Myrtlewood, did she?" Rosemary asked Neve.

"Well, she did a long time ago when I was growing up," said the detective.

"Sherry, what's Mei's last name?"

"Lee," said Sherry.

"That's funny," said Neve. "That's my mother's maiden name."

Rosemary waited for the penny to drop.

The detective looked at her, startled. "That's my aunt's last name..." She clamped her hand over her mouth and looked at the little girl. "But how?"

"Sherry can explain in more detail," said Rosemary. "When she came back from the fae realm all those years ago her family had totally forgotten about her. It took a long time for them to remember her again, even after she'd returned."

"It...can't be!" said Neve. "I'm going to call my auntie straight away." She hurried from the room.

"What was that about?" Athena asked.

"It seems this little girl might well be related to our favourite police detective."

"No way!" Athena said, smiling at her mother. "Mei is supposed to be the same age as Sherry, isn't she?"

"Yes, we were good friends, growing up," said Sherry.

"And you never forgot her all those years after she disappeared," said Athena.

"I promised to bring her back," said Sherry. "I've been trying this whole time."

"It's almost enough to make me cry," said Rosemary. "So sweet...Even though you stole my necklace."

"Here you go," said Sherry, reaching around her neck to unlatch the clasp.

"Umm... Thank you," said Rosemary, taking the precious pendant in her hands. "This is turning out to be quite a good day after all."

Athena beamed at her.

"But don't think I haven't forgotten how you ran away with that boy," said Rosemary.

"Don't remind me about *him*," said Athena.

"You haven't escaped being grilled by me yet," said Rosemary. "Just wait 'til we get home. Also, you're grounded indefinitely."

"I probably deserve that," said Athena, crossing her arms. "And I'm kind of going to lie low for a while anyway. But please let me see my friends." She draped her arm around Elise, who smiled.

"I suppose I owe them that," said Rosemary. "They shouldn't have run through the gap in the veil either, but I suppose they did help, and it shows how loyal they are. Even that Beryl girl."

"Beryl? What did she do?" Athena asked, shocked.

Rosemary filled Athena in on the help provided by Beryl.

"She probably only wanted to do that so she could prove how much better she is than me. She just wanted to have something to rub in my face."

"That's a little bit harsh," said Rosemary.

"Well, that's Beryl for you," said Elise. "But she really did help."

"I suppose I'll have to thank her," Athena muttered bitterly.

Dain stepped out of an interview room, followed by Constable Perkins.

Rosemary clutched the anti-Dain protection bundle around her neck.

"Hey," Dain said. His smile was still disarming, regardless.

Rosemary had barely said two words to him before Constable Perkins ushered her into the interview room for her turn. She grudgingly followed the grumpy old officer and was grateful when the interview didn't last too long. As expected, it was just a series of baseless accusations and ridiculous questions from Perkins, but after a while the constable gave up and let her go.

By the time Rosemary returned back to the lobby all of the teenagers had been picked up by their respective families. Though there was still the remaining matter of the foundling children.

Gretchen had gone home with Prue, and Mei was talking excitedly with Neve. Rosemary looked at the four other young children.

Harry, with the bright red mane, said he was six, and little Elowen had white-blonde hair and seemed about four or five. They were currently in the corner of the reception, playing with a small basket of toys that Detective Neve had found.

The twins, with their strawberry blonde curls, were probably less than two years old and didn't speak. Athena had taken the liberty of naming them Thea and Clio, and was sitting with them both propped on her lap.

It was adorable, however the fact remained that they had nowhere to go, and Neve didn't have a bed ready for Mei, her newly discovered cousin.

"What are we going to do?" Rosemary muttered.

"I suppose we could call Child Protective Services," said Neve, approaching Rosemary. "Until we can track down the remaining families."

"But who knows how long they were in there? They don't age in the fae realm, remember?" said Rosemary.

"It would be better if they avoided foster care," said Dain, who had clearly been eavesdropping. "Believe me. You never know what kind of luck you'll get. Besides, they might well be highly magical, especially after so much time spent in that realm."

"They can come back to our house," said Athena. "We've got room."

"Wait a minute." Rosemary felt a rising panic at the thought of suddenly being responsible for all the foundlings from the fae realm. "Hold your horses. I've got enough work looking after one delinquent child, let alone a whole barrel of kids."

"I'll help you," Athena insisted. "Maybe that can be my punishment. It will teach me how to be responsible, or something."

She smiled down at the twins who were falling asleep on her lap.

"Well, I suppose it wouldn't hurt to have them around for a few days," said Rosemary.

"That's the spirit," said Marjie. She'd arrived soon after Rosemary had called her to let her know they were all back safely and had been hanging back, minding the little ones. "I'll help out. Herb can spare me for a few days."

"And what about you?" Rosemary asked Dain. "Where will you go?"

He shrugged.

"Oh dear," said Athena.

Rosemary gave her daughter a warning look, hoping she wasn't going to verbally abuse her father too much, especially not around so many young children.

"Why don't you come back to our house, too," said Athena.

Rosemary was so shocked she almost fell out of her chair.

"Just for a few days," Athena continued. "We might even be able to see if there's some kind of magic we can rustle up to protect you from your little cream problem."

Rosemary almost choked. "You've got to be kidding me!" she said to her daughter. "I thought you were angry at your father for everything he did. And what's all the fuss about cream?"

"I'll explain about the cream later, but we all make mistakes and bad choices, don't we?" said Athena, giving her mother a meaningful look. "I haven't forgiven him, not completely. But I think I've started to understand him a little bit better. He hasn't had the most normal life, or the most stable childhood. So can he come, or not?" She folded her arms.

Rosemary grinned. "Of course he can come to our place, as long as he stays firmly away from our wallets and doesn't steal anything."

Dain raised his hands in innocence. "I promise. A few weeks shackled in a tower in the fae realm has really given me a new appreciation for the freedoms of life, and I don't want to abuse that."

"It's settled then," said Athena. "Let's all go home to Thorn Manor now. Are you coming, Neve?"

"Me?" Detective Neve said.

"You can bring little Mei," said Athena. "And all the other kids too. They need somewhere to sleep and we have plenty of room."

Rosemary bit her lower lip, worried about the mess she'd left the place in. Surely, nobody would mind a bit of chaos, given the circumstance.

"Oh," said Neve. "I hadn't thought about that. Maybe I could come over. I'd just have to call my girlfriend."

"Nesta's welcome too. I'm sure we can accommodate all of you," said Rosemary. It was true that Thorn Manor was huge enough to fit all of them, and plenty more besides. Although Rosemary was mentally trying to figure out how to fit them in comfortably, as both east and west wings were notoriously dusty and shabby the last time she'd gone in there, let alone the huge experimental jumble she'd created when cooking up possible ways to get into the fae realm in her many failed attempts.

"We can always make some makeshift beds in the living room now that all of those plants have been cleared out of the house," Rosemary said. "I'll just have to move a few tables of potion equipment."

Neve didn't look too convinced.

FORTUNATELY, the house seemed to have heard the call, and by the time Rosemary and Athena and the others arrived back at the manor, all Rosemary's magical paraphernalia been tided away, and the door to the west wing was open for a change.

Rosemary peeked in to see it was no longer a dusty mess, but was sparkling and gleaming as if it had just been cleaned by a maid service and was perfectly well maintained. Even more conveniently, a large nursery had appeared that Rosemary was certain hadn't been there before, complete with five little beds. A few adjoining rooms held queen sized beds.

"How does it *know?*" asked Athena.

"I don't know. But I think it's best we treat it with kindness," Rosemary replied, tapping the wood of the door.

The little black kitten scrambled out from under one of the small beds where she'd clearly been investigating. Athena scooped her up.

"I've missed you," she said, nuzzling against the cat's head.

"Sweet little Serpentine," Rosemary cooed, reaching out for a pat.

"You've named her properly!" said Athena, beaming. "And you chose my preferred name."

"That's right," said Rosemary. "May I formally introduce Miss Serpentine Fuzzball Thorn, her Royal Cuteness."

Athena giggled.

"This is very organised of you," said Nesta when she arrived, after following Neve into the nursery. "How did you know?"

"It wasn't us," said Athena. "The house has its ways."

"Now I know why they say the Thorn family magic is so strong," said Neve, clearly impressed.

Marjie arrived with baskets of Ostara buns and chocolate eggs for supper, which Athena was almost as excited about as the young children seemed to be, sleepy though they all were.

While their guests adjusted to Thorn Manor, Rosemary and Athena retreated back to the kitchen. Athena put the kettle on for tea – both the electric one and the old fashioned one – to make enough for all the additional visitors. Meanwhile, Rosemary made a saucepan of warm milk with cinnamon and honey for the children.

As the smell of sweet spice drifted through the kitchen, Rosemary smiled at Athena. "I'm so glad to have you back."

"That was quite...an adventure," said Athena.

Rosemary looked at her daughter. "Don't go running back to the fae realm, now," she said sternly.

"No. I'm relieved to be back. You know, I quite like our strange little magical life here."

Rosemary's smile widened even further. "You know what? You're right. Aside from all the risks and danger and creepy things, which I decidedly do not like, everything else in Myrtlewood is just fabulous!"

EPILOGUE

As Rosemary and Athena slept peacefully in their beds that night, a woman stood on a hill under the light of the waning moon, overlooking the village of Myrtlewood.

Her eyes gleamed in joy at the news – such good news. Her contacts had come through, finally. A girl had entered the fae realm, and not just any girl, the one she'd been looking for all these years.

"Right here under my nose," she said to herself and cackled in glee.

There was finally a path in sight, a way to cut through to the realm, and this held the key to unlocking many years' worth of plotting.

"The power will be ours," she said to her companion, who hung back, overshadowed by trees.

The woman raised her arms, her dark hood sliding back slightly to reveal pale hair that gleamed pearlescent in the moonlight as she began chanting the ancient words, not heard for centuries.

Down in the fields of Myrtlewood, all was quiet.

Then, as if from nowhere, a gust of wind swept through the back of the old Twigg farm.

The barn that had stood there for a hundred years suddenly burst into flames.

Agatha Twigg looked out her back window in horror as the bright orange fire engulfed the structure before turning an unearthly pink.

"Oh dear me, Marla!" Agatha called out to her niece. "Ring the authorities. Something big is coming!"

Order Myrtlewood Mysteries book 3 now!

A NOTE FROM THE AUTHOR

THANK you so much for reading this book. I enjoyed writing about Ostara, the Spring Equinox and the fae realm.

If you have a moment, please leave a review or even just leave a star rating. This helps new readers to know what kind of book they're getting themselves into, and hopefully builds some trust that it's worth reading!

If you're keen to read more, you can order Myrtlewood Mysteries book 3 now!

You can also join my reader list or follow me on social media. Links are on the next page.

ABOUT THE AUTHOR

Iris Beaglehole

Iris Beaglehole is many peculiar things, a writer, researcher, analyst, druid, witch, parent, and would-be astrologer. She loves tea, cats, herbs, and writing quirky characters.

Printed in Great Britain
by Amazon

31408894R00172